INFINITE DIMENSIONS
CROSSROADS

INFINITE DIMENSIONS

CROSSROADS

MICHAEL BEN-ZVI

SHIRLEY CHAN

JENNIFER GRAHAM

CAITLIN MCKENNA

MACKENZIE REIDE

JENNJETT MEDIA

Infinite Dimensions
Crossroads

JennJett Media
New York, NY USA
www.jennjettmedia.net

Compilation copyright © 2017 by JennJett Media
All individual stories © 2017 by their respective authors
Copyediting by Caitlin McKenna
Cover design by Michael Ben-Zvi
Interior design by Mackenzie Reide

ISBN 978-0-9994136-09

Table of Contents

Preface

The world is going through difficult times. One question among many is what role writers have to play, particularly in the world of speculative fiction. What stories can we tell that will inform our choices when it seems like everything is going off the rails? And can we as a society make the right decisions to set ourselves on a better, more hopeful path?

Over the past several years, our team of authors has been meeting as members of a New York City-based science fiction and fantasy writing group, *4th Dimension Writers*. Most of us have been published in one form or another, and all of us have ideas or works in progress. For years, we would exchange critiques and share our work, writing in different genres and pursuing our own independent visions.

It seemed at the time that dystopian fiction was dominating the film and book market and everyone was convinced the world was circling the drain. The smart money would be to capitalize on that trend. Over a year ago, we decided the time was right to launch a project of our own, a collaboration of short stories whose main theme was one of "hope." It was an exciting direction for us, a catalyst to perfect our writing while saying something important and working together toward a common goal. It was also a project that could serve as the basis for future science fiction/fantasy anthologies centered around a shared theme.

Of course, a few things happened along the way. For one, the world became increasingly . . . well, chaotic. The dystopian post-apocalyptic stories that were once novels and movie plots seemed to be playing out in the news and social media. Reality was catching up to fiction.

As the five of us were developing our story concepts, we realized the tales we wanted to tell weren't about hope at all. They were about choices: characters forced to a point of decision in settings of great difficulty and challenge. Without intending to, we had each independently realized that it was more important to tell the world that we needed to make better decisions. Knowing we have a choice is perhaps the most hopeful message we can deliver.

This is how *Infinite Dimensions: Crossroads*, our first fiction anthology, was born.

We know that five short stories won't transform the world by themselves. What matters is the difference it has made for us: collaborating and leveraging our respective talents and experiences has made this project possible. We plan to expand upon our experience with future collaborations in the *Infinite Dimensions* series.

Keep making good choices. A better world depends on it.

December 2017

Michael Ben-Zvi
Shirley Chan
Jennifer Graham
Caitlin McKenna
Mackenzie Reide

Acknowledgments

This collaborative effort would not have been possible without the many people who helped to support our writing. We thank our beta readers, our advisors, friends and family, and all those who supported and offered words of encouragement in this endeavor.

With special thanks to: Chris Africa, Frank Cernik, Chaz Baker, Samantha Fleschner, Shareen and Miranda.

Humanity
Michael Ben-Zvi

For a long time, "Humanity" was a title and a concept in search of a story. What I wanted to do was create my own Star Wars *saga, a mostly hard science space opera universe of epic adventure with room for multiple stories to tell, yet with transhumanist and futurist concepts geared to a contemporary audience. I eventually realized such a setting would be an opportunity to explore how one falls into a life of—for lack of a better word—evil, and how someone finds his or her way out from such a life. Movies will often take the easy way out and have the character find redemption only through their death. But what does it take to go on living—even against the backdrop of war that only promises more death? How does one rediscover their . . . humanity?*

If Mala Roi remembered one lesson of value from the hell that had been her homeworld, it was that focus could save her life. And she knew she would need all her energies focused for the task that was to come.

She tuned out all extraneous chatter around her. She could hear the status feeds through her sharelink, the words of the others on the flight deck while she stood at attention in her battle armor. She could hear her name and rank spoken in passing. But her thoughts were entirely on the mission, and what would come after if they succeeded. When they succeeded, she thought with determination—determination and focus. She would need that to survive. She always had.

"White Knife! White Knife!"

She could hear the roar of the crowds, the stadium filled to capacity. They had come for the sport: bored scions from the Estates, merchants from the Plazas, working folks from the Shallows, miners earning their precious allotment of sun-time to visit the surface and the Battle Pits. All social classes across the spectrum of the Eternal City of Tannapor, united in their desire for blood.

All to see her, the White Knife, kill again. Or perhaps this time it would be her, the young woman with the unending appetite for violence, who would be finally claimed by the Pits after five years of victories. Five years of glorious kills. *How many dead at this point?* she wondered. She had stopped counting after the first fifty.

"Focus!" she heard Six yell at her in his gravelly voice. It was the only name she knew him by, and she only knew that from his tattoo. No one's birth names meant anything here in the Battle Pits. Those names, those lives, were long gone.

"I hear you," she said, not even looking at him. Her attention was entirely on the open arena, where she would soon be stepping out. Another opponent, most likely another convict serving out his sentence or a miner forced to erase his debt bondage. Some would be brutal, some totally out of their depth; all would be desperate, just as she had once been. That was before the routine settled in, before the killing had become normal. She stopped paying attention to much else long ago. The barren cell where she slept. The bulky clamp around her neck to track her movements. The parties where the Gamemasters and the patrons would put her on display, dress her up in ridiculous outfits for their amusement. Or sometimes not dress her at all, for other amusements.

"You're not hearing me, Knife." Six leaned in. He was older, heavily tanned and weathered, training fighters for the arena for at least as long as she'd been alive. "I know what you're planning."

"I don't know . . ."

"Shut it," he said. "Don't say anything. You still have to go out there. And they've lined up someone particularly nasty this time. Some freak pumped full of off-world muscle biotech. Secondhand stuff, made him all twisted inside. He killed four women before they clamped him and brought him here. Brought him here to kill you."

That got her attention. *Do the Gamemasters know?* she wondered. The diplomatic transport from the Harmonious Order would be at the Port of Jiballa for only another day. The guards would be drunk after the bout, especially the ones who'd wagered on her. She'd figured out how to hack the clamp and jam its signal. Just a two-klick run in the dead of night to the Port . . .

"You focus on this like it's any other fight," he told her. "Never let them think this day is any different. This guy is big, bulky and full of blind rage, but he doesn't have your speed. Or your drive."

"I know," she said, gazing out upon the expanse of the arena. "I saw him train earlier. Didn't know the muscle was all fake."

"It'll feel real enough if he slams his fists into you, so don't let him."

"I won't." She thought to turn around, to look at Six and . . . she wasn't sure. Say something. Like what? Goodbye? Thanks for taking in a frightened gang youth and molding her into a killer?

"Are you going to wish me luck?" she asked him, finally looking over her shoulder, seeing just how old and beaten down he really was.

"With the fight? You don't need it. I've taught you everything you need to know. Beyond that, I don't know anything else."

She heard her name called, and she stepped forward. Barefoot, draped in just a few loose spidersilks with some leather padding. And her knife. It was all she'd ever needed.

The fight didn't frighten her, nor her plan to escape. It was her defection to the Harmonious Order of the Mind that was the real gamble. Even if she successfully stowed away on their ship and cleared the system's jumpknot before being discovered, they could still kill her on sight, or worse, return her to Jiballa. She'd heard stories about life in the Harmonious Order, stories meant to terrify. But anything had to be better. She had skills she could trade. And she was desperate. Desperate enough to believe the stories. And if they were true . . .

She would welcome the new life they had to offer her, a life where she was no longer the White Knife.

She looked about the flight deck of the dropship *Determinado*, a phalanx of blanks standing around her at full attention, along with six Armada officers. Like herself, the officers were all fellow fleshborns. Biostatic, geno-optimized, fully Leashed and combat synched. All good and proper *civitas* of the Harmonious Order. More proper than she was, without a doubt. Her adjunct, *Oficira* Breeshall, and the *Determinado's* flight crew were all born to the Order, never having known any other life than that under the Leash. Not like her, or the rest of the Jagger Corps. The Jaggers were, by their outsider status, accustomed to lives of violence.

Our disharmony is our greatest weapon. That's what Parran had told her. He'd meant it as a joke, but the words proved more truthful than he realized. The Jaggers existed to do things that other *civitas* might struggle with, even with the Leash to guide and encourage them, tasks that couldn't be trusted to a blank. Even the Order needed help in keeping order.

She was Mala Roi today, but that was not the name she'd been born with, no more real than the White Knife. Or the Blood Angel. Or the Butcher of Tannapor. Officially, she was *Jaggero Secondo* Mala Roi, her rank and identity with the Jagger Corps. Her old name, the name of her birth, that no longer existed. She wasn't that person anymore. Too many choices made since then.

Mala looked at Breeshall's calm porcelain face, her golden hair tied in accordance with the Order's military protocols. Breeshall wasn't that much younger than her, yet she seemed so childlike and unperturbed. So much at peace. Like she had no inkling that this mission was the start of a war a long time coming.

"We are on approach, *Jaggero*," Breeshall informed her. "Society carriers are maintaining their distance." The *Determinado* had separated from its jump carrier and was making the descent to their destination.

Mala nodded in acknowledgment. "They're trying to figure

out what our intentions are." A subtle smile curled at the corner of her mouth. The enemy would soon know what they intended. "What about their units on the surface? Any movement there?"

"No change, *Jaggero*," she said. "It's exactly as our probes informed us. They're limited to an evacuation detail. For the ecoformers."

"Fools," *Leftat* Neshat said from his command station. "A system this valuable, this strategic, and they leave only a small ecoforming colony without any real protection. If these are the kinds of mistakes the enemy keeps making, we'll be victorious by Summertide." The others on deck, officers and blanks alike, stood sharply at attention, a show of solidarity and patriotic fervor.

"Valuable to us, *Leftat*, not necessarily to the enemy," said Mala. Neshat was technically in command of the craft while in flight, even if she was the overall mission commander, so for now she had to indulge his need to project his authority.

"It looks so bleak," said Breeshall, staring at the grayish, cloudy planet growing larger in the holofield projection. "Nothing at all like home."

"You haven't been offworld enough," Mala replied. "Lots of worlds like this in the Diaspora. Worlds gone fallow." Ketheritt, like all of the Diaspora worlds, had been made habitable to bio-static humans, though not entirely pleasant in its current state. The planet had been ecoformed by the Transcendants during the later years of their "rule" over humanity, shortly before their departure to . . . no one knew where.

"I wonder who used to live here," said Breeshall.

"What?" said Mala, turning from the holofield as the planet grew larger, until the gray pall of clouds obscured the entire view and the external scopes switched to infrared for easier navigation.

"The original colony, from Old Earth. There's nothing remaining in the *Archivo* about the planet's history from the Transcendent era."

"Because it doesn't matter, *Oficira*," said Mala coldly. "They didn't survive on their own, not without the Trancendents or contact with the other worlds." *Too soft*, she supposed. *Not like Brightholm. Or Jiballa*, she considered, painfully. Or with grudging acceptance, Aris and the other Society Worlds.

During the long centuries of the Post-Transcendence, while the rest of the Diaspora rebuilt from the ashes and some rediscovered the stars, Ketheritt lay abandoned, its terraformed biosphere going wildly unstable without someone to tend to it. It was only in the last century that expeditions from the Society Worlds arrived on Ketheritt and brought the ecosystem back under control, tamed and guided to match the Society's aesthetic ideals.

"Is that all the Society wants?" asked Breeshall. "To fix a broken planet?"

"It's their way," said Mala. "They can't help themselves. They love to fix things. It's in their nature to interfere where they shouldn't."

"So they knew nothing about the jumpknot connections when they placed the colony?"

"I'm sure they knew about it, *Oficira*," said Mala. "They just didn't consider it important. They think in terms of science solving problems. Strategic value doesn't even factor for them."

"And that is why—" Neshat chimed in proudly.

"Yes, *Leftat*," said Mala, cutting him off. "By Summertide."

He was right, of course. The Society Worlds would lose. In the years since they rediscovered the jumpknots, they assumed they'd have the universe all to themselves, to remake the Diaspora as they saw right and proper. It never occurred to them that some of the worlds they reconnected might see things differently, and challenge their vision for the future.

"What's happening on the surface?" Mala inquired of the scope officer. "Has the colony detected our approach?" She remembered his name, Jenghett, another fresh-faced *oficira* who looked even younger than Breshall. Neshat was no doubt perturbed that she hadn't directed the question to him, the flight commander. He wouldn't show it, of course. Any burst of anger or breakdown of military protocol would be dissipated by a release of dopamine directed by his Leash.

"No visible response, *Jaggero*," *Oficira* Jenghett replied. "Our emissions are still within the margins. Stealth doesn't appear compromised." She nodded in acknowledgement and said nothing. Mala could hear the nervous timbre in the boy's voice, almost squeaking as he talked. She wondered to what degree Jenghett's Leash had to overclock his brain to give him a semblance of courage and combat discipline. Without the Leash, the boy would no doubt have soiled his uniform at the first sign of missile fire.

She would have preferred leading a larger, more battle-hardened assault platoon than the team she'd been given, just herself and a few of her seasoned Jagger comrades. But she understood the *strategistos'* insistence on a lean mission emphasizing stealth, boosting beneath the notice of the Society Worlds Guard Fleet. The rest of the Jagger Corps were spearheading the push against the Society Guardians in the Ingressa system, five jumps distant, while Mala Roi and her strike force were dispatched here.

There was also no need to draw attention to the fact that from the Ketheritt system, twelve Society-allied systems lay within striking distance. Seize at least three, and the Society Worlds could be cut in half. Or attacked directly, if the *strategistos* so wished.

Her team, the *strategistos*, even the other Jaggers, were all assuming the Society was completely oblivious to the Order's plans—that the Harmonious Order was too distant a concern, cut off by stellar cartography and distant jumpknot bridges. No threat to their own decadence and comfort. Their disordered, purposeless lives.

This was the Order's vision, the ideal of a united humanity, living under the Leash. The Order had to grow, or it would inevitably fray at the edges, and then strangle itself under the imposed isolation of the Society and its allies.

There could be only two choices for humanity in the wake of the Transcendence. Either the Society or the Order. There were no alternatives.

Too much introspection, she realized, her mind drifting elsewhere when her focus should be completely on the mission. She had learned to sense those shifts in her thoughts when her Leash was subtly influencing her, keeping her norepinephrine levels balanced, bringing her back into alignment with her purpose on the *Determinado*.

Mala directed her attention again toward Jenghett. "Are we close enough to identify their contingents on the surface?" He was startled by her question and quickly turned to his station, where several smaller holofields were arrayed with data from the external scopes.

"We . . . um, we're still gathering intel, *Jaggero*," he answered, doing his best to appear poised while he and the rest of the flight crew started strapping themselves into their acceleration harnesses for the planetary descent. "There's definitely a single Messenger-Class dropship on site, big enough for a full Guardian phalanx and to evac all the scientists."

And cargo, she thought to herself. Seizing the planet was the primary objective of her team, but there was always an important, if unspoken, secondary directive in place whenever a world was rediscovered. In any system visited or changed by the Transcendants, there could always be old technologies left behind, knowledge long forgotten that could be found and repurposed. Such a discovery on the moons of Brightholm had led to breakthroughs in neurotech and the creation of the Leash, the very founding of the Harmonious Order itself. And in wartime, a similar find could be the key to victory. Energies that could tame planets and reopen jumpknots could also potentially destroy both.

"Nothing smaller?" Mala looked over the young officer's shoulder, trying to make sense of the scope data herself. The heavy dropship at the colony didn't concern her, which only reconfirmed what she suspected about the presence of Guardians on the surface. But one or more smaller, separate craft would tell her more about the importance the Society placed on this colony.

"Nothing we can detect, *Jaggero,*" said Jenghett. "They must be maintaining a stealth presence on the surface, just as we . . ."

"They?" Neshat joined in the conversation. "What do you mean, *Oficira*?"

"The Sentinels, *Leftat,*" Jenghett replied as he stood at attention, as best he could while harnessed. "Surely that is what the Lady Mala . . ."

"That will be all, *Oficira*," she commanded him. She hated that title, of all the names she'd been given. Lady Mala. It seemed ironic, almost an insult, considering the egalitarian ideals of the Order. Another way of indicating she wasn't one of them.

But indeed, it was the Sentinels that concerned her. The strike team could face off against a single phalanx of Guardians with ease, especially with stealth and drone support on their side. A Sentinel was a different matter entirely, and part of the reason she was here.

She knew that the enemy would not leave Ketheritt unprotected, or completely ignore its strategic import. For all their philosophical detachment and talk of diversity, she knew that the Enlightened Sentinels, perhaps alone among all the Society Worlds' institutions, understood the urgency of the competition between the two cultures, and how seriously the Order regarded the need for expansion. There would be at least one Sentinel accompanying the evacuation dropship, maybe two or three. She doubted they would send much more, not until they regarded the current state of hostilities as an outright war.

So at least one Sentinel. It seemed a good balance. One Sentinel, one Jagger. A fair battle, more fair than most that Mala Roi had known in her life.

The *Determinado* touched down at the bottom of a wide ravine, free of the overgrown vegetation and mutated fungi that had come to dominate Ketheritt's ecosystems during the long centuries of neglect. Mala Roi was the first through the air-ramp, suited up head to toe in her ebony Jagger Corps armor. A quick mental command and her suit's liquid exosupports flowed into place to augment her limbs and torso. A second thought command and the armored suit's helmet lowered and locked in place over her head, the pressure seals solidifying into a rigid ring. At first, she was in total darkness and briefly slowed down her breathing. It took several seconds for the helmet's neural mesh to connect with her own brainware, and for the lifesystem's breathing tube to extend fibrils through her nostrils, allowing filtered oxygen and tailored sensory-enhancing pheromones to flow into her lungs and bloodstream. The suit went through its quick configuration cycle, adapting the exosupports and biofilters to Ketheritt's atmosphere and gravity. It didn't matter to her that the local gravity was 30% heavier than what she'd become used to, or that the planet's air had become choked with locally evolved pollens and other con-taminants. Her armor would adapt, giving her the strength and agility she needed to fight.

She stepped down the dropship's ramp onto the craggy surface of the ravine. The air overhead was as thick and gray as it appeared from orbit, the dense clouds refracting the light from the system's orange dwarf sun. Without her armor, the oxygen levels would be dangerously low and she'd sicken within days from breathing in heavy particulates. No images survived in the Order's *Archivo* on what Ketheritt had looked like when the Transcendants first finished their work, or whether the resulting world had matched their intended plans. But looking around, Mala couldn't help but feel a sense of colossal failure about her, that perhaps the almighty Trancendants had had their limits, unable to build worlds to last the ages.

Looking up at the ravine's edges, she saw gargantuan, twisted roots spilling over from the vast charcoal-gray woodlands that now covered this region. The comm static from her platoon network filled her ears as her blanks disembarked behind her, their own battlesuits now calibrated. The regular *soldatoi* of the Grand Armada of the Harmonious Order didn't have the same augmentation that armor of the Jagger Corps possessed, but they didn't need it. The Armada relied more on heavy weapons and remote support, while the Jaggers were optimized for close combat. Armada armor was less adaptable, but it carried heavier shielding and could absorb more impact. Jaggers needed to be lighter, more mobile.

Blank units on the other hand, were more likely to be shot at. Which was why they used blanks to begin with. Run low on troops, and you could always print more. The Order's municipal fabricators were at full capacity, churning out new *soldatoi* to be flooded with memories, once the decision had been made to commit to the war. It wasn't that blanks were uniquely expendable. When serving the Order, *everyone* was expendable. Some with skills, like Mala and her fellow Jaggers, were a bit less so. *Civitas* who came out of a matter printer were definitely more so.

Many of the Order's neighbors found the practice of print-and-flood citizenship abhorrent, like a form of ancient slavery. But there was nothing really horrible about it, or so Mala thought. Everyone was equal under the Leash, all committed to the same desire to pursue the Order's collective goals. In theory, it shouldn't matter if a *civita* could trace their lineage to a biological parent or if they were just printed to fill a need by one of the Order's planning committees.

"Fan out," said Mala. "Surveillance pattern *Prima*. We'll observe before committing to action."

"The order was to seize the Society encampment, *Jaggero*," said the disembodied voice of *Leftat* Neshat. She disregarded him immediately. Regulations gave Neshat authority while in flight, but once on the surface they were officially engaged in the mission, which made Mala Roi the field *Komandanto*.

"The order is that *I* give the orders here," she snapped at him. "I'm not revealing our numbers until we know if there's a Sentinel presence onsite."

"That will mean delays," said Neshat. "Armada Kommand was insistent that we take prisoners and gather our intel quickly . . ."

"Then we won't waste time by discussing it here," said Mala Roi. "We are committed to war, *Leftat*. We're under military protocols now. Which gives the *Komandanto* the authority to judge any deviation from protocol as an act of treason. Do you care to guess who has command authority now that we've made planetfall?" She smiled cruelly, picturing Neshat's youthful arrogant face quivering, realizing in his zeal he may have exceeded his reach. She could understand his arrogance. Neshat, like most Armada officers, wasn't just fleshborn, but born under the mother sun on Brightholm. It was only natural, in their minds, that they would be superior not only to the blanks under their command, but to people like herself—those not born to the Leash, but who chose it later in life.

The word "Jagger" in Nu Esperese, the primary language of Brightholm and the Harmonious Order, technically translated as "foreign soldier." But in common use, it stood for "alien" or "outsider," always with an unsavory connotation.

Jaggero might have been a title of status, but to many, that status marked her as not belonging. Even a harmonious order was an order built upon layers within levels. Order sometimes demanded hierarchy.

She commanded two of the nearest blanks to follow her, dispatching the rest to take the path leading directly up from the ravine along the forest wall. The *Determinado* was outfitted with the latest in stealth screens and low infrared-signature gear. Given the Society's light presence on Ketheritt and the movement of ships aiding in the evacuation, she was confident they had landed unseen. All attention would be focused on the threatening Armada fleet near the system's secondary jumpknot. No one would notice a single dropship breaking formation in the middle of the chaos. The planet's turbulent atmosphere, timed with the sun's flare season, had further worked to their advantage, as expected. Mala wasn't worried about the Society's Guardians, too busy overseeing the evac teams. Sentinels were a different matter entirely.

Mala Roi and her two escorts cleared the winding path out of the ravine. She felt the ground grow spongier under her feet. The ancient basaltic rock had become overgrown with a thick, black moss, and fat, twisted vegetation and roots wound outward from the canyon's edge. The roots grew thicker as they went farther into the forest. Bulbous mushroom-like growths peppered the tops of the roots like barnacles. The giant roots stretched off into the distance, where she could see the tall canopies of gray and violet obscuring the horizon. The Society colony was somewhere in the midst of that forest canopy and she and her escorts would have to navigate those woods while keeping their signatures hidden. Their armor exo-supports had taken over their movements and were now piloting them at a faster clip than their own natural leg muscles. While her armor handled her ground speed and approach, she took the time to deploy an all-spectrum scan and listen in on the Society's comm traffic, wanting to know at the very least what everyone was saying. And hoping none of it was about her crew and the *Determinado*. They were speaking in Changlese, but Mala knew enough to listen in, with her brainware helping to translate to fill in the blanks.

"We need to move . . ."

"We didn't bring enough forces to determine . . ."

"You have your orders . . ."

"The Armada's just sitting there. What are they waiting for?"

"They're baiting us. This whole thing's a setup."

Then there was one voice, something in the pitch that triggered reactions from the other speakers.

"What do you see, Sentinel-*Zhu*?"

Sentinel! So there was at least one for certain on the planet. That was one question answered. Would they fight her, and more to the point, could she emerge victorious?

"We may have company soon," a female voice spoke in reply.

Mala Roi recorded the voice and ran it through her *Archivo* memory. *Zhu*, a title of respect, of mastery. This wasn't a first-level initiate, but someone of true authority within the Sentinels. The search against their Society intel came up with a match. The decision to scout ahead and defer attack had paid off, and then some. Ressa Kaya Frey! The daughter of the *Dìsān Gāo* of the Enlightened Sentinels herself. It was no longer a question of whether the Sentinel would challenge her. Now Mala needed to determine the best way to draw her out and engage her directly in combat. Claiming the Ketheritt System for the Order might have been the primary mission, as well as seizing whatever Transcendent technology might still be functioning on the planet. But the chance to kill a Sentinel-*Zhu*, the only child of the Third High Master—the blow to the morale of the Society Worlds would be devastating. An opportunity like this could not be allowed to pass.

"Lady Mala," one of the blanks addressed her, using her honorific instead of her military title. She did a quick recall on the platoon idents in her mission profile. *Privita* Aden Secondbrother. A common surname among the municipally issued, not a number like someone printed and flooded to fill a civic goal, but one slotted for a military rank.

"*Privita?*" she responded.

"Do we have the authority to engage Guardian forces at the encampment? I am fully rated in close quarters marksmanship, and *Privita* Fourthdaughter," he gestured to his companion to his right, "just received her marks in scrambleware offense . . ."

"Belay that," she answered curtly. "Observe and report is our primary objective. Leave the Guardians to the remotes once we've ascertained their numbers. Engage only if identified."

"*Plenumo*," said Secondbrother. *Compliance.* A common salutation among blanks in the Order.

"Will you require assistance, Lady Mala?" asked *Privita* Fourthdaughter. "With the Sentinel?"

Require assistance? Mala Roi would have laughed out loud if such a response had been appropriate in the middle of an operation. "You have no experience against a Sentinel, *Privitas.* You can do nothing."

To call a Sentinel dangerous was an understatement. They didn't think of themselves as warriors, but they had perfected their own unique fighting style and combat conditioning, minimizing reliance on technology and external tools. Human history among the stars was proof enough that technology could fail and knowledge could be lost.

She also knew the fables about Sentinels that abounded in the outer Diaspora: tales of witches and mindreaders who could pull the deepest secrets from a subject's memories. These were just stories, but Mala knew that the Sentinels were trained to observe the minutest details of a person: patterns in their voice, how they stood, the motions of their eyes. They were even trained to be sensitive to the state of a person's biochemistry, able to gather information from sweat, breathing and even a subject's bioelectric field.

Any blank or *civita* of the Order could be flooded with combat sims, then suited in a battleshell and sent off to war. From what Mala could tell, the Society regarded war differently. The Sentinels saw themselves as peacekeepers and spiritual guides first, upholding the codes and norms of the Society and directly engaging with its citizenry. They were both celebrated as public figures and whispered of as objects of mystery, and like the Guardian Legions, they served to fight in wartime and engaged in lawspeaking and public service in peacetime. But the Society Worlds had known nothing but peacetime for the last three hundred e-years.

Body. Mind. Voice. Soul. Heart. Flow. The Path of the Enlightened Sentinel, for life and for combat. But in none of those mantras did they ever say the word "kill". That, more than Neshat's overconfidence, was why Mala was certain of the Order's inevitable victory. The Jagger Corps and the Grand Armada did not exist to perform public services. Every Leash-bound *civita* was expected to fill that role. Her purpose was to fight and to kill for the Order. The Society Worlds, for all their technical prowess and recovery of old lost knowledge, couldn't adjust their thinking to that reality, no matter how adaptive they claimed to be. To them, killing was a tragedy. To Mala and the Jaggers like her, it was not only a brutal necessity, but sometimes it could be righteous. Even beautiful.

And that was why the Society Worlds would lose.

Mala Roi moved silently, her armor an extension of her mind and will. She locked onto the signal source, using hand gestures to silently command her escorts to fan out and maintain an equivalent silence. The gray roots and vegetation grew denser around them, taller, covering them with a canopy overhead. Purple flora sprouted among the twisting roots, competing with other, more alien plant life. Green shoots and grasses, products of the Society ecoforming, predominated the deeper they went into the forest. All part of their long-term plans to reclaim the planet, Mala observed, to replace the malignant, locally evolved ecosystems with ones more human friendly, to rehabilitate Ketheritt as a locale for permanent human settlement.

Rehabilitate. That was a word the Society liked to use. They didn't punish, they rehabilitated. They didn't impose order, they encouraged healthier outcomes. To her, the Society was no different from the Harmonious Order in trying to impose a vision on the Diaspora for what the human species should ultimately become. The Order was just more honest in what they saw as the means to make it happen.

They took several steps farther before Mala raised her hand and motioned the party to stop. The forest had become thicker around them, denser knots of green and purple vines and roots. She switched to grouplink to signal her blank escorts.

"Stay alert," she subvocalized. "We're on the perimeter." It was an observation as well as a warning. They were entering the outer

Green Zone of the Society colony. With Society military tech, it was difficult to tell the difference between machine and biology. Insects could be target drones, vines could be active tripwires. Guardian Legionnaires could be camo-cloaked and waiting.

Then she saw through the roots the bright lights and more distinguishable sounds of ships and human speech. Ketheritt Station. Bulbous pods, some organic looking, others clearly synthetic, sprouted in a circular formation among the tree-like forest growths. At the heart of the colony was a large clearing, where a squat, spheroid dropship sat on four broad landing legs. Messenger-Class, one of the largest used by the Society Guard Fleet. Crowds were gathered around the craft, teams of scientists and colonists carrying gear and belongings, queuing up as directed by several individuals wearing pearl-gray combat Skins and helmets.

Guardians, thought Mala Roi.

Around each suited individual was a flock of what looked like small birds, and some of the Guardians were accompanied by short, squat quadrupeds. Flocks and Rovers. Living bioweapons. She knew the Guardian approach to offensive weaponry. Side-arms and rifles were long considered an outdated technology, consigned to backwater worlds out on the fringes. Better to have your weapons an extension of your own mind and body, so the current thinking went. A Guardian Legionnaire could command up to a dozen Flock drones or a Rover with just a thought, while their Skins absorbed and deflected any combat damage.

She registered at least twenty Guardians, with an unknown number still aboard the ship. A full platoon. There were the ship defenses she'd have to consider. There'd also be flight crew, engineers, almost certainly mission specialists and science advisors to work with the colony recovery teams. Any Transcendent artifacts found so far would already be packed and prepared, ready to be loaded once the civilians were safe. Hence the importance of the timing of the attack. And then . . .

Mala spotted the woman talking to one of the Guardians briefly before she silently oversaw the onboarding of the civilians. The Sentinel. Ressa Kaya Frey herself. Her target. Her kill for the day.

She didn't have the gray padded combat Skins of the Guardians. The woman looked almost naked from a distance, her own Skin formfitting and blending in seamlessly against her deep tan complexion. It was only after a few seconds that the skinsuit rippled in response to her movement, and took on patterns of gray, green and purple to mirror her background. Unlike the Guardians, the woman had no apparent Flocks or a Rover. She didn't even appear to have foot coverings, nor did she wear a helmet like the Guardians. Both her head and feet were bare, her hair cropped short. Mala Roi magnified her eyesights and identified the glint of a knife strapped to the woman's thigh. A fiberknife, the traditional weapon of the Sentinels, other than their own minds and bodies.

How similar it looked to her old blade, she remembered, struggling not to drift back to the Battle Pits of years past.

She would have to create a distraction, lure Sentinel Frey away from the Guardians and any support she'd get from the evac ship. *But what more perfect distraction could there be*, she thought with a satisfied smile. They had their intel, knew the numbers of the enemy on the planet, where their target was. The goals of their reconnaissance were achieved. It was time for the next phase.

"Prepare to signal the *Determinado* on my mark," she commanded Secondbrother. "Send target coordinates. You'll act as spotter. Strike launch is Go."

"*Jaggero*," Secondbrother acknowledged. "Our orders to engage?"

"Maintain this position, *Privita*," she continued. "Both of you. *Leftat* Neshat will assign further instructions once engaged."

"M'lady?" said Fourthdaughter.

"I'm taking out the Sentinel," she said. "Signal now."

It took less than a second for the targeting signal to go out, followed by multiple flashes of light as plasma remotes engaged the strike zone. The blank platoons were already deployed along the forest perimeter and would be following up the *Determinado's* artillery launches with their individual weapon strikes. Branches and leafy canopies erupted in flashes of fire surrounding the ship, and the civilians let out cries of panic, ready to break their loading formations to find safety. The ship's shields rippled to life, absorbing most of the plasma bursts. Their scattering was the distraction Mala needed. She bolted from her position, her exoarmor augmenting her leg muscles. It propelled her forward, eyes targeted on Frey.

She could feel her brain coming alive, her Leash priming her for battle, elevating her oxytocin and vasopressin levels, dampening her fear and narrowing her focus. Focus, focus . . .

"Focus," came a female voice, impossibly boosted over the echoes of the plasma bombardment. "Board quickly. Ignore everything around you. We will protect you. That is our bond."

Sentinel Frey, Mala realized. Projecting the All-Voice, encouraging calm to the civilians as well as her Guardians, none of whom were prepared to fight a war, but were committed by duty to protect their charges. The civilians were not Mala's concern. The ship only mattered to the degree to which it could support or augment the Guardian forces. Seizing the planet was what mattered to the Order. But for Mala, the only goal that mattered now was killing the Sentinel.

Tuning out the flames and screams around her, she closed the gap between herself and her target. Her wrist sheaths engaged—the monoblades extended outward from her right arm, the plasma burner from her left. The Guardians were focused on the civilians, so none of them were registering her. Their focus was on the sky, not the ground. And that was exactly what she needed.

Then Frey's attention immediately jolted away from the firefight and turned toward Mala. The woman moved impossibly fast, leaping just beyond Mala's reach and the aim of her burner. Mala was able to get a good look at her now. Indeed, she was barefoot, with those elongated toes the Arisi had engineered for themselves for easier freefall maneuvering, her tight-clinging combat Skin now shifting to a dark green. Her knife was out, but to Mala, it seemed a ridiculous weapon to use against an armored opponent equipped with a plasma burner. The advantage in range was hers.

Something leaped out at her, just in time for her periphery scanners to alert her. One of the Rovers had locked onto her. It was a mass of fur and four spindly legs, with a set of powerful jaws and a shell-like harness that wove about its upper body to a hard cover over its eyeless head. The harness had its own burners and the Rover lit them up as it leapt at Mala. She registered the sweltering heat as the plasma engulfed her, but her bodyshield engaged and protected her, giving her time to leap free. The burner blasts confused the Rover's visual and IR receptors, giving her a second to react. Her wristblade extended to its full arm's length and she slashed outward, close enough to slice through the Rover's skull and jaws. The bioconstruct's body twitched and fell to the ground.

The air buzzed around her as several of the Guardians became aware that a Jagger had attacked their camp. Swarms of Flock drones were now targeting her, but her scramblers were up, befuddling the Flock long enough for her to refocus on Sentinel Frey. Only Frey had leapt back, climbing up one of the knotted trunks, and then dispatching a cloud of tree spores from one of the branches in Mala's direction. Her targeting sensors were momentarily scrambled, confusing the spores for another Flock attack, and she struggled to reacquire her target. Lacking precision, she aimed her burner in the direction of the branch. There was a bright flash and a thunderclap as splinters of fibers and vegetation burst outward. Mala could see Frey had already jumped clear of the blast.

At this point, the Armada *soldatoi* were encroaching upon the colony site, their burners lit, keeping the other Guardians fully engaged. Mala heard Neshat's orders over the sharelink frequency, and identified *Privitas* Secondbrother's and Fourthdaughter's pings. The battle was engaged while the Guardians urgently covered the civilians' rush to safety. Weapons fire and Flock drones dispatched from the Guardian dropship joined the battle, along with additional support teams emerging from the ship, nearly doubling their initial count of enemy forces to two phalanxes.

That is the Armada's responsibility, thought Mala, trusting her people to carry out their assignment. Her focus went back toward locating the Sentinel.

She heard a squawk over her sharelink, interrupting her thoughts. The ping didn't register with any idents in the Armada platoons.

"Jagger," came the voice of Ressa Kaya Frey, her tone almost taunting her. It was in untranslated, unaccented Nu Esperese. "Come and get your prey. Assuming you're the hunter you think you are."

Trying to goad her, bait her into making a mistake. She wouldn't let her emotions get the better of her. The Sentinel had to know that. It was the Society Worlds who encouraged that kind of weakness and disharmony. She had focus. She had clarity. She had the benefit of the Leash. It gave her Order.

With that, she reacquired her target's location and set off in pursuit.

Where are you, bitch? thought Mala Roi as she scanned for her quarry. The feeds from the firefight faded into the background, the flashes of distant plasma fire growing dimmer as the forest cover grew denser. She switched her eyesights to an all-spectrum scan, but couldn't detect a heat trace anywhere at ground level.

She remembered the long hours of training sims, her and Parran Dex, preparing her for potential encounters with a Sentinel. They did things with their bodies—without the aid of implants or bioware—that made them subjects of legend and wonder throughout the Diaspora. But they were still just mortal beings, human like anyone else. They could be killed.

Her thoughts quickly strayed to Parran, off with the First Armada at Ingressa. Parran was a powerful warrior, the most skilled of all the Jagger Corps. For all the brutality and violence she had known on the streets of Tannapor and the Battle Pits, she could never be the natural that Parran was. He could stand so silently for long, interminable moments, just waiting for an opponent to strike—then suddenly erupt in a fury of energy within seconds, only to then coil the chaos back and return to a calm repose. It was fascinating and frightening to watch. And so achingly beautiful. Just like him.

"You have to move faster," he would admonish her every so often. "Don't be so flamboyant with your maneuvers. You're not in the Pits anymore."

"And what of it?" she would say back.

"This is combat," he reminded her. "It's not about looking pretty or putting on a show for the crowds. Your job is to kill and do it quickly. There's no audience to watch, no bosses to rate you or send you back to fighting the dogs. It's just you and your enemy. It's brutal and ugly and it has to be done quick. The longer the fight goes on, the more you tire and the better the chance your opponent has to overpower you. And believe me, the enemy is thinking the exact same thing!"

She would look at him crossly. "Is that what you thought the Pits were? Just playacting? I had over a hundred kills before I got out."

"I know . . ."

"And I remember every one! Every move, every weakness, every time they almost got the better of me . . ."

"I said I know."

"Good. You know I want to be the best, but don't ever think that where I was before I came here was just silly games and nonsense. It was fight or die, even if it wasn't a war."

"Fine," he would say. "As long as you accept that war is something entirely different. Death might be the same, but how you kill isn't. So stop being so damn proud, *Jaggero*, and take the training. You're being intentionally inharmonious." The way he said it. Inharmonious. Like it was a joke, their own private joke.

"Besides," she said to him, moving closer, into his personal space, "you never complained about my technique in the past." Her hand went to his hip, slowly feeling the muscles in his thigh. Parran was a native Arisi, and had even had some Sentinel training, though he hadn't completed the Path. He knew the culture of the Society, their way of thinking, better than anyone in the Armada. That was what made him such a perfect weapon against them, and a valuable resource to train others. Like most Arisi, he was naturally tall and sinewy, though his time on Brightholm had given him added muscle and bulk to match his height. He was like an ancient marble statue from Old Earth, the kind of art they used to depict gods, long before humans had become gods themselves.

"Not here," he said.

"Why?" she replied. "They don't watch us. They trust the Leash."

"But they review the feeds after training," he said, "to monitor our progress. We can't let any emotional spikes stand out." He then looked at her with tenderness, gently stroking her cheek. "Later. They're still getting used to you, learning to trust you. It'll be easier in time. You only just got implanted a month ago."

"And after you tweak . . ."

"Don't," he said sharply, the tenderness gone. And she held her tongue. She remembered that there were some things she wasn't supposed to speak about out loud ever again. It would ruin them both if it were ever revealed.

"I'll be careful," she said.

His tone was gentler again, revealing the man she knew he had to keep hidden. "After meal break, we can request sauna time. It'll be safe then."

"Yes," she said softly. "Until then." It would feel like an eternity, waiting for his touch. It would never be safe, but it would be better. That was enough to sustain her.

She steadied herself, knowing the risk she was taking letting her mind go to such inharmonious places. She could feel the Leash slowly refocus her mind on the task at hand, and she was grateful for its guidance and certainty. Just as she was grateful for the subtle differences with her Leash and those of her fellow Jaggers, giving them the relative autonomy that *civitas* of the Order could never have. She could be subtly nudged to focus on essential tasks and duties to the Order and the Corps, the Leash reinforcing loyalty and a sense of duty and belonging. But she and the other Jaggers could still maintain the independence of thought necessary to conduct their tasks beyond the real-time direction of the MasterMind and the Protocols.

It wasn't freedom. She wouldn't use that word. She couldn't even consider it. She was just . . . independent. A part of the reality of being a Jagger. Of the Order, but never truly one with it, not like those born to it.

It was what bonded them together, their status as outsiders, their familiarity with the ways of war and violence. The attraction they had felt, her and Parran, was only natural, despite the rules and the Protocols that forbade intimate relationships between Corps members, especially between a *majoro* and one of his *kamarados*.

The Leash urged her attention forward, onto her more immediate responsibilities. She panned her eyes up toward the treetops, hoping to find something . . .

Something found her. Something fast and twirling in a circular motion as it was lobbed rapidly from one of the upper branches, right toward her head. Mala's sensor suit pinged an alert and she dodged quickly out of the oncoming path of the . . .

Tree branch! The Sentinel had managed to carve a weapon for herself, a projectile to hurl in Mala's direction. A simple plank of wood wouldn't have been enough to incapacitate her, she thought, not even thrown at great speed. Her armor would easily protect her. The Sentinel had to know that.

Unless the goal was not to injure her directly, but to force her to jump out of its way. Exactly to the place and moment where . . . Mala felt the air moving behind her, the shifting pattern of the skinsuit blending against the tree trunks, along with the quick glimmer of the knife. Her armor went rigid where the knife thrust beneath her ribcage. She winced at the impact, but felt her armor adapt to absorb the blow. She wasn't cut, not from this angle. But had it come down more forcefully, with greater speed, the rigid molecular edge of the blade would have successfully sliced through her protection before it could configure properly. She twisted around to throw the Sentinel off her balance before she could deliver a more direct cut.

Up close, Mala could now see the Sentinel clearly. Frey's close-shorn brown hair blended well with her light brown complexion, her bright blue eyes providing a flash of unexpected color against an otherwise drab and muted environment. Tall and elongated, she seemed almost slight, but Mala knew looks could conceal strength. In addition to the skinsuit, now rippling to match its wearer's movements along the tree trunks, Frey was adorned with a pair of shell-like protrusions that curved around both her ears. Earwigs of some sort, Mala assumed, maybe with neural interface tech to help direct the skinsuit and communicate with others. Not quite as low tech as she'd been left to believe. What also provided relief against Frey's tanned face was her bright smile. An actual smile.

"Nothing personal," Frey said to her. "You did come here to kill me, after all."

While still twisting to escape her grasp, Mala responded with an exo-boosted blow to Frey's torso, knocking her back and allowing Mala to jump to a safe distance and aim her burner. But Frey was too quick, her skinsuit absorbing the punch and her impact against the tree behind her. She was able to jump clear before Mala's burner ignited and engulfed the trunk in plasma flames.

"Good recovery. But you'll have to be quicker than that," said Frey, coming in over Mala's link. She tried to isolate the signal, to get a fix on her new position. But the Sentinel had used the flames as cover to jump and hide. Mala resisted the temptation to respond. Getting into a conversation with a Sentinel was a dangerous move. Their training included sound modulation and subliminal imprinting to subtly manipulate opponents with their voices alone. She had to assume any communication would not only be a taunt, but a means to subdue her.

"You're a Jagger." Mala heard Frey's voice. "You're not one of them. Everyone else on Brightholm and the Sister Worlds were born not knowing any better. But you chose this life. You chose the Leash. How horrible was your life before this, to make you actually want to give your mind and soul away?"

Mala wanted so badly to shout back at her, to tell her what she could do with her precious mind and soul. She didn't know her or her life, or anything about the choices that brought her to the Harmonious Order. She scanned around her, waiting, watching for the next attack. What was Frey leading her into? Another ambush?

She kept moving forward, the flashes of light and rumbles from the colony battle now completely obscured. It was just her, the dim twilight of the orange sun and gray clouds overhead, and the dark twisted forest with its gray and purple growths. The sprouts of green had long been left behind. Just her and what was left of nature on Ketheritt. That and the Sentinel.

Looking up again at the canopy, she noticed the rustling. There were no birds on Ketheritt, or any surviving arboreal life. The only large mammal moving among the forest canopy had to be Frey.

She was tempted to aim her burner again and take her down from the ground. But if Frey was camouflaged and emissions-cloaked, she'd have a hard time getting a perfect lock on her. Frey might use the blast as an opportunity to attack while Mala was blinded. She smiled as she accessed her topological map of the area, formulating a plan. If she could keep pushing Frey along in the current southern direction, the canopy would start thinning out before it hit a nearby riverbank. Frey would have no choice but to come down from the trees if she wanted to get by her. And that's when Mala would be ready.

Mala Roi wandered on for several moments more, observing

the lower density of trees and roots, the thinner cover of the canopy overhead. She avoided looking upward, not wanting to reveal to Frey that she knew she was being observed. Mala smiled. The Sentinel probably believed she was leading her into an ambush, but it was the other way around.

She continued following along the remnants of several root clusters, until she could see the river up ahead. Her audio sensors were tuned to subsonic frequencies, able to hear the subtle movements from the sparse treetops overhead. Frey was running out of canopy to hide among, which made Mala certain that the Sentinel's attention from up high was focused on her movements down below. Very gently, she flexed her left wrist, and her armor gauntlet loaded new ammo into her burner. Now, instead of flammable plasma gel, she was armed with high-yield *batalilo* explosive penetrating rounds.

She stood a good distance from the riverbank, still not looking up, waiting until the rustling overhead grew still. Waiting several seconds, she flexed her left wrist again, ensuring the explosive rounds were primed. She counted to five, and then sprang into action.

She didn't aim her left arm upward, but targeted the heart of the tree trunk. Four *batalilo* rounds bored into the tree at high velocity, and half a second later, the base of the tree trunk shattered in a bright flash of light and heat. Mala was prepared and her body shield flickered on, absorbing the impact of flame and shards of wood. She had aimed at just the right point to bring the tree down, her audio sensors locking in on Frey swearing in Changlese as she desperately tried to leap to safety as the tree collapsed beneath her. The upper trunk and branches fell before

Mala, as she watched Frey trying to jump to the weaker branches of the smaller trees surrounding her. But the Sentinel was moving on instinct, and was unable to find a branch that could support her weight. One branch after another snapped as she leaped lower and lower, trying to find a safe spot. But it slowed her down, giving Mala time to load another *batalilo* charge. Frey was still too quick to take a direct hit, but her arboreal coverage was limited. Mala was forcing her to the ground, with the river at her back, leaving her no place to run.

Frey fell as predicted, stumbling to her knees. Mala quickly loaded a standard burner gel round and fired again, but even stunned after the explosions, Frey hadn't lost any of her agility or speed. But she definitely seemed less certain of herself now.

"That was . . . clever," said Frey, in her own voice, not over the link. "You're more dangerous than I thought. I'll remember that."

Mala booted up her audio filters, just to be safe from any subliminal manipulation. She couldn't resist the opportunity for a retort. "You won't have long to remember." And she aimed her burner again.

Once again Frey seemed ready. She rolled clear of the blast, then lifted herself up in an impossibly high jump while Mala attempted to reacquire her target. Frey came down feet first, her fiberknife unsheathed and slashing outward. The blade skated harmlessly across Mala's helmet visor, but the close contact knocked her backward. Losing her balance, she almost fell down but managed to recover, just in time for Frey to land in front of her and sweep her right leg outward, knocking Mala Roi off her unsteady feet to land on her side.

The Sentinel moved in quickly, trying to go for the display

panel on Mala's left gauntlet, but landing on her left side gave her the chance to roll over with her right arm extended. Her wrist blade deployed, Mala slashed outward, scraping Frey's skinsuit, which had now shifted to a dusky orange to match the tinged sky. The suit reacted to the blade attack, and Frey had to step back to avoid the full impact of the slashing. That gave Mala Roi the time to jump to her feet and re-arm her burner.

Then a bright flash of light appeared overhead. Mala knew it couldn't have been anything deployed by Ressa Kaya Frey. Was it a plasma burst? Was Frey being reinforced by the Guardian Legions?

Mala focused on the light and the trail of vapor in its wake. Not a plasma bombardment, but a launch. The Society dropship was breaking for orbit. It was then she realized she'd taken her eyes off Frey for a half second longer than she should have.

The Sentinel twisted herself in a mid-air leap, coming at Mala, and wrapped her arms around her helmet. Mala struggled in her grip, trying to pry her off, then tried booting up her shields. But the body shield wouldn't initialize with such a large obstruction in the way. Mala desperately clawed at Frey, wrestling with her to pull her off.

Then she heard a pop and the hiss of air pressure changing. A wave of humidity hit her face. Frey had managed to detach her helmet, exposing her to the outside atmosphere and pressure. Warning pings went off as the armor alerted her to the breach and her breathing tube tore free from her nostrils. She gasped as she finally knocked Frey clear, but her helmet was already dislodged, her long black hair unfurling in the planet's gentle winds. She stumbled back and took stock of the situation. The oxygen levels on Ketheritt were lower than optimal, and she'd find herself exhausted after long physical combat. Frey must have respirocytes in her bloodstream to allow her to fight unhindered without the use of a breather. Mala didn't have her helmet's heads-up display, but she still had her brainware to issue commands. She instructed the armor to give her a resp-ox injection, boosting her oxygen levels to give her more energy to fight in the depleted atmosphere. She aimed her burner once again at Frey, waiting for a clear target lock.

She heard the buzzing in her ear, her grouplink detecting the armor breach. "*Jaggero*," said Breeshall in her head. "What is your status? Your armor . . ."

"Functional," she answered sharply, her eyes on Frey, who was standing warily, ready to leap again. "Situation, *Oficira*?"

"We've secured the colony site, *Jaggero*. Minimal casualties on our side, still ascertaining numbers. We've also secured the artifacts. The Society dropship managed a takeoff in the middle of the fighting. And . . . there's a Society jumpship in orbit waiting for dock. They're scrambling our targeting systems . . ."

"Belay targeting," instructed Mala. "Deploy the shield wall and ready the artifacts for transport. Inform the Armada to make maximum burn for Ketheritt orbit."

"Yes, *Jaggero*."

"And dispatch a squad to my location to assist. *Rapida!*"

"Yes, *Jaggero*." Mala didn't let her attention stray from her intended target, not this time.

"It's done," said Frey, tossing the helmet aside, as soon as the connection was cut. "I had to draw you away, keep you focused on me. At least the civilians are safe now. They're probably docking as we speak."

"One of our carriers is en route," said Mala. "They'll intercept your jumpship once it breaks orbit."

"It won't happen," said Frey. "Your Armada carriers are pulling too much mass. The *Tero* is a Corsair-Class, stripped down for maximum burn. She'll be at the secondary jumpknot by the time your ships are in-system."

Mala tried not to let her words get to her. "Ketheritt is ours. We've secured the primary jumpknot and we'll have the secondary knot locked down within hours. And we forced your people to abandon their artifacts. Their escape means nothing."

"I think it means more than you'll admit," said Frey. "The Order's far behind us in Transcendent studies. Your masters are a bit lacking when it comes to creative problem solving. It's what happens when your brains are wired for slavery." Frey's face grew more serious as she spoke. "You forced this on us. We may not have wanted this war, but we intend to fight. We don't have a choice. We know what's at stake. It's horrible enough what your Harmonious Order does to its own people. But we won't let you destroy what makes us all human, not the Society Worlds or our allies. Someone has to say no to you people at some point."

Mala looked at her through narrowed eyes, her burner aimed and primed. "I planned to kill you here today. Strike a blow against the Sentinels. But maybe you'd be more valuable to the Harmonious Order as a prisoner of war. And I'm guessing you have a ship of your own hidden out here somewhere. I wonder how much we can learn from that, never mind you."

Frey's face grew paler in response, and she shuffled her feet. Mala approached closer, but Frey moved too quickly, swiping her leg and kicking up a wave of sand and soil, splattering Mala in the face. And without her helmet to shield her, she had nothing to protect her eyes. With Mala temporarily blinded and firing her burner wildly, Frey used the distraction to make another fast roll, this time aimed directly at her attacker. Her hands came in contact with Mala's face.

Mala could feel some kind of instant connection, a transfer of energy of sorts. She couldn't be sure. *Was that Frey's purpose in dislodging my helmet?* she wondered. Was she trying to make direct contact to gather information on her opponent? If that was the case, she had to make sure Frey made no further efforts to make physical contact with her before her people arrived. It wasn't just her voice she had to fear.

But surprisingly, Frey didn't seem like she had gained the upper hand at all. She'd landed gracefully on her feet, yet she seemed hesitant, even unnerved. If something had thrown her off balance, then Mala Roi had to take advantage of this moment quickly.

She deployed her wristblades again, extending them to their full length. She lunged at her quarry, and Frey jumped aside to avoid being slashed. That gave Mala the chance to jump at her with her leg extended, hitting her in the sternum. The skinsuit hardened on contact, but the momentum of the blow knocked Frey back. She landed on her side, rolled, then leapt to her feet, striking back with a kick of her own to Mala's legs, knocking her to her knees.

"That's enough," said Frey. "Your people are coming soon. Do you yield?"

Mala couldn't believe what she was hearing. "Yield!? Are you stupid?" If this was the Society Worlds' notion of combat, then even the skills of the Sentinels wouldn't be enough to save them. This wasn't a contest. It was war!

Mala was feeling the drain of the low oxygen, even with the resp-ox and the rush of adrenaline. She commanded the armor's exo-supports to boost her legs, letting her jump to her feet. She soared over Frey's head, landed behind her, then swung her left arm to swat her in the spine. The Skin would protect Frey, but the blow would send her sprawling.

Frey was more resilient than Mala expected. The impact made her tumble, but she was able to roll, kick more dirt in Mala's face, then flung the discarded helmet just past her head, which she dodged easily. Frey charged toward her, the skinsuit hardening on impact with the armor as she tackled Mala to the ground.

"Enough! Stay down! Please!"

Mala kept her mental focus, certain that Frey was now trying to use vocal commands to undermine her resolve. But she wouldn't let it work on her. Her Leash was flooding her with adrenaline and a host of neurotransmitters to push her forward. She was determined, committed, driven. It was how she'd survived the streets of Tannapor, the tournaments in the Battle Pits, her desperate escape and defection, and her training and fighting with the Jagger Corps. In each case, her life had been literally on the line. Just as it was here. And she hadn't faltered before. She wouldn't now.

"Never," she said. She rolled over, flipping Frey into the air, then flinging her to the ground. Mala figured at some point the limit of the Skin's ability to absorb kinetic energy would be reached. And that's when she could inflict real damage to Ressa Kaya Frey.

But that moment hadn't been reached yet. Frey and Mala both got to their feet, and Frey pulled out her fiberknife. But she seemed too uncertain, too hesitant. Not just from the physical abuse she'd been taking, but from something inside, like the fight had somehow gone out of her.

"Please. Just stop," said Frey. "I'll keep fighting if I have to. I won't let the Order put a Leash on me. But please . . ." she said, breathing heavily, raggedly, *"Don't make me kill your baby!"*

Mala Roi stopped in her tracks and let the words, the shock of the truth, sink in. Baby? Her baby? Hers and Parran's?

That moment of confusion was what Frey needed. She dived to the ground, rolled between Mala's armored legs, and leapt on her back. She used her blade to wedge open an access port on the armor's backplate. As Frey jammed the knife in and twisted it about, Mala felt the exo-supports in her armored limbs spasm and then seize up. One by one, systems just shut down. The burner and ammo loaders, communications, sensors, everything was frozen. Even the wrist blades wouldn't respond to mental commands. Frey toppled her over, trapping Mala in her own armor, and her head hit the ground . . .

The blackness faded but the ache in her head still lingered. Mala was still trapped in her armor, unable to get up, move her arms, or even call for assistance.

"You're fine," said Ressa Kaya Frey. Mala's vision cleared and she saw the Sentinel standing over her. She wasn't smiling about having defeated her. She seemed, in fact, genuinely concerned.

Mala wanted to reach up and strangle her.

"You were only out for about a minute. You're fine. So is your baby."

Mala glared at her, saying nothing.

"I'm not voxxing you, *Jaggero*. This is truespeech, the honest truth. I swear on the Scholars and on the life of my father. You really are pregnant. I didn't make that up so I could defeat you."

Mala didn't know if she could believe her or not. She didn't know what felt worse, being beaten on the field of battle because of a trick, or being defeated by the truth of her own indiscretion.

"*Jaggero Secundo* Mala Roi," said Frey, shaking her head. "I had to know if it was true."

Mala finally spoke. "Know what was true? And how do you know my name?"

Frey smiled, now seeming to be amused once again. "It's stenciled on the inside of your helmet. And I had to know . . . did you really tamper with your own Leash?"

Mala went pale. She knew the truth, of course, but to hear it spoken aloud, by the enemy no less . . .

"I mean," Frey went on, "that just doesn't happen in the Harmonious Order. Certainly not among the *civitas*. And even among Jaggers, I didn't think it was possible. I suppose you had to, disabling the emotional monitoring and suppression routines was the only way you and . . . the baby's father . . . could carry on your relationship in secret. I guess you didn't figure that would throw off the other hormone regulators. But Saints and Scholars," she said, shaking her head, "do you *know* what they'll do to you if they find out?"

"Shut up," Mala hissed at her.

"I know what happens inside the Order, the rules they have regarding sanctioned reproduction, births determined according to needs and quotas . . ."

"Shut up, I said." Mala's voice grew louder.

"And those rules are especially stringent with foreigners. I'm sure there's all sorts of protocols in place regarding what you can or can't do in the Jagger Corps or the Grand Armada . . ."

"I said shut up!" Mala shouted, like she wanted to tear the world apart.

Frey paused, looked at her, and sighed. "I wasn't making light. And if I could take you prisoner, I would. We can help you; take all the hardware out that the Order put in. But I'd never make it to my ship while carrying you at the same time. Your people would be right behind me. And I won't risk being captured, not even to help you. I'm sorry, but I meant what I said. I'd rather die than let them put a Leash on me."

"I never asked you to help me," said Mala.

"I know," said Frey, then she kneeled down to talk to Mala, almost eye to eye. "You know what will happen, even if you're not punished, even if they let this pregnancy happen. They'll take your baby away right after it's born, raise it in a crèche, and after a few months, they'll implant its first Leash. Your child will grow up never having an independent thought or an unplanned emotion, or any kind of choice or decision."

Mala sat in her immobile armor, saying nothing.

"You hacked your own Leash, so the Harmonious Order and its Protocols can't be that sacred to you. Why do you fight in their name? Why do you even stay?" Frey looked at her more seriously. "Is it because of the baby's father? Are you there for him?"

Mala turned, as best she could in her immobile armor, and snapped at her, "I'm there because I have nowhere else to go! I'm a killer. I'm a very good killer. And that makes me valuable to the Harmonious Order. And you want to know something, Sentinel? I've known nothing but pain for a very long time. The Order may be exactly what you say it is, but everything works, and things get done. Brightholm is a paradise, and that's coming from someone who grew up in a cesspool. All I ask for is to keep one thing that's made me happy, one thing that's mine and mine alone."

Frey sighed again. "You realize that one thing is too much to ask for, as far as the Order is concerned. And are you even sure that's how you really feel about the Order, or is that just your Leash talking, what little of it you still have?"

Mala slumped her shoulders, saying nothing.

"Your accent," said Frey. "You're from Jiballa, aren't you?"

Mala looked up, nodding silently.

Frey shook her head, like she pitied her. "I can see why you'd see the Order as a step up." She stood up and dusted herself off. "They're coming. I have to go. I wish I could do more." She looked down at Mala, her eyes so bright. "I realize I don't know you, and officially we're enemies at war now. But I have to ask you, is this really what you want? This life?"

Mala cast her eyes downward. Frey's pity was almost too much to bear. "It's better than what I had before."

Frey nodded. "I think I understand. Promise yourself something, Mala Roi, if you can. The first chance you get, if you can find a way to escape the Order, take it. I know you'll be fighting your instincts on this, fighting your Leash, but if you can make it to the Society Worlds, we have the means to remove whatever tech they put into you. You can use my name if you need to. I can't promise we're a paradise, but there's freedom, whatever that's worth to you."

The Sentinel turned to leave, ready to run off into the distance, but Mala called out to her first. "Wait!"

Frey looked back.

"Why are you doing this? Why do you care about an enemy soldier? It can't just be about my . . . my baby." She could barely get the words out.

Frey turned to her, looking sadder than before. Mala knew that Ressa Kaya Frey was roughly the same age as her, even a bit younger. Yet she seemed so much older now, more worn down.

"You and I both know what's started here on Ketheritt, and where this is going. The only way for the Harmonious Order to survive is to grow. Your MasterMind would have every world in the Diaspora under the Leash if it could. That's not something my people can allow to happen. So we have to fight. The Path of the Enlightened Sentinel has always been the way of knowledge and peace. It's the tradition my father taught me, and his mother before him. And now we have to take centuries of training and devotion and apply that to the art of war. You called yourself a very good killer, Mala. That's what my comrades and I have to become to win this war. We have to become like you."

She paused. "This battle will be the beginning of something very long and very ugly. So if I survive this war or not, I want to know, while I'm still on the true Path of the Sentinel, that I did at least one very decent thing."

As Frey turned to go, Mala spoke one more time. "Soolein. My name was Soolein. Before." She caught her breath. "I don't know why I just told you that."

Frey's countenance lightened up, and she smiled again. "You made a choice, Soolein. The first of many good ones, I hope. Let the Saints and the Scholars guide your way." With a nod, her skinsuit shifted to match the background, and she headed off along the riverbank and disappeared into the bush.

It wasn't much later that the platoon found Mala Roi and rebooted her armor to get her back to base camp. More carriers arrived in orbit and dropships landed on the surface, all to help take official possession of Ketheritt in the name of The Harmonious Order of the Mind. It was just after the first carrier, the *Ekliptiko*, pulled into orbit that a surface launch was detected. Despite their best efforts to shoot her down, Frey's ship managed to evade being targeted and slipped past the rest of the Armada to arrive safely at the secondary jumpknot. It was treasonous for her to think so, but Mala was quietly grateful that her opponent had gotten away.

No one said anything to her about her failure to defeat Ressa Kaya Frey. She wasn't disciplined or lectured by the *Ekliptiko's* captain, who had assumed operational command of the new forward base on Ketheritt. She imagined any official reprimand would happen back on Brightholm once her debriefing was complete, possibly from the MasterMind itself. Until then, everyone was strangely polite. Of course, politeness was only strange to someone like Mala Roi, someone not born within the Harmonious Order. There, politeness was always on display.

She noticed how *Leftat* Neshat had not taken advantage of the situation, after he had overseen the platoon occupying the Society colony and prepping the artifacts for transport. On Jiballa, someone like him would have maneuvered for political gain, aggrandizing himself and undermining opponents like Mala Roi. But that wasn't how it was done in the Order. The Leash saw to that. Arrogance and ego were kept in check. Duty and commitment to the greater good of society were elevated. No matter how much bigotry and contempt Mala saw beneath the surface, the Leash managed to make Neshat into a somewhat tolerable, thoroughly undangerous human being.

In contrast, there was Breeshall, who consistently displayed attributes of kindness and empathy. Ever since she'd been assigned to Mala, she had been the closest thing to a friend she'd known since defecting to the Order. Of course, she never used the word "friend." In Nu Esperese, the word *civita* translated as both citizen and friend. In the Order, it was simply assumed that everyone was everyone's friend. To choose only a select few for that label was considered . . . inharmonious. And while Breeshall was a friend of sorts, it was also her responsibility to observe Mala's behavior and report any anomalies, which she was completely honest about.

That's how it was in the Harmonious Order. There was no politicking, no deception or hidden agendas. Everyone was exactly who they appeared to be, and said exactly what they were thinking. The exceptions being herself, and Parran.

And could she really trust any of those charitable emotions she was feeling, she wondered. Was it really just the Leash that made her content with her life, or was it the only thing keeping her from truly going mad?

When she had finished her account of her battle with Sentinel Frey—minus a few moments of conversation between the two, particularly toward the end—Mala was given her orders to report to the carrier *Prudenta* for the journey to Brightholm. She would discover then, she supposed, what the consequences of her failure would be. Thankfully, the Order relied heavily on the Leash and the commitment of its *soldatoi* to ensure reports were honest and accurate. One thing she was grateful for was that Frey's disabling of the armor and the forced reboot had led to a loss of the last few minutes of recorded data. Any mention of the baby, or Frey's proposition of defection, were preserved only in Mala Roi's memory.

With the long trip home via several jumps, Mala had the time to check one important thing. A quick trip to the surgical bay during third shift, when there was only a single medibot on duty, gave Mala the proof she needed. She was indeed pregnant. Nine weeks. How Frey had been able to detect that was nothing short of a biotechnical miracle, but at least she knew for certain that she hadn't been defeated by a lie. It took only a few minutes for her to erase the medibot's memory of the visit and any records of the scan. Compared to hacking her Leash, medical records were easy to manipulate.

Sitting in her small, spartan quarters on the *Prudenta*, Mala did that which she hated doing most of all—reflecting on her life. She'd been happy once, long ago, when she was Soolein, when she was a child and her mother was still with her. But that was a long time ago, with much pain, betrayal and tragedy between then and now. Here, in this moment, she had much to consider. Did she dare tell Parran, assuming she even saw him again before she had to make a decision on her own? Did she want to leave her place in the Harmonious Order, a place that was increasingly likely to become untenable very soon? The choices that seemed so open would soon narrow to a precious few, and she would have to make a decision, perhaps by the time she arrived at Brightholm.

Whatever she decided, she knew one thing. Mala Roi, *Jaggero Secundo* of the Jagger Corps, the girl once known as Soolein, was a survivor.

And her child would be one, too.

Fire Star

Shirley Chan

The genesis of this story was the mega millions jackpot lottery and the usual "what if I won" type of fantasy. It has evolved quite a bit since then, as it's not really money that makes the fantasy, but how you choose to live your life.

"I passed Round 2 and they're about to review my medical!"

Eli did her best to smile. "That's so sunny, Kaylee." Her best friend was so excited she probably didn't notice how Eli's teeth show was forced.

"Jeff said it should just be a formality at this point. The parents think I'm too young, but they can't deny my chance. I'll get to go with him."

Eli nodded and tried again to smile. Unlike hers, Kaylee's eighteenth birthday was within the three months of the launch window which made her eligible. Kaylee had included her in every step of the process, the application, medical, referrals. Eli was genuinely happy for her friend, but it was bittersweet that her name wasn't also on the list.

"You should have hit that submit button. They would have made an exception for you," Kaylee said as she sent over the review board's letter of progress.

Eli shook her head. It was a pro/con internal debate that lasted until the last minutes before submission. She didn't regret her decision, but it had hurt. "It's their rules and their system. And the publicity, my family's not ready for that. Anyway, you'll have Jeff," she said, trying not to be selfish. It was the best case for them. "Jeff will take care of you."

"Ha, you mean I'll take care of him. Heart him to death, but he'd forget to eat if I weren't around." Kaylee paused. "You'll be on the next one, Eli. Jeff and I will be natives by then. We'll be your sponsors. And hey, who knows, maybe we'll be sponsoring two people. Maybe you'll come with someone like oh, say, Chad."

Elinor stuck her tongue out. Kaylee had been teasing her about the new guy just because she had made a passing comment about how tall he was. She appreciated the change in topic, but switching from one unattainable to another wasn't much fun. Before she could say anything in reply, her mother's strident whisper came through the bathroom door.

"Elinor Parker, are you in there?"

"Busted." Kaylee made a face.

Eli sighed. "I gotta go, tell me the rest at the meat meet."

"MM on Friday and we can work on Chad, too. Bye."

Eli rolled her eyes, then logged off. She got up from the edge of the tub, took a deep breath and opened the door.

"You were supposed to be watching your great aunt," her mother Vivian was still whispering as she glanced over to the bed.

"She's asleep," Eli whispered back. "I'm supposed to watch her breathe?"

Charlotte almost laughed out loud, but made an effort to keep her breathing even and steady. Her grand niece definitely skewed toward her side of the family. She was so like her namesake in many ways with her "say it like it is" attitude.

She hadn't really been asleep, just resting her eyes and giving Eli a mid-afternoon break. It was a well-orchestrated piece of fiction these past few weeks, but unfortunately, with Vivian out of work, everyone had too much free time and too little privacy.

She listened to the soft bickering as Eli and her mother walked out of the bedroom and closed the door. The tension had been ratcheting up with it being Eli's last year of high school. The Eli of five years ago had plans, goals and self-imposed milestones. Now, she seemed so aimless, and even graduation seemed more of a chore than an achievement.

And with her friends about to leave, Eli had retreated even more into her shell. It wasn't just teenage angst, it was as if pointlessness was the point. Why bother trying if there was nothing to try for?

Charlotte sighed. Eli was too young to feel this way. Perhaps they could all talk to her again later at dinner when her father came home. And definitely talk to her, not at her, not like Vivian was doing now. Charlotte would rest her eyes and give this a bit more thought.

"You're not supposed to be in the bathroom, spending credits talking to your friend." Vivian tried not to wince at the words coming out of her own mouth. When and how did it come to this? When did she become a nagging mother?

Wait 'til you have kids of your own.

They were in the kitchen and Eli was leaning back against the island, arms crossed with her bored face on. Vivian reached over and gently tugged her daughter's long strawberry blonde hair.

These used to be pigtails.

"Honestly, Eli. Watching over your great aunt while she naps is not hard. You know she hasn't been 100% lately." Eli looked up at that and Vivian saw the worry in her eyes. "Yes, we are all worried about her, so why not spend time with GA when you can?"

"She was resting," Eli mumbled as she looked away and walked around the island to the sitting area. Vivian followed and they both sat down on opposite ends of the red couch.

"Well, if you had extra credits to spend, you should be using it for extra study not for extracurricular. You're seventeen, not seven. You know the value of credits." This time Vivian did wince, though luckily her daughter was turned away and didn't see.

She is only seventeen.

"They're my credits, Mom. I logged time on the building cycler. And I've been helping Carlos deliver packages in the building. I haven't been dipping into the family account if that's what you're wondering." Her daughter sat still as a stone. The more agitated she was, the less fidgety she got, as if she was storing up energy to deal with the problem.

Vivian tried again. "Eli, I didn't mean it like that. I wasn't accusing you. It's just I wish you'd pay more attention to your school work. Your teacher pinged me and said you haven't shown her any of your year-end project yet. You know you can't graduate without it."

Eli said nothing and finally shrugged as if she didn't care. Vivian knew that wasn't true. Eli was at the top of her class and they were all hoping that it meant there'd be scholarship money. It was the only way they could afford college.

"Eli, you have to focus, have a plan. High school, then college. We talked about this. In this day and age, you need the advanced degrees."

Eli looked up at that and said, "You and dad have advanced degrees and you're out of work, and Dad . . ."

Vivian bit her lip. "Your father will be home for dinner. He promised." Luckily, her screen pinged. "And this may be a job lead." Vivian got up and walked over to her bedroom to answer her call. "Work on your year-end and we'll talk about it later when your father's home."

He promised.

Excerpt from Elinor Parker's year-end project:

Simon Chi was constantly being compared to his father, Raymond Chi. "Visionary" was used so often to describe Raymond that even his son described his father that way. The legacy of living up to a vision, and the parental pressure, must have been part of Simon Chi's day-to-day routine.

April 18, 2048: Simon Chi on the NewsStream.

Ramona Carson: . . . but your father had no government backing. Everything could have gone spectacularly wrong.

Simon Chi: Interesting choice of words, Ms. Carson, since everything went spectacularly right. Mars is still greening. Green and blue. If our own skies cleared long enough, you can even see the colors.

RC: And isn't that the point? He could have used the tech, the money, and done it here, cleaned up our backyard first.

SC: And which government would have agreed to that? They were enacting laws to ban GMOs and couldn't even enforce the Paris Agreement of '15 or that of Rome in '20. It was an anti-science atmosphere and no one was thinking long term.

RC: Just your father?

SC: My father was a visionary and he hired the best and brightest. Barsoom Inc. has done what no government could have. Look, this is all history. The deed is done and we're eight months from launching *Barsoom 8*.

Dinner meant devices down, dishes up. Though these days, her nephew seemed to be online even when he was offline. Charlotte watched as Vincent moved the food around on his plate. He was barely eating and his eyes were glazed as if he was still watching the screens.

Everyone was surprised when Vincent walked in the door, even though he had said he'd be home. And didn't that say a lot for the state of affairs?

"Was it really bad today, Vincent?" Vivian asked softly as she laid her hand on his arm.

Vincent blinked slowly, then smiled. "No terrorist alerts or storm warnings. Air quality was a 6, but I had my mask on the whole time, I promise."

He was deliberately misunderstanding. Charlotte knew Vivian wasn't asking about the alerts or his commute. "Well, glad to see you here with us, Vincent."

Vincent smiled back at her. It seemed automatic, a prompted, programmed response.

"I wish you'd take them up on their offer, Dad," Eli said as she ate her fish. "To set up home access, then no matter how bad it gets out there, you won't have to commute and we'd get a much better pipe."

"No." Vincent stopped smiling. "I won't have that filth in my home."

As a digital gate, her nephew spent the day policing the net —deleting and flagging any questionable content. From his dazed look, filth was an understatement.

"Didn't the new bot help? I thought there was an upgrade," Charlotte asked. The tremor in her left hand was more pronounced than usual, and she smiled gratefully at Vivian who was cutting up her food.

"The bots were a 10% improvement at best." Vincent shook his head. A lock of hair fell over his eyes and he made no move to push it back. "Every day it gets worse."

"Would they offer you home access again?" Charlotte asked as she carefully speared a piece of fish with her fork.

Vivian pursed her lips and said carefully, "It was a good package with the extra credits."

"Dad, home access, Mom can get faster job-ups. We'll all have better links!" Eli said. She was more animated than usual. "And it's not like I'm a noob, I've seen things online—"

"Like what? Porn? Hate speech? Anything you've seen is tame compared to—" Vincent shook his head. "I'm not going to talk about this at dinner and spoil everyone's appetite."

Charlotte heard Eli mutter under her breath, "It's not like you'd talk about it any other time."

Everyone fell silent. Charlotte tried to think of a more neutral topic. Dinner was more fun when Vincent, Vivian and Eli first moved in with her about ten years ago. Now, everything was tense and no topic seemed safe.

To Charlotte's surprise, Vincent broke the silence by clearing his throat. "Eli, your mother said you still haven't finished your year-end."

Eli paused in mid-chew. She swallowed, then looked down at her plate and muttered, "I'm working on it."

Charlotte rolled her eyes at Vivian, who mouthed back, "At least they're talking."

"Simon Chi, right?" Vincent said, not looking up. He was examining his plate as if to see which piece of food to tackle next. "I'm surprised you didn't pick Raymond Chi. There must be a lot more material on him."

"That's the point, Dad. Everyone knows all about Raymond." Eli was gesticulating with her fork. "It's a lot harder being the guy who comes after, to have to live up to the legacy and all that."

Charlotte winced, and both Vincent and Vivian froze. It took a few more seconds before Eli noticed and then she dropped her fork and flushed beet red. "I, I didn't mean . . ."

"Fish filets." Charlotte finally found a neutral topic. She smiled brightly and said as she chewed, "They must have mixed up a good algae batch. Taste almost like the real thing."

∞

"Thanks for bringing this up."

"Not a problem, Shircara," Eli said as she handed over the package.

"I know the package room is full, but I swear I've barely had time to go to the bathroom never mind the package room."

Elinor smiled at her downstairs neighbor as she authenticated the package. "I'm happy to help." She could hear the baby fussing inside. "She must be getting big now."

"I meant to ask, maybe you could babysit sometime? It'll be good to get her used to real people."

"Sure, Shircara, ping me, I'm around." Eli smiled, and smiled even more when her screen buzzed softly. Shircara was a great tipper.

Eli waved goodbye and walked back to the elevator. Carlos spoke in her ear. "That's the last of it, Eli. Package room is empty and drone drops are done for the day."

Eli nodded. "K, I'll check in tomorrow, same time?"

"Sure, should be lighter tomorrow, mid-week. And hey, don't stew over the dinner thing, your father knows you didn't—hey, stew, dinner." Carlos chuckled.

Eli made a face. Carlos loved his puns and she knew he was only trying to make her feel better. "You didn't see their faces. And it's hard to apologize you know, especially when it's not even on purpose."

"Of course it wasn't. I'm sure your father realizes that. And on some level, he must be used to it by now. Anyway, signing off, deliveries on 500 4th. I'll talk to you tomorrow, kid."

Eli had never met Carlos, their virtual doorman, in person. He lived somewhere in Puerto Rico, which with the travel restrictions might as well be Mars. She liked working for him and maybe he'd be able to swing more hours for her after graduation.

Eli decided against the elevator and walked to the stairwell. It was only two floors and it wasn't as if she was in a hurry to get back to the apartment. These days every interaction and conversation seemed to end in drama. Graduation, year-end, dinner fiasco.

At dinner, after her unfortunate comment, her father had recovered and even laughed a bit, saying he was being overly sensitive. But maybe her subconscious had made a choice to focus on Simon Chi and not Raymond. To reflect back on her dad and his father?

Eli was third generation, and even she got splashback when people found out that her grandfather was *the* Elliot Parker, one among ten. The first human to set foot on Mars, to find water on Mars, to find precious metals; his list of firsts was long. He was also the *only* human on that mission to have a son on Earth. Eight years old and eager to please, the newstreams couldn't get enough of Vincent and the Parker family—especially when Elliot Parker was also the first human to die on Mars.

Raymond Chi's vision and the continued success of the Barsoom missions refocused the spotlight, and her father was able to have somewhat of a normal life. Though how could it be normal to live up to a historic figure?

Her father was so unpredictable and moody lately. Eli felt they were all being extra careful to not trip the wire, which made her dinner comments even more insensitive. How would he react when she made her try for Mars?

Eli walked back into her apartment and saw with relief that her parents had retreated into their room. It wasn't that late, and she could hear them talking softly. They obviously didn't want another round of awkward, either.

She walked softly to the room she shared with her great aunt.

"You're back early," her great aunt said. "Or maybe I'm up late? Take a nap in the afternoon and your whole cycle is screwed up."

Eli smiled. Her GA was sitting up in her bed and reading a paper book. She always waited up for her, and not just because they shared a room. "Shircara in 6B asked if I could babysit."

"Well, that's good. Didn't you say she's a good tipper?" Her GA paused as Eli nodded. "What about that internship she was talking about? Did she say anything about that?"

Eli shrugged as she plugged in and sat on her own bed opposite her GA. "She's still on maternity leave. And it's not like I'm really in the running. I'm not even finished high school and those internships are for college grads."

"It doesn't hurt to keep asking. That Shircara has good contacts. She can probably give you good career advice, too."

Eli made a noncommittal hum. Everyone was a little too interested in her prospects, or specifically her lack of prospects. She knew her parents expected her to go to college, but for what? The same mind-numbing jobs they had?

"Elinor, I know things have been tense around here. But you do know that we all want what's best for you, right?"

Eli sighed and said softly, "How do you know what's best? And what does it matter anyway since it's all impossible?"

Her GA looked at her sharply. "Come here," then patted her bed. Eli walked over and curled up next to her like she had as a small child.

"The world has changed so much since I was your age," her GA said. "And yes, I was your age once."

"Yeah, you still used paper credits and had flush toilets." It was part of her nightly ritual as a child. Her GA would tell her stories of the old days.

"Actually, I was thinking of your grandfather. In many ways, he was a world changer."

"It's because of what I said at dinner, isn't it?" Eli groaned. "I didn't mean to say it like that. I wasn't trying to be mean to Dad."

"Of course you weren't." Her GA rubbed Eli's shoulders. "Your father remembers the virtual streams. And even those were mostly for public consumption. It wasn't the real Elliot Parker." She paused. "I bet your teacher was expecting you to do your year-end on your grandfather."

Eli shrugged. "She said she was looking forward to an authentic telling."

Her GA snorted. "What would anyone know about authentic these days?" She looked lost in thought and Eli waited, not wanting to break the mood.

"I'm glad you picked someone else instead. It's not that I wouldn't have helped you," her GA finally said. "What you said earlier? About things being impossible? We all, including your grandfather, thought his being chosen for the Mars Ten was impossible.

"Your grandfather was what they called . . . complicated. He was not the easiest person to get along with. Mainly because he was always ten steps ahead of everyone else and he had no patience. Once a thing was done, he was onto the next. You never really got his full attention 'cause he was always thinking about the next thing.

"Your father, his wife, his family were just those done things. I'm not saying that he didn't love us or miss us, but he . . . there was always that next thing."

Eli looked up at her GA. She rarely talked about her brother, and when she did, it was often per the party line of "sister to the sacrificing hero".

"Your grandmother couldn't take it. Especially after he chose to leave us, her words."

Her GA had raised her father after her grandmother left to join a commune. So who really left whom?

"Why are you telling me this, GA?"

"Because I am probably the only one who really remembers Elliot Parker, and everyone should know who and what shaped their history and destiny."

Excerpt from Elinor Parker's year-end project:

> Much has been said about Raymond Chi's early association then break with the Chinese government, the tax shelter-like status of his company, Barsoom Incorporated. However, with the spectacular success of *Barsoom One*, he eclipsed earlier pioneers like Elon Musk and Jeff Bezos, and provided a dream for the entire planet.
>
> A dream that Simon Chi inherited and became the executor for. Officially, Simon didn't take over until the sixth Barsoom launch; however, many believed that Simon was instrumental in the planning and foresight that preceded each and every mission

starting with the third.

And while *Barsoom One* was the dream, the subsequent missions, specifically *Barsoom 5* with the Mars Ten, meant there was an executable plan, achievable milestones and goals. No one disputes Raymond Chi's genius, but as was noted by then-President Chelsea Clinton:

Raymond Chi was the one small step, the one who showed the way, but Simon Chi was the giant leap and the one who paved the road.[21]

In their corner of the meeting room, Kaylee was crying and Eli made sure to block her from the others' view as much as possible. Kaylee was not a pretty crier: her face was all blotchy and her eyes were red and puffy, but she was quiet about it. Though judging from the looks coming their way, the news was already spreading.

Eli's mother had pulled Kaylee's mother aside and they were talking together not too far away. They looked worried, but they and everyone else at the MM left Kaylee and Eli alone.

"They said I was too genetically compatible with others on the list," Kaylee said as she cried. "They wanted more genetic diversity with their payload."

"Bureaucratic trolls," Eli said as she rubbed Kaylee's arm and passed her a tissue. Was she a bad person that she wasn't as upset for Kaylee as a good friend should be? Eli wasn't sure how she might feel later, but right now, it was mostly relief that Kaylee was not leaving after all.

"I was going to go in for nano injections to boost my oxygen intake and temp tolerance. I had it all scheduled."

Her family must have been so sure of Kaylee's chances. Nano injections weren't cheap, nor were appointments easy to come by.

"What about Jeff?" Eli asked. She looked around again and Jeff was definitely not in the room. As one of the few blondes, he usually was easy to spot. She did see Chad talking with his younger cousin. Eli looked away quickly before she was caught staring.

"What about Jeff?" Eli repeated. "Is he still . . ."

"He's still on the list." Kaylee looked up and said fiercely, "He's committed to me. We filed an appeal but it's not likely to go anywhere. It's all bullshit anyway. They're biased against couples."

Rumors had been circulating that people with emotional bonds were rarely chosen. The idea being that pre-existing pair bonds fostered the "us against them" mindset, and decreased the chances of promoting the genetic diversity a thriving population would need.

"You should have applied as a single." Eli couldn't help saying it. They had debated this over and over again and it wasn't that Eli wanted to be right, but she was right. "After you get there, who cares how you have your babies. You could go artificial."

"Never," Kaylee hissed. "Jeff and I will have *our* baby, not anyone else's."

"Better get working fast then, there's only a few months before the lift," Eli said. "I guess the alternative is to store his sperm." Eli paused when she saw how appalled Kaylee was. "Well, it's true, unless he's giving up his ticket and staying here with you?"

"Don't be slow, I'd never ask him to do that," Kaylee said, then lowered her voice, "Jeff went to see his uncle."

"The payload specialist? The one who fast-tracked your application?" Kaylee and Jeff's entire family were obviously working behind the scenes.

Kaylee nodded. "We can't talk here, Eli. There's a meeting in a few days at my place. Come over." Kaylee reached over and squeezed Eli's hand. "When the time comes, you will be there too. To hold your godchild on Mars."

Excerpt from Elinor Parker's year-end project:

> With an almost exponential number of people per manned mission (*Barsoom 5* and the Mars 10^6; *Barsoom 6* with the Mars 100^7, *Barsoom 7* with the Mars 500^8), Simon Chi has shown that survival is no longer the barometer. The launches every 24 months alternated people with equipment and supply payloads. These have become an established routine and an expectation, with each launch improving and building on the techniques of the previous one.
>
> *Barsoom 8* and the Mars 1000 will be Simon Chi's legacy. This is the point where future historians will stop speaking of missions and start talking about migrations. Applications are still the only point of entry, with each and every applicant carefully screened for the best possible combinations of vigor, skills and potential.
>
> **January 29, 2048: Simon Chi on the NewsNow**
>
> Paul Dance: How do you answer your critics who say the application and selection process is unfair?
>
> Simon Chi: The process is the process. Everyone can see the quality of successful applicants at #GotoMarsLive. We're not hiding anything, including the selection process.
>
> PD: But there are plenty of people who say they're being

rejected because of the most trivial of reasons, like a family history of obesity when they themselves are young and healthy.

SC: It's a numbers game—there are more people who want to go than we have openings for. And obesity? Trivial? Hardly. It's not just the short-term needs, it's the long term. Mars is not Earth and we don't yet have the margins.

PD: Yet? Does that mean there will come a day when—

SC: When it's not so much of a quota and selection? When even I in my old age can go and breathe Martian air? I'm not dead yet. I'm not dead yet.

∞

Charlotte knew who it was before she opened the door. Mara always knocked the same way, a rapid and nervous tattoo, like the woman herself.

"Hello, Mara," Charlotte greeted their neighbor from across the hall. "If you're looking for Vivian, she's down in the gym banking credits."

"Hi, Ms. Parker," Mara said as she licked her lips. "I was actually wondering if . . ."

"If you can have some potable?" Charlotte sighed. "Did they turn off your water again?"

"I just ran out, I only need a liter to reconstitute dinner. I, we, get paid tomorrow."

Charlotte motioned for Mara to wait, then walked slowly to the kitchen. She tried not to shuffle but didn't think Mara was interested in how she moved. She opened the pantry and pulled out a small bottle. It was one of the older bottles, so they could afford to lose it.

Charlotte watched as Mara's eyes fixated on the bottle. Mara reached for it but Charlotte curled it into her body. "Lecture first. Promise me that you're getting a filter unit when you get paid. One like we have to catch rain."

Mara looked away and said softly, "I am saving for one. After the rent and the water bill. It's not like the electrical where I can bank it in the gym."

Charlotte nodded, then handed the bottle over. "You'll dehydrate if you bank too much in the gym. Get a filter unit. It's going to save you credits in the long run, you know that." Charlotte put her hands over Mara's and the bottle of water. "Keep the bottle, use it for your first filtered potable."

Mara bit her lip and nodded. "Thank you," she whispered and ran back into her apartment.

"We're missing a bottle," Eli said as she rummaged in the pantry.

"No, we're not," Charlotte replied, trying to find a comfortable position on the sofa.

"But I know we had eighteen here on the shelf."

"You miscounted, or your mom took one down to the gym with her."

"But, I . . ."

"You miscounted or your mom took one down to the gym with her," Charlotte repeated while giving her grand niece a serious nod.

Her grand niece's eyes widened and then she nodded back. She pulled out the tool chest and started laying out the tools.

"The new filter finally came. I figured I might as well replace it since Dad won't be here to do it." Eli turned away and started unscrewing the back panel of the window unit.

"No sitdown tonight?" Charlotte asked, watching Elinor. Her brother's namesake was capable and smart. Pretty, too. It was too bad that his fame didn't mean more fortune.

"No, Dad pinged and said he's staying at the office tonight," she muttered as she peered into the guts of their filtration unit. "It's the Water Don't, Subways Won't again."

Charlotte shook her head. "As if hacking the subways would change water policies. They're only hurting their own. Not like those in control would be caught dead riding the subway."

Elinor "hmmed" and shrugged: the ubiquitous teenage sign of "I've heard this before and am only pretending to pay attention".

Charlotte's lips twitched. Was it really so long ago that she'd made the same noise and gesture at her own parents? Not that she blamed Elinor, who was much more patient than she had been at her age. Charlotte knew she was repeating herself more often, just like her grandmother and mother. It wasn't just the aching joints or the occasional dizzy spell. Genetics rule, no matter how cruel, and aging was not for cowards.

"The Tarps. They own more water rights than anyone in the city. They're not going to be riding the subway," Charlotte said. "I heard their younger kid is in Sierra U. The one where they still have classes on site."

Elinor nodded and continued to work on the filter unit. Charlotte suppressed a sigh. It was probably for the best: not only could they not afford it even if Elinor got a scholarship, Vincent had had a horrible time at Columbia back when they still did day classes. He said people would sit there and just watch him, as if doing so could bring back Elliot Parker and they could share in the glory.

The adults had all assumed that Elinor would go to college, but assumptions and dreams were not the same thing. Charlotte didn't know why they never really talked about it. Probably they were all wary of Vincent's reaction. Since he wasn't here, Charlotte tried the other one. "And the Desmonds, I heard their oldest is on the next Mars launch."

Eli paused for a microsecond; if Charlotte hadn't been watching, she would have missed it. This time Charlotte did sigh. It wasn't as if she was surprised. Charlotte knew Eli's best friends had applied. It was not easy for her being the third-generation Parker.

"How's the year-end coming along?" Charlotte asked.

"It's coming," Elinor replied, paying more attention to the filter unit than it merited.

"You do remind me of your grandfather. Always very focused on the task at hand." When Charlotte squinted, she could almost see Elliot in the shape of her niece's head. She also moved like Elliot, as if she needed to demo Newton's laws. The Parkers all moved that way, deliberate and reactionary.

"Done," Elinor proclaimed as she screwed the back panel back in place. "That should last us another six months."

Charlotte nodded, and then had to bring her hand up to stop the movement. She didn't think Elinor noticed, but it was getting harder to stop the tremors.

Elinor put away the tools and turned on the filter unit. The hum was soothing, one less life essential to worry about.

Elinor turned to face Charlotte and said solemnly, "Though I would of course be more careful counting and rotating the bottles when I collect."

They both looked at each other and Elinor was the first to

smile. Charlotte knew she had an identical smile on her own face. Genetics rule.

Excerpt from Elinor Parker's year-end project:

In his rise to be CEO, Simon Chi was not a mere figurehead. Most would say that he earned the role. He worked in and contributed to almost every division of Barsoom, Inc., most notably in its research division. In the '30s, he led the transformative studies in water reclamation and ecological balancing that made such a difference here on Earth and for the company's ultimate goal.

Simon Chi's TED Talk: "Water, Water, Everywhere", August 8, 2036

The red planet has fascinated humankind long before they knew it as a planet. Mars was named for the Roman God of war, its red color thought to be the blood of the battlefield. The Chinese have a different name: Fire Star.

And fire was long considered one of the four key elements: fire, air, earth and water. With water being its diametric opposite. Our research at Barsoom, Inc. has led to direct applications that can rebalance the water table here on Earth and create the water we need on Mars.

It may be oxymoronic, but we can turn the Fire Star into the Water Star.

If this is the only way to earn credits, then so be it.

Vivian breathed to the rhythm of her pumping legs and the metallic version of the *Ride of the Valkyries* sounding in her head.

The trick was to not pedal so hard that she needed to rehydrate, which would cost her credits for the water, but not too slow or she wouldn't make her quota. Of course, being unemployed, she had all the time in the world and it was nice to get out of the apartment.

Even with the excellent referral from her last contract, the pickings had been slim. Vincent at least had some job security, but Vivian knew that the job and the commute were taking their toll on his health. And what kind of examples were they setting for Elinor? Both unhappy and unfulfilled? No wonder Elinor had no interest in graduating.

Vivian checked the meter. Elinor must have done her stint earlier in the week, as their apartment's quota was banked. Vivian queried and got an affirmative for 10C. Omar's wife must have gotten a short-term gig, otherwise she would be here pedaling, too. Vivian switched the cycle to 10C and set the alarm for the allocated credits.

If this is the only way to earn credits then so be it.

She had just banked the first credit when the door to the gym opened and he walked in. Vivian looked up and gave a polite nod and smile. He did the same and walked over to the weight bench in the corner of the gym.

The new guy had caused a bit of heart flutter and plenty of chatter among her condo clutch. Vivian tried not to stare as he stretched and then reached for the free weights. From the way he handled them and his well-toned arms and chest, he was obviously very familiar with weights. This one wasn't cycling for credits.

He looked to be in his fifties, though with DeAge and SkinSoft, it was hard to tell. As he settled down on the bench and began his arm curls, he met her gaze and smiled again.

Vivian blushed for being caught staring. She hoped he would think it was the exercise.

"Hi, I'm Bruce. I just moved into 20."

20, the penthouse. The building had had a going-away party for the Watsons when they decided to move to Sudbury, Canada, to live with their daughter. To get away from the municipal madness and the smog, they said. Their son Bruce took over the ownership. Bruce owned a mid-sized digital security business, WhiteHat, and by all accounts was doing quite well.

Vivian realized that she'd been silent a beat too long as his smile faded. She quickly tapped her ear and pretended it was the music. "Vivian. 8B."

"Vivian? Good to meet you." He was smiling again. "I haven't met many of the neighbors yet."

It was her chance to get some answers on the guy and be the news bearer. The penthouse was nice, but why here? Surely he could afford better? Except she was terrible at this sort of thing. Vincent for all his reticence was the small talker; he had learned early to deal with the media and the glory sniffers.

"We have a monthly networking event in the common room. Next Thursday night. You're more than welcome," Vivian blurted out.

"Yeah, I got that notice." He switched arms. It must have been at least twenty kilos and he wasn't even breathing hard. "Anything I should know? Rules for the gym?"

Vivian blinked. Other than the corner with the free weights, theirs was a small gym with two rowing machines and the ten cyclers. She shook her head. "No rules really. Use at your own risk and book ahead for busy times early morning and late evenings."

"8B, the Parkers, right?" Bruce said. And before Vivian could reply with her standard, yes, Vincent Parker, the first Martian orphan, Bruce surprised her. "Mom said to say hi and that your family is invited to visit anytime.

"She really liked your aunt, Charlotte, is it?" Bruce asked. At Vivian's nod, he continued, "Yeah, Mom kept going on about the building and the neighborhood. She said your aunt probably is the last original owner left in this place. Mom didn't want to leave, but the smog and the weather, plus Dad's healthcare. Now sunshine 200 days out of the year, automated attendants, plus the grand-kids, a no-brainer as they used to say."

Vivian stared. It didn't seem so out of line now, since they were having a conversation. And he was worth staring at. It wasn't that he was fit or that he was especially good-looking—he was notice-able. If Vincent's face wasn't plastered all over social media, no one would give him a second look. Bruce, on the other hand . . .

"Why are you here, then?" Vivian couldn't stop herself from asking. "You could live anywhere." Vivian waved her arms.

Bruce smiled. "Because neighborhoods rise and fall, because I'm still healthy enough, because I don't need sun and I'm looking for a change of scenery."

Change of scenery? He would choose Brooklyn over sunny Sudbury? The gym in the basement over a penthouse apartment? Before she could reply, he switched positions and now had one knee on the bench to do arm pulls with the weight. In addition to well-sculpted arms and chest, he had a great butt.

"I've seen you here before, during the day." He met her eyes in the mirror. "Not working?"

Vivian shook her head and continued to pedal. None of the other gym goers were as talkative.

"By choice?"

Vivian shook her head again, more slowly this time.

"What can you do?" he asked, turning so that he was facing her again, and started working his other arm.

Vivian cleared her throat and said, "I have a degree in digital management and cyber optimization. I balance and remix digital package delivery with encryption keys for—"

"Maximum efficiency. That's your elevator speech?"

"I'm good at it. I'm a digital payload specialist."

"Better." He dropped his head and started another set. "Want a job?"

Vivian's mouth dropped open. WTF?

"You'd still have to go through HR and pass the security checks. The team will need to test your skill set, too."

"Why would . . .? You don't even know me." Even as she said it, Vivian couldn't help the small bubble of excitement. A job, a real job, not a contract. With the income, they could send Elinor to college. Maybe get GA better medical care.

Bruce looked up at her and shrugged. "Any number of reasons, being neighborly, paying it forward, because I can." He put the weight down. "And I like the scenery."

"Sex is the root of all evil." Kaylee's uncle Joseph was a short man who used his hands a lot while talking as if to distract from his lack of height.

"I thought it was money," Eli whispered, more to herself than anyone.

Chad chuckled from where he sat to her left. "Money was invented to buy the sex."

Eli glanced over and smiled a little. One more thing to know about Chad, he had great hearing. Eli had been surprised to see him here, and even more when he said hi and sat next to her. Sitting on her other side, Kaylee and Jeff had nodded to him and included Chad in some small talk while they waited for the meeting to begin. Eli hoped that her arm wasn't bruised from where Kaylee kept pinching her.

"The who, where, when and why," Joseph proclaimed. "These are intimate details that should not be under the control of any government or anyone."

This whole evening had been one surprise after another. Her mother didn't give her the third degree about leaving the apartment, just told her to check the air quality and wear her mask. And then this. Who knew that Kaylee's uncle had such Puritan views?

"Pair bonding is an evolutionary advantage, a nurturing principle to ensure the stability of the family unit."

Eli looked around to see most of the crowd nodding. And it was a crowd, at least fifty people. She didn't think they could fit that many people in Kaylee's apartment. Some, like Chad, she recognized from the MM, and Kaylee said there were even more on the Subnet watching.

Mention of the Subnet had made Eli a bit nervous. She didn't think her father would be happy to hear about her being anywhere near the Subnet. But everyone here seemed perfectly normal, and while his views might be a little extreme, Joseph didn't sound like a terrorist or a criminal.

"To claim genetic diversity as a necessity and use that to override the emotional ties of committed couples is to use morals and questionable ethics to uproot and control lives."

Kaylee had stopped pinching her arm and was leaning into Jeff, who was stroking her hand. Earlier, Jeff had been talking about his preparations for the trip, but it was also obvious that he had no intention of leaving Kaylee behind. Eli didn't understand how they were going to get over this paradox.

"And who makes these rules? Why should we allow moral laxity to prevent our reach for the stars?"

"And now the reveal," muttered Chad.

"Barsoom, Inc. and the Chis may have been the first, but they're not the only. Paired Up is ready, willing and able to accept the committed and reunite those who should not have been separated. No one will be forced to choose between a partner and a life."

"Jeff will go as scheduled and then Uncle Joseph will get me a place on the *Ark*." Kaylee hugged Jeff even tighter. "He'll be waiting for me when we land."

A handful of people left after Joseph finished speaking, but most stayed and were quizzing him. Eli stayed because she had questions, too. She couldn't quite believe that it would be so easy. She thought there'd be more restrictions, but when she was introduced to Joseph, he beamed at her, acting as if her spot was guaranteed.

"It's the Parker in you, Eli," Kaylee had whispered in her ear. "And that's not a bad thing."

The four of them were standing in a small group by the wall, nibbling on some kelp sticks. Chad had stuck to her side throughout and Eli was almost used to his presence. It turned out that Jeff knew Chad from one of his online classes from before he moved into the 'hood. That meant Chad was maybe three years older than Eli, another thing to know about him.

"Why wouldn't Jeff go with you, then?" Eli asked before she thought better of it.

Kaylee's eyes dropped and Jeff's face tightened.

"Because what no one has said is that Paired Up is not one hundred percent," Chad said. "They've had to strip down and speed up in order to make the launch window." Chad nodded at Kaylee and Jeff, then asked, "So, a sure thing with *Barsoom 8* or a roll of the dice with the *Ark*."

"My uncle says everything is fine," Kaylee replied a bit defensively. "It may be a bit primitive, but it's as safe as can be."

Chad shrugged. "I'm not passing judgement, just stating the obvious. If I were in your shoes, I'd do the same thing. Speaking of which . . ." He turned to Eli. "Can we talk for a bit? Privately?"

Eli barely restrained her gasp of surprise. Why would Chad want to talk to her? Kaylee made a shooing motion as if to say, you'll never know if you don't go.

There was not much room for privacy with all the people around, but Chad managed to carve out a corner and stood in front of Eli with his back to the room. He was about a head taller than her and Eli felt as if she was being cocooned. She barely heard any of the other conversations.

"You realize that it's risky?" he asked. He had his hands in his pockets and Eli had the impression that he was nervous too.

Eli certainly was: other than her family and friends she had never been so physically close to another person before. There was barely any space between their bodies. If she breathed deeply, her chest might actually touch his. She gritted her teeth to stop herself from doing so.

"The thing is, Elinor Parker," Chad said softly as he pulled one hand out of his pocket and placed it on the wall beside her head. "They'll only take pairs. Committed couples."

Chad leaned down to whisper in her ear. "I want to go to Mars, Eli. And I think you do, too."

∞

Excerpt from Elinor Parker's year-end project:

Mars was always going to be a one-way trip. The resources to send missions there were astronomical, to send missions back, nonexistent.

Over the years, Simon Chi's support of Barsoom, Inc's research division paid off in brands we know as GeneFence™, CommSec™, DrinkMe™, and the T vaccine. These and many other patents and marketables spanned industries and changed the lives of millions on Earth. Beneficial without a doubt but not altruistic, as these consumables fueled and continued to fund the missions. As they will continue to change the lives of those to come: Earthlings and Martians.

Simon Chi's TED Talk: "Human Resources", November 8, 2040

Earth is our home, our origin story. But we as humans now have the means to grow and expand our horizons. Cliché though this may be, just like our ancestors, we must recognize the necessity to settle new lands while we still can.

Ours is a world of limited resources. The only thing that seems to be limitless is human population and ingenuity. The success of *Barsoom 5* proves the latter and while the dangers are real, so are the opportunities. It will be a different life but it can be a good life.

Those prepared for the sacrifices will be embracing a legacy, and will always have a place among the stars.

Charlotte heaved herself out of the sofa and kept her hand on the back until she felt steady enough to stand. The girls didn't notice. Vivian had logged on immediately after dinner to chase a job lead. And Elinor was finally working on her year-end. Vincent was at work again, the second time this week, though at least this time it was to pick up an extra shift.

Charlotte sighed. They all worried about Vincent's mental health. He had always been the opposite of his father, insular and barricaded—the paparazzi taught him that. But lately, he had been even more distant. Maybe Vivian's job lead would be a good one; she certainly seemed excited enough about it. Then Vincent could ease off and there'd be less pressure.

And Elinor seemed, if not happier, then more motivated. Her friend Kaylee's Mars rejection might have been the call to reality that Eli needed. Or maybe it was a boy. Vivian said there was one showing interest at the last MM. Charlotte hoped it was a boy; the girl needed more emotional attachments in her life. Eli was an only child and family could only go so far.

Charlotte shuffled to the bedroom. These days it didn't seem worth it to get out of bed. She knew it was better for her if she kept to a schedule, but all she really wanted to do was sleep. She reminded herself of an old cat she once had. The vet had called it old lady disease. At the end, she was an unsteady bag of bones that went to sleep and just never woke up.

Charlotte kept her hand on the wall as she walked. The trembling was more and more obvious every day and it was definitely affecting her balance. She paused at the bedroom door and looked back at her grand niece. Her brother Elliot would have been amazed and pleased, and he would probably say something extremely inappropriate like how hot she was.

People forgot how Elliot couldn't seem to censor himself—he just said the first thing that popped into his head. He wasn't being mean or intentionally insulting, but he never acquired the knack of conversational flow.

They saw less of that once he was on Mars. Charlotte could tell he was more scripted on camera, and off camera? Well, it wasn't as if the Mars Nine would ever talk about it. Mars dust in the wind.

Eli looked up and asked, "You okay, GA? Need any help?"

She must have been standing in the hallway too long. Charlotte shook her head.

"Night then, GA," Eli said. "Carlos said there's quite a few packages, so don't wait up for me."

"You know I'll be up. For as long as I can."

"Did you fulfill items on my Amazon wish list?" Eli kept her voice low, though her mother was too absorbed on her own screen to pay much attention to her.

Chad shrugged. The man seemed to have a whole repertoire of shrugs. Eli thought this was the "hope I did good but will pretend I don't care" shrug.

"Thought it would be better than virtual flowers. They'd last longer."

Eli smiled; she couldn't help it. Her Amazon wish list was just that, items that were someday items, nothing that she could ever justify. Now, three paperback books—actual books—were coming her way.

"They're much better than flowers. Thank you so much."

Chad smiled back and visibly relaxed. So the shrug and pose was a defense mechanism.

"No way I could get everything on your list, but when I saw the books, they seemed pretty special. Not many go for the paper these days."

"My great aunt. She used to read to me from her collection."

Chad raised his eyebrows in alarm. "The books are for your great aunt?"

"No, yes, in a way." Eli didn't want Chad to get the wrong impression. "My great aunt taught me to read with paper books and she taught me to love these books, too."

"So I scored points with two Parker women?" Chad asked, smiling again.

Eli nodded. Chad was really trying. They might have started out unconventionally, but the more she found out about him, the more she liked. "I think at the next MM, you should meet my mom officially."

"Officially as in 'Mrs. Parker, I'm interested in your daughter', officially?" Chad asked.

Most days, Eli thought what they were trying to do was crazy, but the way Chad phrased it, Eli barely stopped herself from laughing out loud. "You won't get a dinner invitation otherwise and won't meet my GA. She's not mobile enough to come to the MMs."

"Ah. And it's important for me to meet your GA." He cocked his head. "Though I suppose it's really more that your GA meets me?"

Eli nodded again. Smart and understanding.

"Well, then it's a good thing I already banked some points with those books."

"So, young man," her GA said as they sat down at the dinner table. "I have you to thank for those books?"

Eli watched as Chad faced her GA. "Yes, madam. I wanted to give Eli something special. The books seemed more interesting and less ephemeral than other virtual spend."

GA nodded and her mom looked bemused. Earlier, as they were making dinner, her mom had waxed nostalgic about Eli being a baby. Well, she might be six months shy of official adulthood, but she had a plan and a man.

"And when Eli told me about how you taught her to read with similar books . . ." Chad shrugged. "I think I made the right choice."

"You do realize that the books are all romances?" her GA asked.

"Well, *The Mail Order Bride* and *The Beauty and Lord Beastly*, sure, but Eli had to explain about the debutante and the garden implement."

"Smart, a sense of humor and he knows how to use the word

ephemeral," her GA said. "I think our Elinor made the right choice."

"GA!" Eli protested. They all laughed and Eli tried hard not to blush, especially when Chad squeezed her hand under the dinner table. "It was mutual but I think we're off to a good start."

"I'm sorry Vincent, Eli's father, is not here to meet you," her mother said. Unspoken was the fact that he had promised to be home on time and was nowhere to be seen and completely offline. Eli would have been more worried, but this was happening more and more often. Her mother also seemed more resigned than worried.

"Yes, well, they'll meet eventually, as we'll be seeing more of you, I'm sure." GA pointed at Chad with her fork.

Her mom had splurged and used some of their hydroponics allotment, so they had real salad greens. They were even going to have farmed chicken tonight, not vat grown. It was like a holiday dinner.

"I'm sorry he's not here too, especially as he's missing this great food." Chad looked at each of them as he ate his chicken.

"Doing it a bit too brown as they say in my books." Her GA chuckled. "Don't think we eat like this all the time, not unless Eli brings home a new boy every night."

"OMG, GA!" Eli protested again, even as her mother laughed.

"She's right, tonight is a special occasion. More so because I finally found a job." Her mother was all smiles.

"Mom, that's totally sunny!" Eli exclaimed. "Why didn't you say something earlier?"

"I only found out right before Chad came in. So Chad, consider yourself this family's lucky charm."

"Congrats, Mrs. Parker," Chad said. "I'm sure there's more to it than luck." He turned to Eli and said, "Though I suppose if luck works in my favor, who am I to argue?"

Kitty Valderez, NewsStream, September 1, 2048:

Last night, the body of Vincent Parker, only son of Elliot Parker, one of the Mars Ten, was found floating in the Hudson River canal. Family members said that he had been increasingly despondent over his job as a digital gate at Google. NewsStream captured this statement from Vincent's supervisor:

He's always been a bit moody and closemouthed. Probably carryover from the days when he was paparazzi bait. Look, I don't mean to sound insensitive, this type of job gets to everyone. He had regular psych sessions like all the others and the last I saw of him, he was fairly upbeat, said he was meeting his daughter's boyfriend. A family dinner.

An investigation is underway as to the cause of death. Family members are asking the public to respect their wishes for a private service.

Vivian bit her lip and tried not to flinch as yet another building resident came up to offer condolences. It was very generous of the condo board to allow them to have the memorial here. So many people had wanted to come, but they couldn't afford to hire a place.

Vivian looked over at Elinor sitting next to Aunt Charlotte. They were just outside the projected range of Vincent's holo. She looked so much like her father, except she was solid and present. Chad was standing behind her. He put a hand on her shoulder and whispered something in her ear.

Look what you're missing, Vincent.

Google representatives had come earlier with the police and the lawyers. They closed out Vincent's account and gave her his personal items. Vivian was clutching his wedding ring; she would have to give it to Elinor.

Did you really want this to be her last memory of you?

Elinor was calm now, but likely their whole floor had heard her earlier.

"How could you not know? Were you so wrapped up in your own life that you didn't know he was hurting? Didn't see?"

Vivian had let Eli scream and rant. Then she, Eli, and Aunt Charlotte had joined in a group hug, and they had all sobbed together. Weren't the words applicable to all of them?

How could you leave us, Vincent?

"The crowd seems to be thinning out, Vivian," Bruce said as he walked up to her. He was looking extremely somber in his dark jeans and turtleneck.

Vivian had never seen him in anything but his gym clothes, and she started to laugh. Bruce immediately stood in front of her, blocking her from most of the crowd. "What? What is it?"

"It's just I've never seen you so covered up. I always look forward to seeing those biceps."

Bruce glanced at his arms, then smiled and looked Vivian up and down. She was wearing a long black maxi. "And your ratty

T-shirts were always so much more interesting. Did you know your blue one has a small rip just under your left arm?"

No guilt, no regrets.

Vivian sobered up. She shouldn't have brought up the gym, not here. "I want to thank you for helping today."

Bruce had hired guards to screen the guests and corral people. He made sure she, Elinor and Aunt Charlotte weren't being overwhelmed. All done in his role as condo board president.

"I didn't know Vincent well, but I would have liked to." Bruce must have seen something in her face. "Don't look so surprised, Vivian. I think every boy wanted to be Vincent, to have a famous father like that."

"He always hated it."

Bruce nodded. "It couldn't have been easy. And then his job. I couldn't have done it."

No, but you wouldn't have done this either.

"Please come and have dinner with us," Vivian said as she touched Bruce's arm. "You haven't really met Aunt Charlotte or talked to Elinor."

No guilt, no regrets, you left me first.

"No, GA, you'll stay here. We'll take care of you." Eli cried, tears streaming down her cheeks.

Elinor was kneeling by her bedside and Vivian was sitting on the end of the bed. Charlotte knew it would be a difficult conversation, but it was also the right decision.

"It's the end, sweetie, look." Charlotte held out her trembling hands. "The shakes are too bad, I can't control them."

"We can take care of you, we can help you." Eli looked at both her and her mother.

Vivian looked unhappy, which was generous of her, but they had already talked about the realities. Vivian shook her head as she reached over to touch Eli's shoulder.

"It's more than just helping. Your great aunt is going to need 'round the clock care."

"It's for the best," Charlotte said. "They'll take good care of me there and you can come visit." Though really, Charlotte didn't think there was much time left for that. It was going to be messy at the end and she had already talked to Vivian about keeping Elinor out of it.

Charlotte wanted to touch Eli too, this grand niece who was more like a daughter. Words, not touch, would have to be enough. She wanted to make sure that Elinor understood.

"I don't want you to spend your life taking care of me," Charlotte said. "Your life is going to be spent on Mars, as it should be."

Elinor wiped her eyes and blinked in surprise.

"Yes, of course we know." Charlotte almost laughed at her grand niece. She had the same exact guilty expression as her father and grandfather did. Well, if there was an afterlife, she could tell them how their legacy was going to complete the circle. Ironic, that.

"We were waiting for you to tell us," Vivian said gently as she started to stroke Eli's head.

It is going to be harder for Vivian, Charlotte thought. She wouldn't be here too much longer to miss it, but there was still no tech good enough to reach through a screen and touch a person millions of miles away.

"I was going to tell you guys, but nothing was confirmed, and then Dad," Elinor hiccupped.

"It's okay, Kaylee's parents told us." Charlotte reached out her hands again and this time Eli held on to one and Vivian held the other. "It's a good plan. Better than staying down here. They can't deny you, Eli. Not you, or any of the others."

"I wish you could come with me," Eli whispered. "You too, Mom."

Vivian shook her head. "No, baby, Mars is meant for you. It's in your blood. You finally have a plan."

"It's your time and your life." Charlotte smiled. "When my time comes, Vivian will send my ashes. Keep some for yourself if you want, but scatter me near where they did his."

Mars dust in the wind.

Kitty Valderez, NewsStream, December 10, 2048:

We've had a report that Charlotte Parker, the sister of Elliot Parker, has been taken to a hospice for end-of-life care. Family members say that she never fully recovered from her bout with the Tela virus last year and her condition has steadily worsened.

In her youth, Charlotte Parker had been vocal in support of her brother and vehement in her denial that he was anything but a hero. Elliot Parker died on Mars after repairing the water recycling unit that some of the crew alleged he broke in the first place.

This is the second life event to hit the Parker family this year. Earlier, you'll remember that Vincent Parker was found dead in

the Hudson River canal. Investigators concluded that Parker had
jumped off the defunct Brooklyn Bridge, adding to the increasing
suicide fad plaguing our city. Last year, there were over 10,000
documented cases and officials have pledged better monitoring
and patrols in an effort to stem the tide.

The light level was low. Elinor came awake slowly, hearing and feeling more than she could actually see. The deck was vibrating beneath her and the straps were digging into her arms. They had given everyone simulations but nothing had really prepared her for the boredom or the cramped quarters.

Her neck was stiff, but she slowly turned her head to the left and could make out the beds all around her. Kaylee was still sleeping in the bunk above hers. Not even her uncle's influence could get her better quarters. There just weren't any.

They told everyone to keep activities at a minimum when in sleep shift, and even separated couples so they wouldn't be tempted. Another bit of hypocrisy for a group claiming to support the pair bond and not be a sex regulator.

Though in truth, everyone was too tired and anxious. The day shift was spent walking the perimeter to maintain muscle tone. There wasn't much conversation as breathing was difficult; the oxygen levels were kept deliberately low to tune up their nanos, or as Chad scoffed, to save credits.

It was only one of the many cost-saving details they all noticed. Elinor had never been on board any of the Barsoom ships, but she had seen the virtual tours. Everyone had designated cubicles and there was plenty to occupy the mind and the body. The Ark was gray and they had a routine.

Elinor always woke before the alarm, and she wondered if Kaylee was dreaming of Jeff and their reunion. A kiss goodbye and then two blast offs within forty-eight hours; at least she had Chad with her.

At least I have Chad with me. Elinor turned that thought around in her head. It was a good thought, wasn't it?

The last six months had been so chaotic and emotional, at times it seemed like Chad was her only anchor. But realistically, they'd barely had the time to really know each other. Their "courtship" was public but their agreement was private. Paired Up would only take committed pairs.

The alarm blared, and seemingly out of nowhere, the subject of her thoughts was helping her undo the straps.

"Gravity didn't cut out this cycle," Chad said. "2,866 circuits this time, beat that, Eli."

Smart, a sense of humor and he knew how to use the word ephemeral. Eli decided to risk it and reached up to cradle his cheek. "I don't want a competition, Chad. We made it here and have a fresh start. It can be real, can't it? A fresh start, together, can you promise me that?"

He didn't shrug this time. Instead he moved closer and touched his forehead to hers. "However we got here, we're here and we're in this together. So, I say yes."

Final excerpt from Elinor Parker's year-end project:

Submitted, grade pending

After ninety days in makeshift shelters, Elinor Parker and her group of one hundred were granted entry to the Mars Station. Elinor Parker is the granddaughter of Elliot Parker, one of the original Mars Ten. *The Ark* is the first non Barsoom, Inc. ship to have made it to Mars, and given the activity on the Subnet and other channels, likely not the last.

Critics of Barsoom, Inc. and Simon Chi publicly questioned the Mars Station's resistance in admitting these new migrants. The company denied issuing any directive and maintained that security and the safety of those in both parties were the main reasons for any delay.

Vivian Parker, Elinor Parker's mother, started the #FreeMars campaign and garnered a groundswell of public support and sympathy for her daughter's plight.

Vivian Parker: They can't leave them out there. His company doesn't own the whole planet. They have no legal authority.

#FreeMars has reignited the debate amongst world leaders about sovereign rights and ownership. The first such World Congress in '40 ended with a set of recommendations that has yet to be confirmed and ratified. Vivian Parker will be the guest speaker at the next Congress, scheduled to occur in three months. Simon Chi will also attend, making one of his rare public appearances, though no word yet on whether he intends to speak.

Charlotte Parker, the great aunt of Elinor Parker, was too ill to be interviewed but issued this statement: Another world-changing Parker, her grandfather, Elliot, would have been so proud. We're all so proud. Don't look back, Elinor.

Elinor Parker's first Martian interview from inside Mars Station:

The Ark brought enough supplies and equipment for our needs and more. We bring energy and commitment. My grandfather helped build this place, and he gave his life to make Mars a better place for everyone, everyone. We deserve this chance. We are the human resources, the hope, the passion. We are the fire on this star.

Better or Worse

Jennifer Graham

I wrote "Better or Worse" as an origin story for my Big 7 universe, a place where megacorporations rule. The story shows one woman's struggle to hold on to what she has in a tumultuous world overrun by corporate greed.

Another earthquake.

Sabreen Toppin jumped out of bed, grabbed her go bag and ran to the arch that allowed entry into the living room. She braced herself, praying that her position near a load-bearing wall would be the safest spot in the apartment.

Alarms blared in the distance. She continued the count she started the moment she grabbed her bag. *Eight seconds.* Cracking noises filled her ears. *Nine seconds.* An explosion boomed far away. *Ten seconds.* The building lurched to the left.

Quakes in the New York City area were nothing new. 1's and 2's were felt across the river in Jersey on occasion. This felt way bigger. A 6 maybe.

Seconds later the quake subsided. Sabreen took a deep breath, and willed her heartbeat to slow down. Feeling calmer, she opened her eyes. She needed to contact her office. The Office of Emergency Management had a new construct that would simultaneously contact all essential personnel in the event of an emergency. Her ringtone, the theme from the latest superhero movie, should be playing at top volume from the cell on the charger next to the vidscreen—where the wall used to be!

Sabreen closed her eyes again and ran a mental checklist of what to do after an earthquake, a few tips she'd learned at a conference she attended years ago on the West Coast. One, she had no injuries. Two, there was no fire, and anything that might catch fire had fallen away with the kitchen. Three . . .

Her train of thought stopped as a woman's scream started from a high floor and plummeted toward the ground. She scrapped the checklist, opened her eyes and groped inside her bag for her bright yellow Tec jacket and matching pants, donning them over pink silk pajamas. The jacket needed a minute to power up. As long as the cell towers still stood, they would be her only means of mobile communication. In the meantime, she needed to get out of her third-floor Brooklyn apartment.

The lights had never come on—the power was out, but morning sunshine shone brightly around her. Sabreen eyed the front door, but the new cracks in the floor made her nervous. She'd made her way to the bedroom when a slight vibration next to her wrist told her someone was trying to make contact. The name 'Munro' appeared on the small screen near her cuff.

She hesitated. Her fiancé, Munro, should be here. Instead, he was off running an errand for his father, the mighty multi-billionaire Carlo Jennings. The last one, he promised. With his own company finally solvent, he intended to make a clean break from his father's business, Zenith Galactic.

He rarely called when his father sent him on money-making missions. It must be important. Sabreen tapped the window on her sleeve to answer the call. Then she yanked the fire escape ladder from under the bed.

"Ro, I don't know where you are but we're having a situation here in Brooklyn. A quake. Bad one. I need to get out of the apartment, then call my office." As she spoke, she opened the nearest window and secured the hook end of the ladder to the sill. After a check that the way was clear, Sabreen threw the chain-linked rungs outside.

A sigh of relief came through the speakers built into her collar. "Honey, I'm glad you're okay." His voice sounded strained, but deliberate. "I need you to do something for me. I need to send you some data."

"I'm wearing my Tec suit. I lost my cell." He would know the suit had no storage. Sabreen swung the go bag over her shoulder. While one leg hung over the sill, a creak ripped through the building, confirming her need for a speedy departure. Items on their dresser—a tube of lip balm, two styli and a cylindrical perfume bottle—rolled slowly onto the floor. The remaining structure leaned. It might stay up for a while or collapse at any minute.

"I can't have this on me when they find me. I only trust you with this. It's the reason for the quake. Please."

Her heart pounded like a locomotive. Indecision could seal her fate, but the plea in Munro's voice made her pause. "This isn't for your father?"

"No . . . not anymore."

She hopped off the sill and ran to the dresser. In the rightmost drawer she retrieved a memory stick and slipped it into the port inside her right sleeve. Somewhere a pipe burst, and water gushed like a waterfall. Sabreen never turned to see if the river came from her apartment. She only heard the sounds as she ran back to the window and eased herself outside.

A gentle beep from the tiny speakers in her collar meant Munro had sent the data. She hustled down the ladder, quick and careful. Three stories up was not the worst position to be in, yet a fall from this height could still break her neck.

Halfway down, she glanced over her shoulder across the East River. The destruction was palpable. Black smoke billowed from unseen fires in the north. Two skyscrapers leaned against each other like a failed attempt to start a falling domino show. *It's the reason for the quake.*

No way was this natural. The third disaster in a month, plus the market was headed for an all-time low. She almost wondered if her company, Fukushi Corp., was behind this. They headed over ninety percent of the world's emergency management offices and a large number of rescue and recovery teams. This disaster would make them a significant profit.

Sabreen had dismissed the idea by the time she reached the ground. Fukushi had no resources to cause such devastation. There were more powerful companies than the one she worked for. Companies like the one her future father-in-law owned, Zenith Galactic. There were few other companies with comparable resources. If Zenith had orchestrated this incident, Sabreen doubted Munro had enough resolve to quit working for his father and turn the patriarch in to authorities all in the same day.

On the ground, Sabreen bent over and grabbed her knees. She took a deep breath to steady her nerves, then straightened up as she linked her suit to her phone account.

Three video feeds, nine calls and four text messages. The videos were from her parents. Video quality sucked on the tiny blue-and-white screen on her sleeve. She needed to return one of the calls or messages—all from work—first, anyway. An incoming call beat her to it.

"Finally, where are you?" her boss, Samuel Musgrove said, then barked a request to someone in the background.

Everyone's confidence in her safety annoyed her. If they could see the state of her building, they might feel differently. "I'm still in Brooklyn, outside what's left of my home."

"Good. Most of the transportation infrastructure is down. Ferry's the only way to get across the river." He paused. "I'm sending a drone to your location. Point it at anything you think needs our attention. Then make your way to the Navy Yard office."

One side of her building had been opened to the elements. Cracks ran along edifices throughout the waterfront. Each structure needed to be inspected for stability. Absently, she fingered the memory stick under her sleeve. What had Munro's father gotten him into?

Sabreen hesitated. She had promised to stop asking questions about what he did for his father if he promised not to work for Carlo Jennings after they were married. This time, he'd involved her whether he liked it or not. She accessed the stick and tried to open a few files. They were encrypted. She needed an app to open them. From the look of the file sizes, the information was too much to take in on the tiny screen anyway.

She chanced accessing the smallest file; it opened without decryption. An interdepartment memo about the start date of project Mole Driver. A name stood out. Brightshores. Zenith Galactic's biggest competitor and major energy supplier. An odd situation for a rival company, but Zenith needed fuel and resources to continue its off-Earth projects.

A drone arrived overhead. It hovered for a second, then landed at her feet. A bright red circle with a white plus sign and a matching capital F was centered on the drone, displaying her company's logo. She squatted in front of the black six-square-inch device and adjusted the settings so it would follow her instructions.

Just over the top of the drone, Sabreen spied two men dressed in black body armor that looked very out of place. No identifying logos anywhere. While others stared in shock at the ruined cityscape and some made their way away from unsteady buildings, these men only stared in her direction. Sabreen continued to tinker with the drone, acting as if she'd never noticed them. It gave her time to think. Again she wondered what Munro had gotten her into.

The path behind her led to a dead end. She could try to make a run through the damaged building, a dangerous prospect when parts of the remaining walls were still tumbling to the ground. In the opposite direction, the East River was a possible escape route. She could jump over the rail and swim for it, getting the drone to send an alert of her situation. A rescue team would find her. Immediately she dismissed the idea. Rescue teams were busy enough. Plus, answering questions about how she'd ended up in the water might force her to reveal the data in the memory stick. She had to talk to Munro before that happened.

That left one option—straight ahead, past the two men and into the street. Sabreen stood. "Up. Stay low over my head." The drone hovered as she commanded. She kept the two men in her periphery as she strolled toward the street. The pair were almost on top of her when she said, "Follow. Sharp turn. Bank low."

She ran straight ahead. The drone swerved and swooped, close to their heads. It would never hit them; the collision avoidance system was too advanced for that. But it made the startled pair dodge out of the way, giving her time to race for the street. The drone followed, as it stayed within a two meter tether, her body the central point of its arc.

Sabreen sprinted into the street. A few lingerers stopped staring at the buildings and turned concerned gazes toward her. They need not worry. The danger was for her alone, and whatever data she carried. She left the river and the Manhattan skyline and rounded the corner, the similarly clad men pounding the pavement behind her. At the end of the block a tall woman sporting a single braid, dark shades and similarly dressed as the pursuing pair, leaned against a van. The woman jumped to attention when she spotted Sabreen. A gun came up from the woman's hip holster and Sabreen swerved between parked cars and more startled pedestrians.

The gunfire never started. Too many witnesses, plus a drone overhead to record everything. They had no idea the camera was off. She ran through a thick crowd, soon realizing the drone was a beacon for her location.

"Camera on. Untether. Go to Sabor Chef Warehouse. Wait by south entrance."

The drone shot away. It would hover over the warehouse entrance and stay there until she arrived. Three blocks for her to lose her pursuers and regroup.

Sabreen slipped away from the crowd and made her way past scattered throngs of people. Most she assumed were from the surrounding high rises. She recognized a few confused neighbors.

Many buildings still stood, but ominous cracks told her they were unstable and threatened to collapse at any moment. She fought the urge to do her job and warn them that milling about in the street was dangerous. Drawing attention to herself could get bystanders hurt in the crossfire.

Phones buzzed around her, an annoying trill, and she knew the OEM had sent out an alert. People would know where to go and get advice on what to do. She pressed on with a brief look behind. There was no sign of her pursuers. Overhead, nothing tracked her from the air. Maybe all the people in the street had acted as a deterrent. But then a yelp. Behind her the woman with the gun had shoved a lady holding a baby out of the way.

Sabreen ran across one street and then another. Finding a burst of energy, she ran even faster. A left turn at the corner and the warehouse was one block away. The scene that greeted her stopped her in her tracks.

Most of the street rested in a sunken pit filled with rubble. Buildings on both sides were crumbled ruins that covered the remains of the sidewalks. Smoke rose from the pit and sparks flashed from live wires. There was no way to get around it, and a climb over the ruins risked electrocution.

After a split-second decision, Sabreen ran on. She had to go an extra block and double back to reach the warehouse. If the heavy surveillance did not deter her potential assailants, she hoped to lose them in the fifty or so aisles of the massive food store.

She ran past blaring alarms, fallen trees and several people. They either shuffled away, to an emergency staging area she presumed, or milled about awestruck by the destruction. A few glanced in her direction, curious about the two women racing through the street, but still caught up in their own shock.

The tall woman was still in pursuit as Sabreen rounded the corner. She had to slow the woman down. A large branch the size of a baseball bat rested on the sidewalk. Grabbing the branch, she waited by the corner of the building. There was only one other person running, so when the sound of rapid footsteps reached the corner, Sabreen leapt away from the building and swung. The branch connected with the tall woman's head. She gave her head a little shake, then fumbled at her holster. Sabreen spotted the gun. She feared the woman's qualms about shooting in public were gone and swung again. This time the woman went facedown on the pavement, dazed but conscious. The weapon skittered a foot away.

Sabreen fled. For a moment she considered grabbing the gun, but without the element of surprise she doubted she'd win any fight. Besides, if the weapon had a biometric lock, she would have wasted precious time. Holding onto the branch in case the other two pursuers decided to show up, she sprinted faster than before.

This better be the last time, Munro. The mantra raged in her head. Although he'd promised the data had nothing to do with her future father-in-law, that did not mean the manipulative senior Jennings was not involved. Carlo Jennings played emotional strings like a virtuoso. He would state his case in such a way that guilt and loyalty compelled Munro to do his father's bidding. "Your older brother has his business to run. He's a busy man. And your younger brother has a learning disability. He can't handle this project. You're the only one I can count on." If that did not work, a speech about his mother would ensue. "If only Manda was alive. She knew enough about the business to lend a hand."

That would lead Munro into a sleepless night. Memories filled his nightmares about the day his mother died. An explosion. Gunfire. His mother's body smothering him as a lone shooter, some disgruntled employee, found them huddled in Carlo's office and opened fire.

Munro had been three years old, and though his mother had saved him from physical harm, it still troubled his mind. Carlo never witnessed his troubled nights. By morning, Munro would agree to Carlo's request, then disappear for a week. She always knew where he went, but what he did was anyone's guess. Whenever he returned he was apologetic, showering her with tacky souvenirs and amorous kisses. He would vow to be done with his father's requests, once his business was up and running.

She wished her fiancé had finished with the senior Jennings ages ago.

Rounding the corner, she sped past closed storefronts. Her parents had the right idea, retire early and get out of the game. They divided their time between the family home in Barbados and a vacation home in Colombia, while they ate flying fish, played road tennis or debated whether or not to take the new longevity serum. Their hi-tech corporate jobs had given them enough to sail away before the economic downturn. Unlike her parents, Sabreen had landed a city job, run by the government until the OEM went private. It was scooped up by Fukushi, like scores of other emergency management offices. Around the world, businesses bailed out government agencies and took over operations, at a price. Job security was a distant memory as companies merged and downsized.

She hustled at that reminder. *Just get to the drone and lose the tail, then stay at the satellite office for the night.* The smoke hit her halfway down the block. Something was really burning. It smelled like wood and plastic and food.

The Sabor Chef warehouse was on fire.

The warehouse occupied an entire block. The two-storey cube had a whitewashed façade with evenly spaced windows on the second floor, customer entrances on the north and south sides, and loading bays for vehicles and drones on the east. On a normal day, people, drones, and self-driving mini-trucks would utilize every entrance to deliver or pick up food.

This scene was drastically different. Smoke rose in thick black plumes from the east side of the building. News drones buzzed high above the building like a swarm of flies. She recognized a few foreign news outlets from their company logos.

Sabreen reached the south entrance of the building and found the OEM drone hovering obediently over the sliding doors. She told the device to record images of the building at all angles and circle back to the main office. It lifted into the air to perform its tasks.

The fire had yet to reach the southern entrance, but Sabreen had no intention of waiting for the flames to arrive. Sabreen jogged away. The satellite office was a fifteen-minute walk from the burning warehouse, but she did not want to risk running into the tall woman or the two men before she got there. Plus, anyone following the news could pick up on her location.

She spotted the local coffee shop she frequented, Quick Coffee. The owner, Vervain something or other, was always friendly. After throwing the branch to the side, Sabreen waved her hands in front of the camera over the front door. Then she brought out an official OEM badge and shoved it toward the camera. The lock clicked and she let herself inside.

"Hi, Vervain?" On the shelves, cups and bags of coffee were overturned. Plaster from the ceiling dusted the floor. The shop was otherwise intact, but looked empty.

"Sabreen, is it?" Behind the counter, a full-sized holographic image of Vervain frowned in her direction. The owner was monitoring her shop offsite.

Sabreen nodded and put away her badge. "You have privacy capabilities? Maybe you should turn them on. The fire across the street was probably started by looters."

Vervain's head did a little shake, as if that piece of news had jolted her awake. Her hand tapped at the air. The front door clicked again as it locked. "You can see out but no one can see in. The window and door are soundproofed and fire resistant."

Sabreen still smelled the faint scent of food and burning building materials. The window might be fire resistant, but not airtight. Sabor Chef's sensors should have picked up the fire and activated fire safety protocols, but the building was still ablaze. A purposely set fire? An unnatural earthquake? With the economy tanking and gas and oil reserves the lowest in fifty years, things were bound to get worse. What was she walking around with that could make any difference?

"What are you doing there?" Vervain's image wavered for a second, then came back. "You said there's a fire. Is that building even safe?"

"I'm fine for now." Actually, she had no idea. At least no one was chasing her at the moment. "Are you okay?"

"I reported to an emergency station in the park a few blocks away. There's a tent city growing out here. Hold on." The sound muted as her image spoke to someone off to the side. "Sorry about that. I'm still operating my shops in Philly and DC. I am safe here, right?"

"I'm sure it's the safest place around." The best answer she could give without more information. "How can I turn the vidscreen on?" It was mounted high on the wall behind the counter.

Vervain's image tapped at the air and the vidscreen came on. "If you need me, just say my name. The shop will let me know."

"Thanks." Her image winked out.

The news reported limited information was coming out of New York. The scene switched to the UK. Sabreen watched a group of young men pounding on a car with a couple inside. There had been something about a food shortage on the news feeds yesterday . . .

She could not worry about overseas right now. A major food warehouse, one of seven for the city, was out of commission. If food warehouses were unable to deliver to residences, small shops, like Quick Coffee, would be targets next.

Sabreen flinched when she turned back to the window. The two men were back, furtive glances searching the street. One man looked back toward the warehouse entrance and checked the sky.

Looking for my drone, Sabreen thought. Her heart pounded in her chest, but neither man gave Quick Coffee more than a cursory glance. When they were gone, Sabreen let out the breath she held and called her office.

"Sam . . ."

"Got the drone's vid feed. Same thing's happening here. Food Sync warehouse is almost ashes. Did you see looters?"

"No, I . . ."

"These guys went in, stole a truckload from the warehouse,

then split. Next thing, building's up in flames. We think they're lowering the supply so they can sell what they have at super-high prices." Sam cursed, then yelled at someone to get rescue teams downtown. The office sounded chaotic, with bells and shouts going off intermittently in the background. "So, Sabreen, why can't I see you? Still calling me on your suit?"

Sabreen took a deep breath. "It's going to take me a while to get to the satellite office for a face-to-face."

"Why? What's going on?"

"Saw someone with a gun. Thought I should I get off the street. I'm staying in a coffee shop until I think it's safe." Not exactly the truth, but not a lie.

"Okay." He paused. "Marie, get me some coffee!" Sabreen could imagine Sam walking over to one of the many screens around his desk as he checked out scenes around the city. "Okay, I can send a security guy over to you in about an hour. One guy's all we can spare."

"That's fine . . ."

"Good." Sam was offline before he finished the word. Anything else she had to tell him would have to wait. Sam was already onto the next crisis.

A delicious smell filled the air as a mug of hot chocolate rose out of the counter. "Thank you, Vervain." Luckily, the power worked but the air conditioning was full blast. A warm drink would be comforting right now. She wrapped the mug around her chilled fingers and took a sip.

On the vidscreen, subtitles played across the bottom of the screen. A reporter spoke of the assistance companies were sending to the city. Sabreen's heartbeat sped up when she read the news caption. "Brightshores Search and Rescue sending teams to New York City".

The bulk of Brightshores' business concentrated on old-world energy industries, like underwater drilling or propellant manufacturing. They had a small search-and-rescue operation that centered around missions on the high seas, usually in or near their platforms. Big cities weren't their expertise. That they had mobilized teams to lend Fukushi assistance so quickly after the earthquake made Sabreen suspicious.

Rumbling from outside drew Sabreen's attention to the burning building. A fire helicopter hovered over the building. A few seconds later, it doused a steady stream of liquid over the raging flames. That should stop the flames from spreading. Sabreen took another sip from her hot chocolate. It might be her last for a while if a severe food shortage was imminent.

A rap at the door made Sabreen jump. She saw a woman with her hands cupped against the door, squinting to see through the one-way shaded glass. The person wore the same two-piece black formfitting suit as her pursuers. The logo of a fist holding onto a scale at its fulcrum was at least different from the three anonymous people who'd chased her earlier. Another outsourced security firm. No one with enough funds called city police anymore for assistance. They were always understaffed and even called private firms themselves to help with cases.

Sabreen's suit received an incoming message. Checking the tiny monochrome screen, a message from Sam appeared with details on the security officer. The crude photo matched the woman on the other side of the glass.

"Hello, Officer Devonish," Sabreen said when she opened the

door. The officer had short curly black hair that stopped at her earlobes and complimented her mocha complexion. Boots thudded against the hard floor as the woman strutted in with the confidence most private security officers possessed.

"Are you ready to go?" While the officer scanned the room, Sabreen relaxed at the other woman's professional manner. At least the sidearm strapped to the woman's side remained there.

"Yes." She adjusted her go bag.

The ground rumbled. A clump of ceiling fell in between them and Sabreen jumped back; the officer never flinched. Just a small aftershock.

Sabreen moved to the doorway, then stopped, making sure there was no sign of her pursuers. The street was clear except for the newly arrived firemen and a few gawkers.

The shaking subsided before Officer Devonish spoke. "Is there a problem?"

"No, of course not. How are we getting out of here?"

"I came on my bike. It's parked on the corner away from the fire."

Still she hesitated. Riding on a bike in a bright yellow suit was far too much exposure. "One moment." She put down her go bag and went behind the counter. "I feel like a target in this yellow suit." She retrieved a crumpled gray jacket tucked on a shelf under the counter. She had seen Vervain throw the jacket back here on the few occasions she worked in the store. It had a coffee stain on its pocket and the sleeves stopped before they reached her wrists, but it would serve its purpose.

She set the temperature regulator to keep her suit cool. At least, if they—whoever they were—searched for a yellow suit, the

Quick Coffee jacket would make it harder. There was nothing she could do about the bright yellow pants. As Sabreen retrieved her bag and moved to the front door, Devonish gave her an odd look. Sabreen ignored the other woman and stepped onto the sidewalk through an inch of water that sloshed over the street.

"So there was a looting problem?"

Sabreen followed the officer's gaze. On one side of the street, storefronts were intact. The only sign of possible looting was the charred half of the smoldering building. If any theft had occurred as in the Food Sync warehouse, they were long gone by the time she'd arrived.

"I saw someone with a gun." Devonish's skeptical glare told Sabreen she should divert the conversation. "Where's this bike?"

Devonish nodded right. Sabreen walked ahead, wondering if she should let Devonish take the lead for protection but not wanting to appear skittish.

"Bike's right there on the corner, ma'am."

Sabreen waited by the bike, her gaze up making a nervous scan of the area. People either milled around or walked on to their destinations. No assassins, kidnappers or memory stick thieves lurked within striking distance.

Instead of approaching her bike, Devonish walked ahead into the street and crouched next to a vehicle.

"Shouldn't we get going?" Sabreen asked. She hugged herself, feeling too exposed on the street corner. Were Devonish's security skills good enough to defend her? So absorbed with her own safety, Sabreen failed to notice what caught Devonish's attention. She stepped away from the bike to follow the other woman's gaze. What she saw made her gasp.

A lifeless arm poked out from underneath the truck parked at the corner. Another woman lay on the street, her neck bent at an awkward angle. Sabreen saw no way it could have been an accident. "She's wearing a Sabor Chef uniform. My boss said looters hit a Food Sync, then set the place on fire. Maybe she got in their way." Both fully automated food stores kept a handful of people onsite for help-desk and maintenance purposes.

"Looters again." Devonish's voice was flat and skeptical as she crouched next to the body to inspect it. She pulled her phone out. "I'm calling a CSD to record and secure the scene. Then we can go."

At the mention of a crime scene drone, Sabreen loosened her straightened hair from her ponytail, using her hands to comb it closer around her face. She wished she had a hood. Devonish's eyebrows furrowed, obviously confused at the gesture, but she said nothing as she stood.

They waited by the officer's bike for a minute that felt like an eternity to Sabreen.

A familiar low hum approached them from the sky. Devonish squinted upward, her hand shading her eyes. "It's here. We can leave." Devonish mounted the bike, thumbed the biometric lock on and released the wheels. She donned her helmet, then stopped to stare at the sky. "There's another one."

Sabreen refused to look and concentrated on Devonish's surprised features. Their eyes met and Devonish's expression turned from surprise to irritation. Let Devonish think she was hiding something. The truth would take too long to explain. "We should go." Sabreen grabbed the spare helmet attached to the bike and climbed on the back.

Sabreen understood her behavior was strange. If a drone flew low overhead, a normal reaction was to look up. She was not about to explain that she wanted to hide her face from the drone, that if it had less than one hundred percent of her identity confirmed, it would take longer to alert whomever was chasing her—she hoped. The officer might be confused about her behavior, but did it warrant such anger?

She was not about to explain what her fiancé had gotten her into, that the current world of corp execs was more cutthroat than the Senate of ancient Rome. It was ridiculous to explain her situation when she was not sure why people were after her to begin with. Maybe the corporate need for good PR would keep her pursuers at bay while she traveled with another woman, a potential witness.

They took off. A few blocks later, Devonish stopped to let an emergency vehicle pass. The sound of the drone had disappeared, so Sabreen peeked at the sky. Far away, drones hovered in the distance, but nothing nearby.

"It flew away the minute you got on," Officer Devonish said, obviously sensing what she was looking for.

"Who'd it belong to? Did you see a logo?"

"Zenith." Silence ensued. Devonish shook her head.

Sabreen had tensed at the company name. A minute went by and Devonish had yet to pull away from the intersection. "What's wrong?" Sabreen asked.

Devonish ignored her question and revved the engine. "Just sit tight." She paused before shouting, "And if you must know, I hate when corp types use security officers for their own personal issues."

Sabreen rode along in silence. Let the other woman think what she wanted. She had to figure out what was going on before she involved anyone else. Was Munro in trouble? Was his father? No matter what, she trusted Munro when he said this was the last special assignment for Zenith. She had no desire to do anything to jeopardize that or get him in trouble.

The Zenith drone was troubling. Did Carlo Jennings care so little about his future daughter-in-law that he'd sent an armed corporate lackey to abduct or mug her for the data she carried? At least they hadn't shot at her when she was out in the open.

Farther away from the river, the destruction was less apparent. Still, a few people determined to make their way out of the city piled into vehicles and added to the traffic on the street. She spotted stacked suitcases and unhappy children in a number of back seats. Devonish weaved around the traffic until they arrived at their destination.

The building was a one-storey square nestled between two thirty-storey structures. The front consisted of a garage door on the right and a regular front door on the left. All the buildings on the street seemed unaffected by the quake. "OEM coordinator Sabreen Toppin, zero four zero nine. Open the garage door." Somewhere, camouflaged in the brick-faced edifice, mics and cameras sent her voice and image to the building AI for identification. After a few seconds, the garage door rolled up and Sabreen went inside. When Devonish pushed the bike in beside her, Sabreen turned to the other woman. "You don't have to stay. Thank you for getting me here."

Devonish held up a hand as if she recited a pledge. "I'm supposed to get you here safely and make sure you're safe here. Those are my orders and I will carry them out to the best of my ability as a security officer. Or until I get new orders." The woman pushed her bike farther into the garage, parallel with the Fukushi vehicle, a standard black car with the +F logo on each front door. Sabreen heard metal scrape and knew the car had received some scratches.

Sabreen shook her head. "Close garage door." The building recognized the tone of her voice as a command and rolled the door closed.

After a survey of the next room, she found it was the same as she'd left it during a training exercise a year ago. A vidscreen took up half of one wall. There was a basic steel desk set, with a table and chair that faced the front door and window. Opposite that was an armchair/futon combination that was actually comfy the one time she'd slept on it. In the back was a small bathroom consisting of a toilet, sink, and narrow shower. A window over the toilet was the only other exit. It led to an alley and a common courtyard for one of the neighboring buildings.

After a stint in the bathroom, she returned to the main room to find Devonish at the window, seated in the armchair combo and keeping watch on the street. At least the officer intended to do her job. It was one less thing Sabreen had to worry about.

The desk had a set of drawers and she opened the top one to remove a laptop. Once connected to the wall vidscreen, she logged into the OEM system. A three-by-three grid of scenes from various parts of Brooklyn appeared on the wall. She connected with her boss and performed her duties as coordinator. She discovered areas in need of assistance, buildings that had fallen after the initial event, or fires that flared to life hours later. Rescues were dispatched and security teams assembled to protect food stores. Thankfully, the automated seawalls, built to withstand storm surges from Category 5 hurricanes, had kept most of the waters between New York and New Jersey off the land.

After three hours of steady work, the situation was stable. She contacted her boss. He dabbed sweat off his forehead before he turned toward the vidscreen. "Yeah!"

"Sam, I'm going to take a few minutes to call Munro."

"Sure, take fifteen. When you talk to him, make sure you mention that if his old man wants to send us some volunteers or donate some equipment, Fukushi Corp and the city of New York would greatly appreciate it."

Sabreen took a deep breath and flashed a wry smile before signing off. Trying to explain that Munro was not his father was a waste of time. Nervous, she sat back and hugged her arms, hoping that was still true. That he still meant to break away from that tyrant. Officer Devonish remained stationed at the window, eyes on the street.

A search of the drawers turned up a privacy filter that Sabreen attached to the laptop screen. She went into their joint cloud account, downloading three encryption apps. After disconnecting from the net and the OEM network, Sabreen slipped the memory stick from the inside of her sleeve and connected it to the laptop. Decryption failed with the first app, but the files opened when she applied the second.

There was a file named Engineering and another named Schematics, while the others all resembled serial numbers and were meaningless to Sabreen. She opened a numbered file at random and found interoffice memos, the Brightshores logo at the top of every page. A test for something called the Mole Driver was scheduled almost a year before. Execs were hopeful about its success. Another file revealed reports on projected fuel production from a new subterranean source.

She viewed the schematics file again. Brightshores, the leader when it came to drilling platforms, had invented a mobile drilling rig. Other files revealed more technical jargon that left her utterly befuddled. The information in the last file left her shocked. She shook her head at Brightshores' callous disregard for public safety. The epicenter and the new source of fuel were the same location.

Sabreen opened a window with four local newsfeeds. The devastation around the mouths of the Hudson and East rivers was overwhelming. Two more buildings had fully collapsed in Brooklyn, while several lay crumbled in New Jersey. Lower Manhattan was being evacuated until foundations were checked and buildings secured. The OEM office had set up camp just outside the devastation perimeter. Even the Statue of Liberty was in danger. Cracks had been found near the ground level.

"All's quiet!"

Sabreen jumped, then realized Devonish was standing right behind her, a wicked grin on her face.

The grin turned to a sneer when the officer tried to glance at the vidscreen protected by the privacy filter. With the privacy filter on, all the officer could see was shade. "Heading to the head." Devonish walked away, closing the door to the bathroom once inside.

With five minutes of break time left, she dialed Munro. She thought he would make her wait, but Munro picked up a second after she sent the call to his emergency phone.

"Thank goodness," he said after a sharp exhale. His hazel eyes stared back at her on the screen. "Don't tell me where you are. You're okay, right?"

"What did you get me into?" Rows of chairs lined the background, filled with people. The sounds of several voices added to the frantic atmosphere. She recognized the Philadelphia International Airport behind him.

"The answer to everything. We just have to keep it out of their hands a little bit longer. You still remember where I'll be tomorrow?"

Sabreen nodded.

"Good. Meet me there first thing." He looked to her right at something offscreen.

"Wait, whose hands am I keeping it out of?" He still had to give her answers. How could she help if she only knew a small part of what was going on?

Munro's head whipped around as an explosion shook the building in the background.

"Ro, what's that? Are you okay?" All annoyance ceased; she just wanted Munro safe.

"I'm fine. Just meet me tomorrow." Behind Munro a ceiling light fixture crashed to the floor, people scattered, then the connection winked out.

Sabreen sat back, hugged her arms and took a deep breath. She knew he was resilient enough to get out of the airport in one piece and meet her tomorrow morning. Still, she feared this whole errand was meaningless, that the Brightshores data was merely a lure meant to reel Munro in to some more nefarious scheme.

No, his father had sent him on a mission like so many times before. Carlo Jennings wanted the information but not until tomorrow. Was he in cahoots with Brightshores? Would he bury the information? Or did he mean to steal the schematics and create an improved non-earthquake-causing design?

Sabreen examined the files again, but found nothing to indicate the Mole Driver caused earthquakes. Still, half the locations were places earthquakes had occurred in recent months.

"Looks like the Brightshores logo." Devonish's mouth was less than an inch from her ear.

Sabreen inhaled sharply at the sudden interruption. "Privacy filters are placed on vidscreens for a reason."

Devonish straightened. "Yeah, usually to hide things."

Sabreen closed the files and tucked the stick back under her sleeve. "You know, I'm pretty safe here. The building will let me know if someone approaches or tries to get in. Why don't you take off?"

Devonish pulled out her phone and shook her head. "Work order says I'm assigned to you for twenty-four hours or until consigned to another assignment." She shrugged. "Sorry."

"Look, I have to work for two more hours. Why don't you rest in the car while I work?"

Devonish's face turned pensive. "I'll make sure the building is secure, then unfold the chair by the window and take my nap. You just wake me when you're done working. We'll switch places."

"Okay." At least she would not have to worry about Devonish for two hours.

The officer circuited the building to perform her inspection. Sabreen contacted her boss, explaining that she had to leave first thing in the morning due to a family emergency. Resistant at first, he acquiesced when she promised to get Zenith to donate some supplies. She worked for four more hours and finally called it a night. Despite Devonish's tough-woman attitude, she was still asleep. Sabreen let her rest and went to the garage to sleep in the vehicle. She was exhausted. Tomorrow would be a busy day.

∞

Someone pulled her legs out of the vehicle.

"Wake up. Someone's here!" Sabreen shook the sleep out of her head while Devonish shook her torso. "Wake up!"

"What? Okay." She managed to sit up. "I didn't hear the building." She checked the stick next to her wrist. Still there.

"They're not near the building, they're across the street."

"Show me."

Devonish sped away into the next room and Sabreen followed. "There. At two o'clock."

Sabreen looked down at the small screen on her suit's sleeve to check the time. Had she slept through the afternoon? It was 6:45 am. Then Devonish pointed out the window and she realized the officer was not talking about time.

"Where are they?" she asked, not sure where two o'clock was on an old clock.

"Over there. See the black sedan, tinted windows? It wasn't there last night. Pretty sure someone's in there."

"Is the security shade on?"

Devonish huffed, exasperated. "Of course. And you didn't wake me like we agreed."

Sabreen ignored the gruff remark. She had to find a way to reach Munro without being followed. Devonish leveled a grumpy stare in her direction. The other woman tucked wayward curls behind her ears and folded her arms. "Are you going to tell me what's really going on? Looter's not going anywhere."

Sabreen ignored the sarcasm and formulated a plan. She could slip out the bathroom window, down the short alley and disappear into the apartment complex, then walk a few blocks to the ferry station. Chances were her three pursuers had thought to cover the back and there was only one way out of the alley. She needed Devonish's help.

"So you're pretty loyal to Fukushi and the people you work for."

Devonish looked taken aback. "Of course. And if you think I won't do my job because I don't like your story, you're wrong. It'll just be easier to complete my assignment if I have all the facts." She glanced out the window and added, "If someone orders your arrest later, well . . ." She shrugged.

"Fine, I need your help anyway. But first you should know Munro Jennings is my fiancé. Carlo B. Jennings is his father."

"He owns Zenith Galactic."

Sabreen nodded. "I don't know if he's working for his father or against him."

"Why would he work against his own father?"

"They have a complicated relationship. Let's just say Carlo B doesn't always do things on the up and up and Munro has a problem with that." She grabbed her right sleeve. "Anyway, the data on this stick proves the earthquake was man-made."

"I knew it. By Brightshores and Zenith?"

"Brightshores is definitely involved. Zenith's role is unclear. I need to get this data someplace without being followed. Will you help?"

Devonish stared out the window. "I can help, but only if you intend to use that information to bring Brightshores and whoever else is involved to justice." After a moment, Devonish turned an intense gaze her way.

"I do. The right person will get this data." She might sit on it while she made sure Munro was okay first, but she would take it to the right authority, once she determined who that was.

"Okay, then." Devonish smirked. "I have an idea."

Moments later, Sabreen watched Devonish drive away in the OEM vehicle. The officer went slow, then sped up as soon as she reached the suspicious vehicle. The other car sputtered to life and followed.

Sabreen scanned the street, looking for her pursuers, and saw no one. She tugged on the legs of the more petite woman's uniform. Unlike her emergency suit, which molded to a wide range of body sizes, the pants ended just above her ankles. She worried about them splitting if she had to run. At least Devonish had said the fabric was supposed to be bulletproof.

Her OEM replacement would arrive in one hour, but Sabreen had no intention to wait. After one more look at the street, she donned Devonish's helmet and went out the front door. This particular street was home to storage centers and light manufacturing offices. Very few residences occupied the route she took. In ten minutes, she reached the ferry service without incident. It took another ten minutes for the ferry to reach her destination.

United Nations Island, formerly Randall's Island, was located north of the epicenter and remained relatively unscathed. On the western side, OEM had erected a tent city to aid those displaced by the disaster. Several survivors had accompanied Sabreen on the ferry, their dazed expressions a testament to their ordeal. They filed past Sabreen and headed for the tents, ushered by an OEM employee in a neon-green Tec suit.

She thought she recognized him as a new employee and made a quick turn in the opposite direction. The helmet was left under a seat in the ferry. If he spotted her, he might want to talk or assign her some task. The only person she wanted to speak with at the moment was Munro.

The UN buildings stood before her in shining glass and steel. Years ago, UN headquarters had been moved to the island for the sake of security. Protection AIs constantly scanned the perimeter for threats. If known criminals approached the building, hidden gun ports opened, shockwave speakers readied, and authorities would be notified. The order of the actions depended on the assessed threat. The moment she left the ferry she was scanned, her identity sent through the AI ringer and then to a security team inside.

Sabreen walked down the length of a food cart court. On one side stood the unattended carts representing the international flavors of the men and women of the UN, while the other side held empty tables with pairs of chairs.

She took a seat opposite their favorite food cart, one that served Taiwanese dishes with freshly made noodles. It was the very same table where Munro had proposed.

She had been staring at a young man at the now-empty food cart as he twisted and tossed noodle dough. Suddenly, Munro had filled her line of sight, on one knee, a ring between his thumb and forefinger.

He slipped the ring on her finger and asked the question. She had a vague recollection of uttering the word "Yes".

Then she was out of her seat, as their arms went around each other and lips locked.

Memory turned to reality and Munro was there. His lips were on hers and for a moment the rest of the world ceased to exist. That there was a man-made earthquake. That people chased her. That her future father-in-law was a megalomaniac who thought his son was marrying below his social and economic class. She was lost in the moment and everything was all right.

But everything was different. The engagement ring was forgotten during her escape, left a foot away from the memory sticks. The extravagant diamond would snag in her hair, and she removed it every night before bedtime. Now it was gone. Some demolition worker would find it or it would go undiscovered in the rubble.

She pulled back and swatted him on the arm. "What is going on?"

He held her shoulders, a huge grin on his face. "I knew you would make it here."

"Munro."

"I was worried when I saw that the quake hit New York. I'm sorry if I didn't show it."

"Munro."

"They found me at the airport. If I didn't get rid of the data, they were going to take it from me."

"Munro."

"I knew it was safe with you."

"Munro!" She screamed him into silence. He stared at her, expectation written on his face. "Tell me what you did and then tell me what you want to do now."

He took a step back and shoved his hands in his pants pockets. After a glance left and then right, he took a deep breath. "Dad sent me to Brightshores. I was at their headquarters in Jakarta. I took the tour. They have a tour if you believe that."

"Munro." He would stall if she let him, his need to protect his father warring with his loyalty to her.

"Right. I went to get data on any recent research projects. Remote access didn't work. I needed to be physically in the same building as their R&D department. They must have ten layers of firewalls. And the encryption . . ."

Sabreen folded her arms.

"Right. I got the data and got out of Brightshores. But I was made. They followed me to the airport. I had a two-hour wait until takeoff and nowhere to go. They were going to corner me and take it back. I knew it'd be safe with you." He grabbed her shoulders. "And then the earthquake. I didn't know the city was their next mining location. I'm so sorry."

She placed two fingers on his lips. "Okay. What do we do now?"

"Yes, Mr. Jennings. What should we do now?"

The woman she'd encountered on the street stood with fists clenched at her sides, sporting a nasty bruise on her cheek. Sabreen saw the glare on the woman's face and knew she remembered exactly how she'd got that bruise. Just behind her a stocky man with a shaved head glared with equal feorcity. No guns in sight, but their stance told Sabreen they were dangerous even without a weapon.

"Ro, did I mention people are trying to kill me?"

Munro took a step back, tugging Sabreen with him. "Dewi Fangestu," he said. "North American head of Brightshores Security."

"We're not trying to kill either of you. Give us the data you stole and no one gets hurt." The woman smiled. It made Sabreen believe her words even less. Even though she spoke to Munro, her eyes were on Sabreen, like a boxer waiting for the next round to start.

Sabreen and Munro glanced behind them where two more men waited.

"This is what you want." Munro held up a stick. For a moment, she thought he'd swiped hers, but the stick she carried was tucked away in an inside pocket. The jacket would need to be unbuttoned in the front for him to have access to it. "Let us go and you can have it. I'll put it down on the ground for you. We walk away."

"I think maybe we search you for copies, just to be sure." At a sharp nod of Dewi's head, the Brightshores men advanced.

Munro gave her arm a gentle squeeze before he said, "You should get to Dad's offices on the third floor."

"We should run. They can't draw any weapons here." Sabreen had no desire to separate again.

"Third floor." Munro gave her a push and ran in the opposite direction.

Sabreen never hesitated. She weaved around the tables and chairs. A sideways glance told her Baldhead was on her heels. Dewi followed, but hung back as if confident in her colleague's abilities. He ran with such an unnatural grace for such a stocky man that stimulants or bioenhancements must be involved. Sabreen lost sight of Munro and the two other men as she zigzagged between tables and chairs. She heard his footfalls get closer. Safety would be at the front entrance with the AI's cameras and the guards. She neared the corner when a rough hand grabbed her forearm, whipping her around to a stop. The bald man had caught up with her.

"Security Officer Devonish. Let her go, then put your hands in the air." The words boomed in rapid succession and with authority. That only aggravated Baldhead, who tightened his grip. He drew Sabreen closer. Any second his other hand would be around her neck.

Two shots fired, so close the air near her face grew warmer as one bullet blew past. In the distance, someone near the tents yelped at the report. Her assailant's grip loosened and she wrenched herself free. His right arm was suspended in midair, while he tried to move it with his left.

"Hands up, lady." Devonish pointed the gun at Dewi, who ignored the command and backed up. "Don't move!"

"An officer has ordered you to stop. Please comply." The words were repeated in a continuous loop, the AI activated once Dewi disobeyed a security officer. Dewi said something that sounded like a curse, then turned and ran. "Warning. You will be disabled!" The words came out of the air; no speakers were visible anywhere. Then an intermittent yowl blared. It was loud, but moving away from Sabreen. Dewi, on the other hand, stumbled to the ground, hands over her ears. Directed sound.

"That should keep her busy." Devonish smirked. "You need me to get you to the right people?"

"I'll get to the right people. Just keep these two away from me."

Sabreen took a step back as Baldhead grunted and reached for her without success.

"He's not going anywhere. The thing about those high-tech prosthetics, one shot in the right place and they just freeze up."

"How did you even bring a weapon without the AIs attacking you?"

"Security officers have an override code. I guess your Brightshores friends didn't want anyone to know why they're here or they would've brought weapons, too. I've probably been reported to my superiors for using it, so I hope I can give them a justifiable reason for it."

Sabreen nodded. "You will." She turned and entered the main building, walking straight to the elevator bank. No one was in the lobby this early. Anyone usually stationed in the lobby had probably gone out to the tents to help.

She took an elevator and stepped onto the third floor, unnerved by the quiet. A sign with an arrow that pointed right indicated the corporate lounges. Zenith Galactic, as well as the other major corps, had a collection of suites, a respite for execs before they addressed the UN. Carlo Jennings would be there. If Munro wanted her to go there, he was not working against his father. All the same, she had no desire to encounter him yet.

The International Council on Corporate Responsibility would meet today. Munro, as a member, tried to attend every meeting. Most people suspected the backroom deals, the system hacks and the corporate spying. No one knew about the community interference, arranged marriages prior to mergers, and the execs in perfect health who suddenly died of heart attacks so eager VPs had to step in. At least, no one thought it affected them, but it did. Munro had joined ICoCoR to change that, though Sabreen suspected Carlo Jennings was the number-one culprit when it came to the corporate underworld.

Sabreen went in the opposite direction, toward the mostly symbolic conference rooms. Most countries let their ambassadors communicate through virtual link, but some still used the facilities in the building. Turning the corner, she found the rooms behind walls of transparent glass. At the largest, two men dressed in uniforms flanked the door. Inside a young man sat, typing at a long conference table, while an older man paced between a window and a huge vidscreen, his white-gray hair a contrast to chocolate brown skin. Kwame Sekou, Chair of the Council. He would deal with Brightshores. She rushed forward, intending to introduce herself and present the stick.

"Halt!" One of the men by the door blocked her path. He held out his hand. "You're not authorized to go in there."

"I have information for the Chair. It proves Brightshores had something to do with the earthquake." She took the memory stick from an inside pocket and waved it in front of the guard.

"It's all right. Let her in." Sekou's voice drifted out of the wall.

The guard stepped aside. Sabreen was met at the door by an excited Chairman Sekou. "This can prove Brightshores caused the earthquake, you say? We've been waiting for something like this. Please, give it to me." He held out his hand.

"What are you going to do with it?"

"Bring Brightshores to justice, of course."

She had seen Sekou's newsfeeds. He tried his best to keep the corps in line, or at least spread awareness about their corruption. There was no better way. Sabreen handed Sekou the stick.

"It will be taken care of. Please, have a seat and help yourself." He gestured to an area of the conference table with a tray of finger food and a pitcher of water, then left.

The young man, who had been staring at the exchange, went back to his typing.

Sabreen had last eaten over a day ago, but she avoided the tray. "May I borrow your phone?" The young man smiled as he handed her the phone. She called Munro and only got his voicemail. How long should she wait for Sekou to return? Was Munro safe? Sabreen mirrored Sekou's actions from before he left and paced.

The guard who had spoken to her entered the room. "Ms. Toppin, can you follow me, please?"

This was it. For better or worse, she would find out if handing the data over to the Chair had been the right thing to do. She followed the guard to the corporate suites. Milky white walls lined the hall; even the doors lacked a window. Corps valued their privacy. Sabreen doubted calls could be made from the hallway without security clearance. The guard stopped at a door with a Zenith logo on it, and faced a clear plastic square panel. A red horizontal line panned down the panel, scanning his face or just his eyes. Sabreen had no idea what type of scanner it was, but its existence made her nervous. The door clicked open and Sabreen fought the urge to run. This had to be a mistake. She should be in the Chair's chambers or some other public meeting place.

"Ah, my soon-to-be daughter-in-law, Sabreen Toppin, is here. Please come in, Sabreen."

Which was more of a shock, Carlo calling her his future daughter-in-law out loud or him saying "Please"? For a moment, the astonishment froze her in place. Scenarios leapt into her mind. There was a gun to his head and anyone who entered would be cut down as soon as they stepped over the threshold. It was really the end of the world and she should bolt, find Munro and head to the nearest underground shelter to wait out the ensuing blast.

Instead, Sabreen hesitated in the doorway. The room was dim. Various men and women, seven execs of major corps, and Sekou, sat around a horseshoe-shaped table. Brightshores president

Yuda Erasmus sat at the head of the table. They all faced a huge vidscreen that took up most of the wall. She recognized one of the Brightshores files from the stick. Jennings waited by the screen, as if he were about to point out something.

"Brighter lights." Carlo walked over and pecked her on the cheek. "Glad you could make it."

Two men lurked in the farthest corner. Sabreen stepped back, recognizing the men she'd spotted outside her wrecked apartment building. Carlo held onto her shoulders. "Don't worry. You gave my men the slip when you left your little office. Took them a while to figure out that officer wasn't you. They were sent to help you get here. Apparently, you didn't need it." He gestured to the two men, who grabbed Erasmus by the shoulders and lifted him from his seat.

"They're not with Brightshores?" Sabreen asked in confusion.

"Hardly." Carlo waved at the pair. "My men are here to ensure everyone's safety."

Yuda Erasmus kept looking from the vidscreen to Carlo, anger creeping into his features. "This is an outrage. That device was safe. It would find and extract fossil fuel close to the mantle. Bring it back safely to the surface. Something else must be at play here."

"How do you know it was safe? What impact study did you base that on?" Carlo stepped into their path. Rage filled his voice.

"Your study . . ." he yelled in equal rage, then shrank back.

Carlo tilted his head and smiled. "My study? You mean the one we did on our project that ultimately showed such a device would lead to devastation? That we scrapped and locked away with the rest of our failed projects? In fact, we had our lead scientist on that project fired for falsifying data. He said there were huge oil reserves underneath Manhattan. That couldn't be the study to which you're referring." He gave his lips a thoughtful tap. "Now, how would you know about all that, Yuda, unless you stole our research?"

Murmurs of shock went through the seated execs.

A moment of recognition followed by resignation passed through the man's eyes. Carlo's smile got wider.

Erasmus shook his head. "You doctored that research!"

Carlo waved his hand and his security men stepped forward.

"This is an outrage! This is your fault! You created this situation by depleting the fuel supply with your damn projects! Colonizing Mars! We can barely live on this planet!" Erasmus ranted as he was dragged from the room.

Carlo ignored the tirade. "What you missed, my dear, was that ICoCoR will become the Corporate Council. Mr. Sekou will become UN Liaison. From now on, the seven major corporations will keep an eye on each other. Make sure we're doing the right thing, ethically, financially, etc. There have been raids on food warehouses, hackers draining corporate bank accounts. Last week, a pharmaceutical company had their products stolen from a manufacturing site after they raised their prices four hundred percent. We see the public dissatisfaction and it's bad for business."

Sabreen folded her arms, shaking her head at the men and women around the table. Every exec had absorbed Carlo's words. Were they more upset over the price increase or that people who probably needed that medicine had stolen it? Either way, Carlo was in charge.

Carlo continued. "As for Brightshores, their resources will be used to correct the damage they've done. Their assets will be divvied up between us. Criminal and civil charges will be brought."

"And the Council will monitor all these proceedings and any future indiscretions that occur. We will remove the chaos that has plagued our world for too long," Sekou chimed in.

Carlo nodded. "Now, I think retiring to our respective offices to hash out any remaining details is the thing to do." He clapped his hands. The execs at the table filed out, like trained seals knowing they were dismissed.

"The Council will be watching, Mr. Jennings." Sekou waited.

Jennings bowed at Sekou, his reaction unreadable. Satisfied, Sekou left. Sabreen furrowed her brows. "Bowing to Sekou? You must be losing your touch."

"Well, I have to answer to the UN." He smirked. "For now."

"I guess this solves your energy issues."

Carlo smiled. "Well, my son did pick a smart one, didn't he?"

Sabreen looked away. At least Brightshores would be dealt with. She had to think of her future. Munro was still out there, on the run. Turning back to Carlo, she started, "Your son . . ."

"He's fine, girl." He went to retrieve a mini-screen from the table. "Munro can have his precious autonomy."

Carlo's eyes focused over her shoulder. Munro was in the doorway. She rushed to hug him. Sabreen spotted another person in the hall and went taut.

"He's all yours, boss." Dewi saluted then walked away.

"Yeah, she works for Dad now. Apparently, he now owns the security wing of Brightshores."

"Best way to find out what else they've been doing. Besides, once I explained about all the evidence we had against Brightshores, she was more than willing to switch sides." Carlo leaned in close and whispered, "If I'd known your fiancée was so crafty I would've asked for her help instead."

"Wait just a minute." Munro's body tensed at the suggestion.

Carlo held up one hand and waved the mini-screen at Munro with the other. "Don't worry, son. Just sign these and you'll have everything you ever wanted. All financial and legal ties will be cut." He turned to Sabreen. "I'm sure you'll do just fine."

Sabreen glared. He'd managed to make the last part sound like sarcasm. "Since you're in charge of fixing Brightshores' mess, the OEM needs more help and supplies."

"Of course." Carlo bowed. Sabreen felt mocked and appreciated at the same time.

She turned her attention to Munro again. He had yet to sign anything. The document terminated his employment, released Munro from all contractual obligations, and allowed him to keep income and certain benefits earned while working at Zenith. Sabreen scrolled down; the end of the document was a non-disclosure agreement barring him from sharing information on anything he'd worked on for Zenith in the past. She rubbed Munro's back until his body relaxed. "Sign it, for us."

Munro's face lifted in a smile that made her heart melt. Raising a finger, he signed the document and handed the mini-screen back to his father. He turned to her and said, "Let's go."

Sabreen glanced at Carlo. He was already on a vidscreen negotiating with another exec. Maybe the other execs would keep him in line. For now, she would concentrate on making her life with Munro. She took his hand and led him away from the suite. "I still have to work, and home might be a pile of rubble."

"Well, I hear you need volunteers and I seem to have a lot more free time." He smiled.

She wrapped one arm around his waist as they walked out together. But the smug confidence on her future father-in-law's face haunted her. Carlo had gotten away with the takeover of the century. Would he really keep the other corps ethically in line? Sabreen had strong doubts. Could she help Munro stay free from his tyrannical grip? In the meantime, she could gather as much information as she could on Zenith Galactic, waiting for the right opportunity to use it to keep Carlo's damaging policies in check. Contacting Devonish was her next step. The security officer must have run across an info agent or hacker at some point in her profession.

A buzz came from Munro's vibrating phone, and she lost him from her grip as he stepped toward a corner in the hallway. "It's my little brother," he said as he moved away facing the corner when he answered the call. When one of his family members contacted him, the need for privacy was automatic. She sighed and hugged herself. Of course, the familial bond was still there, but as she stared at his back, Sabreen vowed to keep their future safe and protect the world from falling into Carlo Jennings' web of control.

Mother of Pearls

Caitlin McKenna

The idea for "Mother of Pearls" came to me as a question: Could an empire enforce its power through means other than the state-sanctioned use of violence? From that premise came the concept of the Chantic Empire, a civilization that maintains power over its vassals not with military might, but through the ability to give or withhold healing to a populace still suffering from the toxic fallout of an ancient war.

When she had forgotten most of her childhood, Eyan would still remember the day her father took her to see the nacre roses. The garden was enclosed in a tiny walled courtyard in the middle of a square pond at the center of the Plaza of Tinkers. The area was a merchant district, part of the middle city, and alive with brightly clad vendors selling repair services, or tools to make home repairs easier for those who preferred to fix their own things. Her father's hand was warm and firmly wrapped around hers as he steered her through the forest of legs, the hem of the occasional traveling coat brushing the cobbles. Her head swam with a multiplicity of voices shouting their wares, both in Chantic and in vassal languages she knew only dimly.

Eyan was relieved when they reached the quiet edge of the pond. An arched wooden bridge gave onto a railed veranda that wrapped around the courtyard garden. Its high walls of white stone were inlaid with vertical mother-of-pearl Chantic script which spelled out something, had Eyan yet been able to read. Her father had promised her that schooling when she was a bit older. Their family was wealthy and in good standing with the court and the throne; Eyan would be afforded an education for any profession she chose.

For now, Eyan's father scooped her up onto his shoulders, tracing the script with a finger as he read aloud:

"In Year 38 of the peace between nations, in honor of the completion of the divine city of New Torj, the Descended Moon Emperor Xiong the First did consecrate this rose garden to be built in the center of the city, so that all may see it and remember."

"Remember what?" Eyan asked, only half listening. She'd just noticed the square hole carved into the stone wall, which her shoulder perch had brought to eye level. She caught the impression of something glinting darkly beyond, with a sheen like oil on water or the inside of an oyster shell.

Eyan's seat wobbled as her father shook his head. "It's better if you see it first." Without waiting for her small trove of patience to exhaust itself, her father moved so Eyan could see through the square hole into the courtyard.

She could have paced the tiny garden inside the courtyard in three steps, but that the entire garden bed was a mass of interwoven vines budding with sharp thorns and serrated leaves that looked nearly as sharp. A few summer roses bobbed their heads above the sea of vines, though not as many as Eyan would've thought to see.

But the thing that made her stare and keep staring, holding her breath like a mouse caught between her hands, was the garden's color. The plants were a deep and total black. Black thorns burst from black branches. The edges of sunlight glittered along black leaves and petals that seemed carved of onyx. Ghosts of color flashed among the black as she moved her head, furtive as carp in a pond. But not the pond surrounding this courtyard—she realized she had seen no fish there. A chill flushed over her skin.

"I want to get down now," she said. Her father set her on the verandah, then glanced through the square hole.

"They are roses poisoned by nacre," he explained before Eyan could ask. "It affects plants differently than us; these roses never seed and they never die. But two handfuls of that soil, were it transplanted into the fields outside New Torj, would be enough to kill everyone in this plaza."

Eyan's lip was trembling of its own volition; her father squeezed her hand. "Don't worry, Eyan, we're perfectly safe. Nacre can't leach through the lead and granite the garden is encased in."

His voice turned somber again. "The first Descended Moon chose this region to build the divine city because it was the cleanest left after the war that tore this land apart. The least polluted by nacre. But in his wisdom he chose to leave this spot as it was, so future generations would remember."

So it was that Eyan Lin Sung first saw the most poisoned spot in the Empire.

Eyan Sung had a quota to fill. She hurried up the broad steps that climbed from the lower city in a spiral to the higher districts of

New Torj, the fading amber light of sunset drawing broad shadows across the cobbled thoroughfare. Even with day drawing to a close, the street was packed with traders on foot and pulling hand-drawn carts home from market, couriers ferrying letters and packages, and the occasional non-Chantic traveler, identifiable by the yellow dust of the road clinging to their cloaks. Anyone else would have had to shove and sidle their way through the mass, taking perhaps ten minutes to travel a dozen cubits. But Eyan was on the court's business. Around her shoulders she wore the distinctive white and red silk robes of a Physician, the satchel of her office slung around one hip. The display of authority had the desired effect: people flowed out of her way like a river around a stone.

The expanse of the Plaza of Temples seemed deserted as she set out across it. A few huddles of late worshippers milled under the eaves of the temples at the plaza's cardinal corners, tossing offerings of coins into the wooden lockboxes at the altars' feet as they intoned evocations to the goddesses Fortune, Prosperity, Peace, and Healing. Eyan curled her fingers against her heart in a quick supplication as she passed the Temple of Healing, a brief obeisance to her vocation.

She returned her hand to its place against her Physician's satchel, steadying it against her hip as she reached what she dearly hoped would be the last staircase on this journey. She was in tolerable shape despite a life spent mostly seated poring over books, but she'd walked almost the entire city of New Torj already today. Dawn had found her in one of the public clinics for the poor, down in the lower city near the dockyards. Eyan hated rising in the dark, but what she hated even more was the smell of these clinics—piss and shit and rotting flesh that more than half the time had already gone beyond her ability to cure. And how patients would clutch at her anyway, begging if their ailments hadn't taken away their voices, *You've got one, haven't you, I see it through your bag there—can't you just, can't you . . .*

She would have to explain, again and again: *Pearls don't work that way. I'm sorry.* That what she carried in her bag was not a miracle, not a cure for their gangrene or cancer or their child's fever. That medicinal herbs and the grace of the Goddess of Healing would have to be enough. That they were so often not enough.

Eyan was past the point where she could not refuse such assignments; it would have been a trifling matter to pass those tickets on to more junior Physicians and reserve the middle and upper city assignments for herself. But her own circumstances had cultivated a certain empathy in her for even the hopeless cases. Especially the hopeless cases. Still, it was always a relief to climb past the Plaza of Sailors into the middle city, where residents were prosperous and called on Physicians for mostly minor ailments.

Her last assignment of the day was an address in one such district. Fumbling the map from her satchel, Eyan squinted at it and turned onto the quiet laneway marked in green ink. The houses here were handsome piles of tan plaster and dark wood, many carpeted with flowering creeper vines that made a manicured jungle of the street. The neighborhood had the kind of quiet ostentation she associated with the middle merchant class, although the cobbled lane itself was so narrow she couldn't imagine a loaded merchant caravan ever using it. There would be a wider mews for carriages in back of these houses, Eyan felt sure. Everything about this area attested to the kind of comfortable, industrious wealth she had grown up around. For a moment she wondered why someone in this district would have put in a request for a visit from a Physician when they were in all likelihood rich enough to keep one on retainer. Perhaps they were a wealthy eccentric who liked to show their loyalty to court and Emperor by patronizing the College of Physicians directly?

I suppose I'll find out, Eyan thought as she found the house she was looking for, brushing vines away from the address plate to make sure it matched the one on her ticket. The door knocker, a polished bronze likeness of a river dragon gripping a ring in its mouth, rose and fell under her hand.

A child answered the door. Through her surprise, Eyan said, "Hello there. I received a call at this address. May I speak to your—" She took a guess. "Your father?"

"Father's the one who's sick," the girl said in a steady voice, though it wavered at the end.

"Your mother, then?" Eyan ventured.

"It's just Father, me, and Aeshok here," the girl said brusquely. She peeled the heavy door open. The room took Eyan a moment to see; the windows were covered by heavy wooden shutters that stole the light. As her eyes adjusted, she saw it was as opulent as the exterior suggested: silk hangings draped the lacquered wooden walls, embroidered cushions had been placed just so on elegant ironwood furniture that seemed designed more for display than actual sitting. On a small but exquisitely carved table, a pipe with mother-of-pearl inlay lay extinguished on a jade ashtray. There was even a small bookcase inset in one wall, lined with leather-bound volumes Eyan guessed were worth more than most scribes earned in a year.

The girl was a study in contrast. Eyan guessed she couldn't

have been more than eleven. Her colored cotton frock seemed too rustic for the resident of such an ornate house, and she wore no shoes, not even house slippers. Oddest of all, she was not Chantic; her black hair was similar, but the dark brown eyes underneath her bangs were too round, her skin closer to brown than tan. Maruan, at a guess. The vassal state of Marua was thousands of leagues from New Torj, but traders still filtered into the city occasionally. The girl's father must be one of them, and a wealthy one at that to afford to live in this house, which made her plain clothes all the more of a riddle.

The girl seemed to become conscious of the awkward silence that had fallen. She stepped back from the door, blinking rapidly. "Please, come in."

Eyan crossed the threshold, accepting the pair of house slippers the girl offered her. (Were they the only pair in the house? Another curiosity.) After this courtesy, the girl stood stiffly in the middle of the room, clearly unsure what was the next proper step in the adult ritual of welcoming a guest. Eyan imagined she could hear the fragile heart fluttering under the child's skin like a trapped bird. She smoothed the red and white silk of her Physician's robe and crouched down at the girl's eye level.

"What's your name, sugar cane?" The girl hesitated a moment longer—unfamiliar perhaps with the Chantic endearment. Eyan had used it out of habit, but now she realized it might mean nothing to a Maruan girl.

But then the too-adult tension dropped away from the girl's features. She bit her lower lip and her round eyes grew moist.

"Azka," she said. "Can you help my father?"

"I'll try, Azka. Where is he?"

The girl—Azka—led Eyan down a short hallway, past a white-washed kitchen that looked like it hadn't been used since the house was built, to a bedroom at the back of the first floor.

The man lying in the gilded four-poster bed within was thin and drawn, shivering despite the layers of silken comforters piled over him. His skin had grayed with illness, but Eyan picked up the family resemblance among him, Azka, and the boy of about five huddled in a chair by the bed, whom she guessed was Aeshok. The man's eyes roved the room, skittering over Eyan like black pebbles tossed across a pond. She wasn't sure he saw her or the room. Still, she bowed as courtesy dictated and announced herself.

"I am Eyan Lin Sung, of the College of Physicians. I have come to treat you."

He continued to stare through her. "Where's Juvan? Has he come back yet, Azka?"

Azka was instantly at the bedside. "Uncle hasn't returned yet, Father," she said. "I called a Physician to help you."

At last the man seemed to realize Eyan was there. "You must have been on the road for weeks," he wheezed. "Thank you for coming this far."

His daughter blew a sigh full of exasperation on the surface. "We're not in the village, Father. This is New Torj, remember?"

Their exchange was heartbreaking; though she had witnessed its like with far-gone patients often enough, it still took effort for Eyan to turn her attention from it. She slipped on a pair of raw silk examination gloves and took off her official robes, hanging them and her satchel on the hook behind the door. Underneath she wore a plain cotton smock, no grander than the children's homespun; the actual business of medicine was frequently a bloody, stinking affair, and if her robes got dirty with blood or shit, the cleaning fee came out of her monthly stipend.

She looked to Azka, feeling very strange to be asking a child permission to examine her parent. "I will examine your father now, is that all right?" The girl nodded.

The smell of unwashed flesh underlaid with something oily and rotten pushed out from under the bedcovers as Eyan peeled them back. Azka gagged and retreated to the chair where Aeshok looked on, his small hands over his mouth. The rotting smell instantly took up residence at the back of Eyan's throat, nestling in the folds of tissue there, but she did not react. Ten years ago she would have vomited. Five years ago she would have wrinkled her nose, at least. But she had smelled as much and worse at the free clinic by the docks.

So it was not the smell that made Eyan gasp, nor the ribs that stood out like quills defining the man's narrow and sunken chest. It was the source of the wasting illness, now exposed and unmistakable even in the low lantern light of the shuttered chamber.

Deposits of nacre bloomed under the skin of his chest and abdomen like terrible flowers, turning the top layers of skin iridescent black. Eyan traced their extent with her eye as she had been trained to, even as she entertained and furiously discarded alternative hypotheses of what the contusions could be. She'd seen buboes, gangrene, hematomas—none of them had that distinctive sheen. None appeared under the skin with no other surrounding markings, bruising, or swelling. The largest blot was the size of her fist, curled under the bottom rib on the right side of his body near the liver. *I wonder if he even has a liver anymore*, she thought, picturing the crystalline tendrils of nacre that must infest the organ, destroying soft tissues as they grew. That spot was probably where the poison had first taken root before spreading to other areas. If the nacre had bloomed in his heart or lungs, he would be dead already.

"That might be a kindness," Eyan muttered. She needn't continue the examination to make her diagnosis: the blight had first rooted in and then destroyed most or all of his liver. The man was drowning in his own toxins, taken by increasing delirium as his heart pumped the poisons to his brain.

Azka reappeared like a shadow at her side. "Can you help him?" Her voice was more controlled than any child's had a right to be, weary more than grief stricken. Eyan heard in that voice an entire history contained, of sleepless nights spent taking care of the man who should have been taking care of her.

Eyan didn't know how to explain it to Azka—her father's condition was not just severe, it was impossible. He had to have been exposed to nacre while still in Marua; there were no deposits in New Torj, save the one that had been preserved in the dark rose garden. In her mercy, the Goddess of Healing Kanin had seen fit to spare the heart of what became the Chantic Empire from that blight. Yet even in the vassal states, where deposits of the thaumatic contagion indelibly marked the soil and water, not even the poorest villager had to endure nacre's effects without a Physician's treatment. How had an apparently wealthy Maruan such as this let himself deteriorate so far, and him with children to care for? A hot anger spiked in her at the idea, making her next words careless.

"Where's your mother?" she asked Azka. "Why are you alone? Don't tell me she left you to care for your father like this."

Curled on the chair, Aeshok burst into tears. He rose unsteadily, fists crammed into his cheeks, bawling like a much younger child, and half fell out of the chair. The boy sprinted out of the room before Eyan had the presence of mind to call him back. She heard a door slam.

Azka looked ready to dart after him, but a moment later the bowstring tension went out of her body. She looked Eyan in the eye and said, as calmly as before, "Our mother's dead."

Eyan's cheeks felt red hot. Of course; she should have put the pieces together sooner. There were still edges to the puzzle she would ask about, later—what circumstances had prevented their father from getting care earlier, especially with the resources their family obviously had—but those questions could wait.

"I will give your father what help I can," she said in answer to Azka's earlier question. "Go comfort your brother. There's nothing you can do here." This last was said kindly, she hoped. Azka nodded with a foregone resignation that clutched at Eyan's heart, and left.

Once alone, Eyan pulled the chair Aeshok had been sitting in to the edge of the bed, sat down, and gently gripped the man's elbow to get his attention. Eyes made large in that pallid face met hers, and this time Eyan glimpsed lucidity there.

"What's your name?" she asked.

He seemed to search his memory. "Toven," he said. "Toven Trivadi."

She inclined her head in a small bow sufficiently courteous for a non-Chantic. "Toven, you are dying." Eyan Lin Sung did not believe in mincing words.

He did not protest, so she continued. "There are large nacre deposits in your liver, and it has spread to your heart and lungs. I could use my Pearl to dissolve these deposits, but I can tell you the damage they have already done to your organs cannot be reversed. At this point, the best I can offer is to remove your pain."

His gaze began to wander round the room toward the end. Eyan wondered if it would be worth repeating any of what she'd just said. But his next words made it clear he understood her. "Juvan said he would take care of my children."

"Juvan is your brother?"

He nodded. "After Mara—their mother—died, I brought them to this house. I thought we'd escaped it, but I . . . I left too late." Toven closed his eyes against a beading of tears, but they rolled down his cheeks to the mattress.

Eyan quickly removed a cloth from her bag and wiped his face. It was a struggle to keep her voice level as she asked, "Escaped what?"

"The plague," Toven said. *Plague* was a common term for nacre sickness among the vassal states. Although every Chantic knew nacre was not a plague but a thaumatic contaminant, halfway between a poison and a cancer, not all people in outlying territories were so educated. Eyan did not correct him.

"How long have you been sick?" she asked.

"A few months," he answered. Eyan began to shake her head and stopped herself. Clearly he was mistaken. Even the worst nacre poisonings she had seen on her regional assignments would have taken a ten-month or more to get so advanced. She made a note of the duration for form's sake.

"It came on suddenly in our village," Toven insisted, as though he sensed she didn't believe him. "Strong, healthy people began to sicken, and a few months or a year later they were dead. Always the plague. Mara . . ." Again he squeezed his eyes shut. "After Mara I decided to esc—to go with the children."

Eyan noted him take back the word *escape*, decided to overlook it in favor of the more pressing question: "Didn't you have Physicians stationed in your village to treat you?"

"Plague—" Toven began, then broke off into a fit of coughing. "Plague had never been a problem in our village before," he finished in a wheeze. "Not til a few years ago. And when we did make the call for Physicians, the Empire—the Empire didn't *send us any*."

A vein of cold crawled down Eyan's neck and back. She stood abruptly, almost cannoning the chair over backward behind her. "That's not possible. The Empire supplies healing to all who need it. Unless . . ." Unless Toven's village had been in rebellion against New Torj. Such a rebellion had not occurred for a century, but the historical examples had formed a vivid part of her training. She still carried with her the memories of villages and even cities cut off from the Empire's healing services, printed woodcuts and engravings of streets overflowing with the nacre-tumorous bodies of people and horses.

"We weren't rebels," Toven said forcefully, seeing her mind. "There is no village in Marua more loyal to New Torj than Acene."

The name did not sound familiar, but then it wouldn't have if it wasn't in the roster of villages with an assigned Physician. Eyan searched her mind for any way Toven's statement could be true. Perhaps their missives for a healer had been lost. Misfortunes happened: hawks took messenger pigeons; couriers on horseback met with accidents. Or perhaps the request had been misfiled. It was possible for the Emperor's agents to make mistakes; they were human, despite what some of the priests of the Four Temples claimed. Though a few years seemed a long time for such a request to go unheeded—

All at once, her thoughts seemed to lock up as the other impossible thing Toven had said finally registered. It was as though her mind was a river some thaumage had drawn all the heat from at once, turning the surface to ice.

"Did you say," Eyan said slowly, "Nacre sickness—the plague—only appeared in your village a few years ago?"

But Toven's eyes had begun to roll distantly around the room again, and this time nothing Eyan said could bring him back.

She spent a few frustrated moments searching for something that would return him so she could ask the question again, but it seemed now truly hopeless. She opened her bag and began what little treatment she could.

The Pearl slipped from her satchel like a drop of moonlight, a silver-white pear shape that she unclipped from its protective velvet harness. Unlike most Imperial property it was unornamented, unpolished, and had no setting; an irregular ripple that must have occurred during its formation ran across the narrower end. No noble Chantic lady would ever have carried such a flawed piece of jewelry on her person. Even a merchant's daughter like Eyan would have been looked at askance and asked why she hadn't had it ground to a finer shape.

But among the many Imperial edicts governing her trade was that Pearls were never to be tampered with in any way. Pearls were healing tools for commanding thauma and the basis of her Physician's art, each more precious than a noble lady's entire jewel cabinet, and irreplaceable. The art for condensing Pearls out of the web of thaumatic energy lying beneath the world had been lost in the great war, along with the ancient civilization that had founded Old Torj.

Cradling the Pearl in her lap, Eyan palpated the dark blemishes on Toven's skin as gently as she could, feeling the extent of the nacreous, crystallized flesh and the coronas of dissolving tissue around them. He loosed an inarticulate groan. She removed her hands and wiped renewed sweat from his forehead. Eyan slipped off her raw silk gloves and took the Pearl in both hands. Raising it to her forehead, she closed her eyes and concentrated on Toven's pain.

A raw red blackness exploded in her mind, sharp and crystalline vines turning to liquid around the edges. It did not hurt as she knew pain—the Pearl transmuted the actual sensations into a form she could feel and manipulate without being rendered helpless by it—but pain impressions still had a way of seeming to twist and rotate while staying still that was dizzying and hideously uncomfortable. Nausea pushed up her throat, and Eyan took small breaths through her nose as she'd been taught until the sensation passed.

She found the glowing lines of energy in Toven's body that controlled when he woke and slept. They buzzed with discomfort; the pain must have kept him in a stupor for days, unable to truly rest. Eyan imagined the red-black thicket contracting, the vines withering until they shriveled into a single point that dissipated into the blackness of a peaceful sleep. As gently as a mother laying her newborn to sleep, Eyan laid her Pearl in the hollow of Toven's chest below his sternum.

In Eyan's experience, pain relief was rarely what made her profession so revered, Pearls treated as holy objects. Tales of clumps of nacre melting away under people's skin like ink in rain made for much better gossip. Yet it was always seeing the pain go out of her patients' faces that made Eyan remember why she had taken up Physician's robes. It made the Pearl worth its great price to her. As she watched Toven's knotted features smooth out, the labor of his breaths ease toward Pearl-induced sleep, some portion of that peace, as it always did, became hers.

Once she was sure Toven slept, she found Azka in the second bedroom, tucking the blankets of a bed almost as fine around Aeshok's sleeping form. Without a word, the girl followed Eyan back to her father's deathbed.

"I don't know how to thank you," Azka said as she watched him sleep. She moved to pull up the bedcovers and Eyan laid a firm hand on her arm.

"Better to leave them down," she explained. "Heavy bedding can impede breathing."

She'd tried to slant the statement so as not to lay blame, but Azka still flinched. "Do you know how long it's been since he's slept through the night?"

"This is temporary, Azka," Eyan said. "The best I can offer is palliative care." A blank look. "That means I can take your father's pain and make him more comfortable, but I can't heal him. He has a week at most."

Eyan Lin Sung believed it was always best to tell children the truth, that they were no less capable of handling it than many adults. She'd always told Jian the truth, especially the uncomfortable kind; it was a matter of trust, and respect for her daughter's capabilities.

Azka's eyes went dim; for a regretful moment Eyan thought the girl would burst into tears as her brother had. But she found the awful strength to nod, and that was somehow worse.

This is wrong, Eyan thought. *Who left these children in this impossible position?* Aloud, she said, "Where is your Uncle—Juvan? Is this his house?"

Azka seemed to ignore the question. "He said he'd be back soon," she said as if that was what Eyan had asked. "Said he'd bring a—" Her face went guarded, and she darted a glance toward the living room. "Medicine," she finished.

There was such hope in that word that Eyan didn't have the heart to tell her the only medicine that could help Toven now were the tears of the Goddess of Fortune. She let the child escort her back through the house with a promise to visit them next evening.

"If he worsens before then, give this to any Imperial messenger," Eyan handed Azka a slip of fine paper marked with her Physician's seal, "along with your address. They'll know where to find me."

Eyan stepped from that claustrophobic opulence into the uncertain night.

The night sky was a narrow river of darkness between the overhangs of houses as Eyan followed the tightening spiral of streets from the wealthy neighborhood above the Plaza of Temples to the Plaza of the Moon, the emperor's citadel. Her apartments were part of a cluster of domiciles near the College of Physicians on the slopes of the acropolis. An hour ago, the thought of her soft bed with the silk sheets would have hastened her footsteps, but now sleep couldn't be further from Eyan's mind.

Hsen, the larger moon, was almost full and its silvery light was more than enough to see by. From this angle Eyan couldn't see Hseia, the fragmented smaller moon, but the faraway sun reflected the halo of pulverized moonrock orbiting Hseia and made it glow like gold dust.

Eyan Lin Sung was an educated woman. She knew the moons were simply spherical hunks of rock, and that the world on which New Torj and all the Imperial and vassal holdings of the Chantic Empire was contained was simply an even larger chunk of rock. A folk story in distant vassal states told that the piece of Hseia that had broken off during the ancient war afterwards formed herself into the divine body of the first Empress, forsaking her consort and children in the sky to help human beings restore law and governance on their world. The legend went that during her reign, Hseia had taken the title of Descended Moon, passing it on to each future sovereign.

Eyan grimaced as she studied the moons. Even in New Torj, many simpler folk believed the old stories. Perhaps it was easier for them to believe that nacre, in all its strange and sometimes terrible manifestations, was a magical plague, the healing art Eyan practiced a kind of miraculous sorcery. The truth was so much stranger Eyan sometimes had trouble believing it herself.

The scholars called nacre the cancer of the world. A thaumatic contaminant, a malignant physical manifestation of the web of energy that organized all matter. Nacre turned living matter into itself until there was nothing left to devour. As far as Eyan knew, there were no vassal states that had escaped a degree of nacre contamination in their soil or water. As the maps spread out from the heart that was New Torj, past the borders of the poorest vassal states, the edges were home to lands so contaminated no one had ventured there in a millennium or more: lands where the air shivered with the residue of thaumatic energies released in the unimaginable conflict between Old Torj and states whose names had been seared into oblivion.

In fact, the only spot on the map that seemed to have escaped nacre's clutches was Old Torj itself, the very city on whose bones New Torj rested. Yet Eyan had read enough history to know this was not because the city had been spared.

Torj was not a Chantic word. There were no surviving records of what it meant, or even root words in Chantic with which to compare it. Other than the name of the city itself, no trace of Old Torj nor the civilization around it had influenced the new empire that rose above its ashes. Even the most conservative historians speculated that Old Torj must have been obliterated, though they differed on how. The most common theory was a thaumatic weapon capable of converting matter to energy so completely that no residue, not even nacre, was left behind. If this was true, the theory went, then New Torj's fortune in being spared the world's cancer was a byproduct of a devastation so total that not even that poison could withstand it. Never mind that no evidence of such a weapon had ever been unearthed; the ancients had clearly had access to thaumatic powers far beyond what thaumages could harness today. After all, it was some kind of thaumatic engine of war that had shattered a piece of Hseia from the sky.

A shiver passed over Eyan's shoulders under her robe, though the early-summer night was warm. Speculation made her uneasy. She liked problems that she could examine up close, manipulate, and if not always solve, then at least attack to the best of her training and with all the information available.

Patients were usually a good source of information: they tended to want Eyan to help them get better, or at least ease their suffering, and she could do that much better when they were honest with her. Yet the girl Azka had been hiding something— protecting her uncle perhaps, this Juvan? And Eyan was convinced that Toven had misdirected her as well—why else give her that ridiculous story about nacre only striking his village in the last few years? It had done nothing but confirm how little the man understood his own illness; the first thing she'd learned in the College was that nacre could not be created by modern thaumaturgy. Nacre was a poisonous byproduct of the release of thaumatic energies on a truly awesome scale; the knowledge of how to harness such thaumatic energies had been lost along with Old Torj.

Vast as some of the nacre deposits plaguing the world were, they were also finite. And dwindling. Every time a Physician used a Pearl to heal someone, the nacre in that person's body leached back into pure thaumatic energy, no longer a poison plaguing the physical world. Bit by bit, healers like Eyan would rid the world of nacre. She believed this in the pit of her heart; it helped her through days like this, when she had to look into a dying man's eyes and tell him he would not be there for his children.

Belated tears prickled at the corners of Eyan's eyes. She wiped them away roughly with the hem of her sleeve, grateful for the concealing darkness.

Eyan let herself into her apartments in the Court of Thrushes, a turn of the spiral or so below the College. It was an overly grand name for a narrow street lined by dormitory blocks of single or double-room apartments intended for junior Physicians. With a few years out of the College behind her, Eyan could have chosen one of the more spacious rowhouses up the spiral, perhaps in the Court of Herons—she'd always liked the graceful mosaic designs decorating the walls in white-and-blue depictions of those long-legged birds. Yet her decision not to move up was reaffirmed as Eyan opened the door, to be greeted by the smell of old parchment, lamp oil, and fermented green tea pervading the two spartan rooms. This was all the space she needed; anything more would have been a distraction.

The drawn shutters cast the entryway in darkness. As Eyan stepped over the threshold, a slip of paper crinkled under her sandal. She lit the lantern by the door and picked up the missive, groaning as she saw the orchid seal embedded in red wax. A letter from her family.

Eyan laid it back on the floor. She bustled about the house, opening shutters on moonlight and lighting lamps. She placed an iron kettle on the hearth to boil, beside it a china cup of loose tea (valerian; it was much too late for anything stronger), then slipped off her Physician's robes and hung them on the hook by the door. As was her custom, she'd already laid out her cotton evening robes on her bed that morning. Eyan gratefully slipped into the cooler garment and caught the kettle just as it was starting to boil.

As the valerian swirled around to steep in the hot water, Eyan realized she could no longer put off the inevitable. Holding the letter between thumb and forefinger, she entered the second small room of her apartment.

All the implements of living—bed, hearth, pots and pans, chamber pot—she confined to the first, larger room; the second room served as her study. Two walls were all books and scrolls, many of them borrowed from the Imperial College Library. They were confined in two ceiling-tall ironwood bookcases lining the left and right walls. Directly opposite the door, an equally massive ironwood kneeling desk crouched in the center of the room, a crimson cushion tucked into the space between the writing surface and the carpeted floor. On the wall, dimly visible in the lantern light, hung an ink-painted scroll depicting Kanin, the Goddess of Healing. She held the four healing implements in each of her four hands: a book on medicine, representing all accumulated medicinal knowledge; an ink brush, representative of listening to and recording patients' concerns; the mythical herb *somang*, representative of all healing herbs; and of course, a Pearl, whose explanation was not needed.

Eyan sat on the cushion with her calves folded under her thighs and gingerly broke the letter's seal with a fingernail. By flickering lantern light she read, in her mother's swirling hand:

Dearest daughter,

Since you have rejected every match we have proposed for you, I can only conclude that you do not wish your parents to intercede for you in this matter. I write this with some disappointment, but, you must believe, no anger. Your father and I wish only for your happiness, and we will support you, within reason, in whichever match you choose.

A snort escaped her. *Within reason.* Leave it to her mother to immediately undermine her professed support. She read on.

Only we must hear an expression of interest from you one way or another soon. Several families with eligible children have been making inquiries, and I see no reason why we must continually put them off with excuses. I would like to once again extend our offer to present you at the next gathering of our peers, in hopes that perhaps your heart may guide you where the firm and loving hands of your parents cannot—

Eyan tossed the letter down in disgust. A coming-out ball. She would've said her mother couldn't be serious, except that this was the fifth or sixth time she'd offered. Never mind that her daughter was nearing thirty, too old for an introductory ball to seem anything but a ridiculously desperate attempt to find a match. Cara Min Sung seemed to believe it was some combination of shyness and lack of opportunity due to the demands of her position that kept her daughter from finding a suitable mate. Even at her most incensed during their intermittent conversations together, Eyan hadn't found the courage to tell her mother the truth.

She wasn't interested in a match. She didn't want a family, not the kind her mother had in mind for her. Jian was all the family she wanted or needed. And the best thing she could do for Jian was to live without the distractions of a spouse and a household, which would only take her away from the studies in thaumaturgy and the healing of rare illnesses that occupied the hours she was not on call.

Her tea should have finished steeping by now. Handling the letter as though it were made of glass, Eyan folded the paper along its creases, pressed the wax seal back together, and tossed it onto her bed. She extracted the valerian dregs from the tea and tossed them out the window into the narrow alley between buildings. She curled up on the bed with her back against the wall and sipped her tea, but the musky-herbal fragrance of valerian didn't calm her like it normally did. The innocent cream rectangle of the letter tugged at the corner of her eye, taunting her for a response. Eyan considered sending it back unopened, but decided even that would be more of a reply than she wanted to give.

She tossed the letter onto the hearth coals.

The rap of brass shattered Eyan's sleep. She jerked up from mussed covers. Several strands of hair had plastered themselves to her cheek with drool, and she wiped them away as she looked around stupidly for the source of the sound. The rapping came again, sharp and insistent as a bone breaking. Her door knocker.

The view through the peephole was solid black. Without unhooking the chain, Eyan pulled the door an eighth of the way open and shone her lantern through. At first the light seemed to reveal no one, until Eyan looked down. The lantern illuminated a form much shorter than the Court messenger she'd expected at this hour.

"Azka," Eyan bleated, then lowered her voice in deference to the late hour. "What in the heavens—"

"Father's worse," Azka interrupted her. The girl's eyes were large and hollow in the lantern light, looking out from under the hood of a light cloak of summer silk. But even now Eyan saw none of the expected tears.

Eyan didn't waste time asking how Azka knew where she

lived—that could wait. "What are your father's new symptoms?" she asked.

"When I left—" Azka's breath hitched. She gulped air and finished. "When I left, his heart was going fast, and he was—he was having trouble breathing—"

"Then there's no time to lose." Eyan threw on her Physician's silks over her cotton robe and found her slippers by feel. Lantern held high, she followed Azka down the spiraling cobbled street to the townhouse she was still unsure they actually belonged in. She considered sending for an escort. If this was a trick on Azka's part—some con to rob her or take her hostage—Eyan could hardly be being more cooperative. She'd heard of such plots occasionally befalling wealthy Chantics who put their trust in the wrong foreigner. Yet Toven's illness had been real. Furthermore, even the most ambitious brigand would have to be mad to interfere with an Imperial Physician.

They made it to the townhouse without incident. The familiar smell of musty sheets and a faint hint of rot greeted Eyan as Azka ushered her into the bedroom at the back of the house.

Eyan heard Toven Trivadi before she saw him. The small, close room seemed to expand and contract with the sound of his labored breaths, as though each one sucked what little air remained from the room. After each strained inhalation came a pause, and each time Eyan's practiced ear expected to hear nothing more. But then would come an exhalation more hideous than silence, as the used air rattled in his throat.

The dying man lay uncovered on the bed save for a thin sheet pulled up over the blackened nacre deposits on his chest and belly. Pole lanterns had been placed at the head and foot of the bed, casting the room in a faded amber glow and drawing long shadows in the hollows of Toven's cheeks. Aeshok had resumed his position in the chair beside the bed. He clutched the heavy bedcovers around him as though they offered protection.

"Hello again," Eyan said, not sure if it was to Toven, the boy, or the room that she spoke. Aeshok still met her gaze, his own dark brown eyes wide. He looked terrified. She patted him on the shoulder, wondering what she could say in a moment like this. *It's going to be all right?* Even a child as young as Aeshok would know that for an adult's lie.

Finally, Eyan settled on, "I'm here to help." *The little I still can.*

With Azka hovering nearby, Eyan pulled a chair up to Toven's bedside. His pulse was rapid and thready, the skin of his wrist clammy with sweat that dampened her examination gloves. She laid down his hand gently and slipped the Pearl from her bag. The deep yellow lamp light transformed it into a drop of amber that felt blood-warm as Eyan placed it against her forehead.

Her eyes were closed in concentration, so she missed the moment when Toven's went wide. A moment later Eyan gasped as he gripped her elbow.

"When you find Juvan—" A vicious cough interrupted him. Connected to Toven through her Pearl, Eyan felt the spasm rack his lungs. It took him minutes to recover, and then he ground the words out, as though he knew they were the few he had left: "When you find Juvan, tell him not to return to Acene. Tell him to take Azka and Aeshok and get as far away from the Empire as they can, across the sea. They'll be safe there."

Eyan resisted the impulse to reply. It was only more raving. Everyone knew there was nothing across the sea but nacre-poisoned wasteland.

"I came as soon as I could," she responded instead. "Are you in pain, Toven?"

"No." He said it without thinking; then awe crept into his voice as he realized the absence of the fog of pain he'd been living in for weeks or months. "No, there's no pain." For a long moment, Toven stared at her, then through her; his grip slackened around her elbow as the breath sighed out of him. Eyan listened at his chest for a minute or so, but this time there was nothing further. She sat upright and used the tips of two fingers to gently close Toven's open eyes.

A piercing wail split the stillness of the room. A finger of ice slid up Eyan's back to hear it, a keening brimful of grief and higher than any adult throat could manage. She turned around to comfort the boy.

But the cry came from Azka. She stood erect and brittle as a dry reed, both fists clenched to her chest, eyes fixed on her father's corpse. Dry sobs poured from her mouth like sand. Her brother huddled in his chair, large silent tears splashing into his lap. Speechless where Azka was dry-eyed, as though together they formed two parts of one grieving child.

"Oh sugar cane, I'm so sorry." Eyan crouched down and gathered them into her arms; Goddess take the regulations against Physician-patient fraternization.

She didn't know how long she knelt on the hardwood floor. By the time Azka's sobs had slowed to the occasional hitch, Eyan's knees had been rubbed sore through her silk robe. Her left shoulder was damp where Aeshok had rested his head.

Azka stepped out of Eyan's embrace, a stiffness in the movement the only indication of the weight she still carried. It came to Eyan, later than it should have, how much Azka reminded her of her own daughter: Jian affected those same dignified, overly stiff movements when she was in pain, as though she balanced a mountain on her shoulders. Then again, perhaps Eyan was so well-acquainted with the shape of her daughter's pain that she had failed to see anything like it in another.

Azka touched Aeshok on the shoulder and said something softly in Maruan. He dragged the heel of his palm across his eyes and left the room, returning with a bundle of white cloth which he placed at the foot of the bed. As he unrolled it, Eyan glimpsed a bundle of deep purple stick incense, along with holders, matches, and brass bells, their tops fitted with leather thongs. A shock went through her as she understood them for funeral implements. In Chantic custom, only priests could perform funeral rites, but perhaps things were different in Marua.

As if in answer, Azka touched her arm. "Please wait outside while we perform this duty for Father," she said solemnly.

Eyan looked between her and Aeshok as he set the incense sticks in their holders and placed one at Toven's feet, the other at his head. "You shouldn't have to do this alone," she said. "I could call for someone, a priest or—"

That was all it took for Azka's composure to crumple. Pushing Eyan toward the door with her small hands, she shouted in a voice that quaked with fury, "Get out, get out! Leave us alone!"

Azka was not strong. But what she lacked in strength, she made up in anger and grief. Eyan retreated to the living room and left her and Aeshok to conduct the rites for their father, her shoulders quaking with unexpected shame.

A gray dawn was beginning to pluck at the shutters by the time Azka came into the living room. For the past few hours, the back room had been filled by soft singing in boyish and girlish voices, and an increasingly strong smell of spikenard incense, but Eyan had resisted the urge to peek.

Azka threw herself down on the opposite couch, a tiredness beyond sleep stamped on her young face. After waiting a decent interval, Eyan cleared her throat and said, "I apologize for upsetting you. It was not my place to say anything."

Azka shook her head. "Please understand. In Marua, when someone d—" she faltered. "When someone leaves this world, his family must prepare his body for the journey. We're the only family my father had left."

"What about his brother, your uncle?" Eyan asked.

"Uncle wasn't here," Azka said, matter of fact.

Eyan leaned forward on the couch, rested her elbows on her knees, and met Azka's eyes. Part of her hated to do this now, when the girl had been through four hells, had seen things no child should have to see. But a tougher, more calculating part knew that with Azka's defenses down, this was the perfect time to get answers to her questions.

"What does your Uncle Juvan do, Azka? Is he a merchant?"

The girl shook her head. "He told us he is a record keeper in the Imperial trade ministry."

"He affords such a grand house on a clerk's wages?"

"This isn't his house," Azka said. "It belongs to a nobleman named—" She clapped her palms over her mouth.

"Come now, Azka." Eyan put on her most cajoling tone, the

one she'd used when Jian was much younger and would refuse to take her medicine. "Your uncle needs to be informed of what happened so he can return and take care of you and Aeshok. If he can be reached through this nobleman, I need to know his name."

The girl dropped her hands, but the voice that emerged was almost inaudible. "Juvan made us promise not to tell. No one's supposed to know his friend is hosting foreigners."

There was no law against Chantics hosting foreigners, and custom permitted it within reasonable lengths of time. She sensed what Azka meant, but didn't say, was the noble had agreed not to reveal he was hosting her family specifically. That brought up more questions about their circumstances than it answered, including one she'd already meant to ask:

"How did you find me tonight? There was no Court courier with you."

Azka was more receptive to this question. "Juvan's friend sometimes sends people to the house. One of them left this." From a drawer in the ironwood end table, she withdrew a slip of fine paper and gave it to Eyan. It was the patient copy of her summons for Toven's treatment earlier that day. The townhouse's address, Eyan's name, and her Physician's license number had been filled into their fields in a scribe's flowing hand. The fields detailing the patient's name and nature of the complaint had been left blank, just as they had on her copy. Eyan hadn't thought much of it at the time; confidentiality was part of the service any Physician offered for those who wished it.

There was something more on this copy, though. Azka motioned for her to flip it, and on the back of the page more characters had been scrawled in a quicker, untidier hand. Eyan read the address of her apartments in the Court of Thrushes. What she guessed was a seal had been stamped in black ink next to the writing. Some type of flower—a rose, maybe.

She returned the receipt to Azka, her mind flickering over something strange in what the girl had said. "You said the nobleman sends people. Are they servants?"

Azka shrugged, her mouth set in a line.

"All right, Azka, you don't have to tell me," she said. "Just tell me where your uncle is. I can have a message dispatched to him this morning."

Her fists crushed into her chest again. "I would, only . . . I don't know where he is."

Eyan sat up straighter. "But you said he works in the trade ministry?"

"He did, but a few weeks before we left Acene his letters stopped coming. The last thing we received from Uncle was the address for this house. The letter said only that it would be empty for us and a key would be waiting. Father looked for him, while he was still well enough to move . . ." She bit her fist, looking in that moment like a much younger child.

Eyan closed a hand around the girl's fist and pulled it away from her mouth, keeping her touch light. "Azka, you must understand I can't leave you and Aeshok here by yourselves. You need a guardian, and someone needs to make arrangements for your father's body. If you don't know where your uncle is, and you won't tell me the name of the man who might find him for me, then I'll have no choice but to report that you and your brother are living here alone."

Azka jerked her fist out of Eyan's grasp and scrambled back

on the couch. "You can't!"

"It won't be so bad," Eyan said. "As wards of the state you'll be well cared for. The Ministry of Child and Family Affairs will make every effort to reconnect you with your uncle, and if he can't be found they'll be sure to find an adoptive home for you in Acene—"

"Didn't you hear what Father said?" Azka asked, as if Eyan were the child in the room. "We *can't* go back to Acene. We'll *die*."

Eyan opened her mouth to argue—to tell Azka her father's sickness had driven reason from him at the end, that he was mad, that he *had* to be. The Empire did not send children off to die. It didn't poison villages with nacre. It couldn't, and what was more, it would never, even if such power still existed. New Torj was not Old Torj; they had learned from the mistakes of the past.

But as she studied Azka's rigid frame, she realized the girl wasn't just heartsick, she was terrified. Azka believed every word she'd said. Eyan couldn't help her by arguing.

"Do you have money?" Eyan said at last.

Azka nodded. "Uncle left forty *luan* for us. We still have most of that."

More than enough money for a couple of months' basic needs. Eyan tapped her knee, thinking. "All right. I have family business to attend tomorrow, and then I will look for your uncle myself."

Hope lit the girl's eyes. "Thank y—"

Eyan held up a hand. "You may not want to thank me yet." She gestured toward the bedroom. "Your father's body will need attention within a few days. If none step forward to claim it, a public undertaker will bury him in accordance with Imperial decrees for dealing with potential sources of nacre contamination."

"What way is that?" Azka asked, her eyes wide.

"Interred in lead-lined concrete," Eyan said heavily, "and dropped into the middle of the sea." Azka sat as if frozen, staring into her lap. Eyan took her gently under the chin and raised Azka's face to hers. "If you want your father returned to Marua and the care of his gods," she said, hating the manipulation but knowing it was necessary to make the girl understand, "you'll do everything you can to help me find your uncle in the next few days. Now, which noble did you say was hosting your family, again?"

Eyan Lin Sung had one last task to perform before she could call this night done.

The back bedroom enveloped her in the kind of silence that came from knowing what was missing. Before her, the sheet pulled up over its head, was the body that had once been Toven Trivadi. The incense holders at his feet and head now held only ashes, but she could still smell a lingering whiff of spikenard. It was almost enough to cover the rot.

It had taken some cajoling for Azka to allow her back in here, but once Eyan explained what she had in mind, the girl had acquiesced. However reluctantly, she must have seen that it was for her and Aeshok's safety.

Eyan breathed deeply to clear her mind and stop the light tremor that ran through her hands as she donned her examination gloves. In theory, there was no danger in being in the same room with a body poisoned by nacre, either living or dead; once ingested, or in rare cases breathed in, nacre was a scourge, but it seemed to pass reluctantly from its chosen host into new victims. In theory, even skin contact with an infected body was perfectly safe.

But theories were just that—theories. Eyan knew, better than most Physicians, that such assurances could never be absolutely trusted. A thousand years and more of Chantic scholarship had done nothing to reveal the process by which nacre replicated itself in the body, or how Pearls reversed its spread. As long as there were gaps in their knowledge, there was risk; there might be methods of contamination that had simply remained undiscovered. So Eyan took care as she pulled back the sheet with gloved fingertips.

The drawn face was ash gray. All the little tensions and movements that animate a living body were gone from the emaciated frame, conspicuous by their absence. The nacre deposits that had killed him stood out even more harsh and black against the pallid skin, like bruises darker than night.

Once more, Eyan removed her Pearl from its bag and placed it on the body's sternum. This time, when she made contact, no red-black creepers jumped out to ensnare her mind; this was a body that had gone beyond pain and suffering. The small comfort she took from that was brief—soon set aside as she began the grim business of tracing the extent of the nacre contamination.

Instead of lines of pain, the nacre registered in her mind as a seething blackness of liquid shapes, continually forming and dissolving away, like oil mixed into water. She pulled her perspective back from the heart of the deposits to the edges, where the shapes rigidified and became crystalline. The boundaries marked where the nacre had been actively devouring Toven's flesh, turning it into more contagion. The places where she would have to start.

In a living person, the process of banishing nacre back into thaumatic energy had to be approached with the utmost care to avoid causing damage to surrounding organs. That, and the often intense pain that accompanied the procedure, meant such healing had to be conducted over weeks or months. But Toven was beyond caring what she did; he was beyond feeling the energies that coursed through his flesh as Eyan channeled her intent through the Pearl and smashed the nacre deposits into shrinking globules that vanished in a whisp of liberated energy.

When she was done, she rested against the side of the bed and wiped the sweat from her brow with a dry cloth. The body should be cleansed now, or near as she could make it. It was no less thorough a job than what a public undertaker would have done, and possibly more. Enough to be safe, or so she hoped. But she knew that all she'd done was buy time.

One of the advantages of being an Imperial Physician was access to a private hospital. The teaching hospital ensconced within the College provided an excellent standard of care, in part to safeguard its own reputation, and in part due to the edict that all healers of the Empire should be in the best of health themselves. It was in this institution that Eyan had completed her own training ten and more years ago. As she passed under the ironwood lintel into the broad courtyard, she supposed that had circumstances been different, this might be an appropriate time for nostalgia. Most graduates of the College would never have had reason to revisit the hospital until an ill friend or a teaching opportunity brought them back, and so would likely be overcome by that uncanny resonance of old memories superimposed on spaces that have since moved on.

The Goddess of Fortune had chosen a different path for Eyan Lin Sung.

She presented her Physician's license to the guard on duty, and he swung open the studded ironwood double doors of the front entrance. They opened onto a comfortable atrium, its wood-paneled walls hung with devotional tapestries of the Goddess of Healing, larger silken versions of the one in Eyan's study.

The charge nurse on duty inclined her head. "Sung-sen. Has it been a week already?"

Eyan nodded to her. "Hello, Chiyi. How is she today?"

The nurse, Chiyi, chuckled. "Bored, I imagine. That child has a mind more active than a basketful of crickets on her good days."

"So it's been a good day, then?" Eyan asked.

"Go see for yourself." The nurse signed her in but didn't bother to remind Eyan of the room number.

She found Jian painting at the low table in her room, her small easel propped up in front of her. Creases marked the coverlet where her daughter had stood on the bed to open the shutters, and the pellucid light of midmorning painted the white-washed walls pale gold. The second-storey room faced the courtyard: paths divided the rectangle of green into quadrants around a jade fountain in the shape of a lotus.

Someone, a nurse perhaps, had propped the door open. For a few moments Eyan watched her daughter paint, her slim sure hands guiding the brush as a look of utter absorption made her face at once more childlike and older than her eleven years. At the same time, she noted at an almost unconscious level the good color under Jian's skin, a tan one shade darker than her mother's. The bed was still made, which meant Jian had not retired to it since the nurses made it up that morning. Her hand was steady as she held the brush, with no incipient tremors of fatigue. This was indeed, as Chiyi had said, a good day.

She'd raised her fist to knock when Jian looked up. Her startled expression dissolved into a wide if close-lipped smile. "*Mata*," she greeted Eyan with the Chantic word for *mother*. "They said you were coming today."

Where another girl her age might have scrambled up, Jian set the brush on its wooden rest and closed a shell case over the inkstone before rising to bow. Each movement was a careful expenditure of a finite supply of energy. But her embrace was warm as Jian put her arms around Eyan. Her mother returned the hug, then stepped back to arm's length and looked over Jian's shoulder.

"How goes the current work in progress?"

Jian turned the easel around to face Eyan. Ink carp swam in a pond that was a few rippled suggestions of water. Jian appeared to be in the middle of adding more detail: scales half covered one fish, drawn in lines of ink so fine they might have come from a single-hair sable brush.

"It's very good," Eyan said.

"It's not finished yet." Jian turned the easel away with finality.

Eyan knew not to push, that her daughter would show her when she was ready. Instead, she patted the bed and the two of them sat down.

"So how are you feeling today?" Eyan asked.

"I've been awake a few hours and I don't feel tired," Jian said brightly. "My knees were hurting a bit before you came, but I think they've gotten much better since last time."

"Good." Eyan nodded, and slipped her Pearl from her bag. "Lie back and let me have a look at those knees."

With the practice of a long-term patient, her daughter lay back on her bed. Cupping the Pearl in both hands against her forehead, Eyan closed her eyes and focused on the sources of Jian's pain.

She supposed another Physician could have performed her daughter's care. There were scores in the teaching hospital alone. But Eyan had been firm after Jian was born—she would take on whatever patient quotas the College saddled her with, volunteer to treat the hopeless cases down at the poor clinic, as long as she was allowed to be Jian's caretaker. It was her responsibility, and more than that—it was an atonement for a mistake she could never undo.

It was not unheard of for a Court Physician to find herself pregnant. The Goddess Kanin in her wisdom had provided mortals with herbs that could prevent a child's seed from implanting in the womb, or even bring off one that had started to grow—though the Empire tacitly disapproved of the practice. The rhetoric went that it deprived Chane of children that would have grown up to be loyal and productive Chantic citizens. However, such medicines were not outlawed, and even if they had been, Eyan doubted that would provide much barrier to an Imperial Physician.

Yet Eyan's professor in Apothecary was fond of saying the only medicine with a hundred percent success rate was *somang*, the mythical all-healing herb. Like all human medicines, contraceptive herbs were fallible. So Eyan had been surprised but not astonished when her belly began to swell a few months into her first field posting.

She hadn't had to think hard to pinpoint what night it must have been. On the eve of her graduation and licensing, all the newly anointed Physicians had gathered in the great hall for a wild celebration. In the morning they would don their silk robes, and with them the solemn cloak of their adult responsibilities—but tonight they were raucous, triumphant youths giddy with release from the hardship of training. Palm wine and betel nut abounded, pipes and dirty jokes were passed around, and Eyan was not at all surprised when her friend Li Ang, whom she'd known since Basics of Anatomy in first level, pulled her aside and asked if she'd like to continue the party in his apartments.

It was more hours of conversation and drink before she noticed he'd moved from his chair to sit beside her on the bed. Then all at once his arms were around her and he was kissing her neck, her collarbone, her mouth.

Eyan had approached sex with Li Ang like an experiment: placing her hands in the places she'd heard were the right places, making the appropriate noises and responses at the right times. It was so novel that she didn't really mind that her engagement never rose above the level of mild interest—certainly not the consuming passion romantic tales told her to expect.

Afterward, Li Ang had lain on his side and stroked her hair, while Eyan studied him as though he were a foreigner come from some country across the sea. The familiar face, narrower than her own and baked brown by an adolescence toiling in his family's fields, had become somehow completely new, his hands made strange by desires Eyan could barely fathom let alone reciprocate.

"I'm leaving for Varost tomorrow," she said at last.

"And me for Dupang," he'd said. A bite of sarcasm infiltrated his voice. "All in service to the Empire."

Eyan knew Li Ang was from a poor family in the outer provinces; he could never have afforded the years of training without an Imperial scholarship, and he'd traded the first ten years of his service to the Empire in exchange. Eyan could pick and choose her postings in the vassal states, could even choose to stay in New Torj if she wished. Li Ang had to go where the Empire told him. He resented it sometimes, perhaps this night more than most.

As if in response to her thoughts, he reached out again and cupped her cheek. "At least we'll always have tonight."

Eyan kissed him, because it felt like the right thing to do.

Eyan thought no more of it until she was well into her first year in Varost. The chilly northern state was well removed from the most heavily nacre-poisoned areas, but even so there were enough cases of frostbite, maulings, and fevers to keep her busy through the short daylight hours. The first suspicion flickered when her blood stopped coming, despite the fact that her diet consisted almost entirely of meat, in the Varosti style. Back home there were tests she could do to be sure, chemically-treated fabrics that could be urinated on to make them change color, but those luxuries were unavailable in the north, even to an Imperial Physician. And she wasn't about to go the village witchwoman so she could stand naked and shivering while the old woman pointed a dowsing rod at her belly and proclaimed what Eyan already knew.

So she kept working as her stomach grew, waving off the solicitations of the Varosti women not to exert herself, to think of the baby. Eyan *was* thinking of the baby: the pharmacy of medicinal herbs she'd brought in her satchel contained an array of women's herbs to encourage a healthy pregnancy, better than anything the Varosti normally had access to; Eyan had started a daily regimen as soon as she was sure of her condition. She wasn't about to cut her first field posting short and get a black mark on her service record because of the wailing of a bunch of uneducated vassals. And when it came time to give birth, with her herbs to control contractions and bleeding, and her Pearl to take away the pain, Eyan could take care of that, too.

She still dreamed about it sometimes—waking out of the blackness to a sharp, stabbing pain, a shard of glass thrusting into her belly that she somehow knew was worse than any contraction had a right to be. Her screams had brought the village women running. The pain made Eyan forget herself enough to be grateful as the witchwoman slipped a scraped caribou hide under her to catch the birth water, called for boiled water and sphagnum moss. Eyan had snatched at her Pearl like a babe clawing for its mother's breast, sobbing and shaking. Concentrating on the gem's smoothness, she'd slowed her breathing enough to form a focus on the red-black strands of her pain, tracing them in a spiral that erupted from the hemisphere of her belly.

All Physicians learned their own bodies as a training ground, but this was the deepest Eyan had ever gone into her own. At first she hadn't understood what she was seeing: knotted black ropes descended through her abdominal organs, coalescing around her womb, *no*, invading it. Then she reached the epicenter of the vortex, and felt in horror the edges of the hideous crystalline deposits wrapped around her unborn child's bones, spreading their filaments into softer tissues.

When her water broke, it was black. The frail girl the witchwoman pulled from her body was yellow with jaundice, whimpering because she was too weak to cry. The afterbirth that followed was a glistening nacreous mass, like a blister of onyx. Streaks of nacre discolored the birth cord where the organ that should have fed life into her daughter had pumped poison into her veins.

The witchwoman applied sphagnum moss to staunch the blood, while Eyan took the astringent herbs from her satchel meant to dry out the veins from inside, but even so the caribou hide was soaked purple-red under her by the time the bleeding stopped. She could have found and staunched the haemorrhage with her Pearl, but the fresh memory of that awful unnatural pain, and terror of what she might find lurking in her womb, stopped her.

When she finally took Jian in her arms, the baby had quieted worryingly. Her skin was tumeric yellow and she had no appetite for nursing. Even after Eyan used her Pearl to clear the worst of the nacre deposits around Jian's liver, giving the damaged organ hope of regeneration, the witchwoman had said she would not live out the week. Eyan Lin Sung promised herself she would prove the Varosti woman wrong.

To keep this vow, she had to break another. She returned to New Torj as soon as she was strong enough, accepted the mark on her record for cutting short her posting in Varost. She'd had no choice: if Jian were to live, she needed the best medical care the Empire could provide, and that was unquestionably at the College of Physicians. And if Eyan were to live with herself, she had to remain near her.

Eyan didn't see Li Ang again till three years later. The time in between had been filled with batteries of medical tests on Jian and herself, as the best minds in the Empire tried and failed to deduce how Jian might be treated. The director of the teaching hospital himself admitted it was a "curious case"—a veiled way of saying neither he nor his colleagues had seen anything like it. Nacre deposits twisted around Jian's bones and joints, making them ache and sending thread-thin filaments of contamination into her soft tissues. But while the spreading strands could be destroyed the usual way with a Pearl, the deepest deposits seemed beyond the reach of any thaumage.

Despite the nature of the birth, Eyan's examining Physicians had not found a trace of nacre in Eyan's womb, or anywhere in her body. Nor could they explain how she might have been contaminated in the first place. She'd drawn on her Pearl's thauma to check her food and drink for nacre the whole time she'd been in Varost and had found nothing. Nevertheless, the tentative hypothesis was that Eyan had unknowingly come into contact with nacre and, in a process unknown to medicine until her case, the poison had accreted around the child in her womb. Eyan had turned her memories upside down trying to determine how she could have been so careless. A vanishingly small amount of nacre would have been enough—a turnip shared from a Varosti housewife's garden, perhaps. But she'd checked all her meals, and Varost was one of the cleanest territories in the Empire.

Nevertheless, the conclusion was inescapable: Eyan was at fault, somehow. She'd let down her guard, forgotten the bone-deep fear of contamination drilled into all Physicians, and her daughter would pay the price with a life shortened and full of pain.

Though she'd kept up correspondence with Li Ang at his posting in Dupang, Eyan told him nothing of the birth. Nor did her parents know, despite her mother's prying as to when she was going to marry and start a family. Although, in a moment of quiet defiance, she'd given Jian their family name in the hospital records of her birth and ongoing treatment, Eyan knew her daughter was hardly the kind of granddaughter her mother would celebrate:

neither born nor adopted within a legitimate wedlock, and so chronically ill due to her own mother's negligence there were days she couldn't get out of bed.

With Li Ang it was different: Eyan didn't want to put the burden of knowledge on him when he could do nothing to help Jian. He was off performing his healing duties in the faraway states, slowly cleansing the world—as she should have been doing if she hadn't erred. There was no reason to punish him when the greater mistake was hers.

But she had underestimated him.

"Why didn't you tell me we had a daughter?" Li Ang's voice, low and angry and baffled, reached Eyan through clouds of pipe smoke and the chattering of other patrons in the restaurant. She'd heard he was back in New Torj through a messenger just that morning, and agreed to dinner at an establishment just off the Plaza of Tinkers in the middle city. Li Ang had always been a bit stiff and uncomfortable in the higher city, even though as a Physician, he could have patronized the most rarefied teahouses without raising any eyebrows despite his work-tanned face and calloused hands.

"W—what are you talking about?" Eyan said stupidly. The heady scents of coriander and frying meat coming from the kitchens made her feel dizzy and thick.

"I'm not a fool," Li Ang said. "Word gets around a place like the College. I only have a week here before my next posting; I thought it a good time to catch up with some friends." He shrugged, his anger making the motion jerky. "When one person tells you a rumor, it's hearsay. When seven or eight people repeat the same rumor, it begins to sound like truth."

A waiter brought their food: a steaming curry in a bronze dish for Li Ang, cold cuts and pickled quail eggs and vegetables for Eyan. She pushed the plate away, not hungry. "How did you know I'd be in New Torj?"

He laughed shortly. "You wrote to me enough when I was in Dupang. You couldn't get fancy rice paper like that in the territories. But don't change the subject."

Eyan exhaled. Under the table, she signed a quick invocation to the Goddess of Fortune. *Please let this be the right thing to do.* "All right," she said aloud. "You can see her. Jian should know who her father is."

"Jian." His voice was subdued. "It's a pretty name. I wish I'd been there to help you choose it."

The tension between them seemed to coalesce into a hard smooth knot in Eyan's belly, as though she'd swallowed a river stone. She'd done her best to keep Li Ang from sharing the regret she felt. It was in the Goddess' hands now.

Jian was excited at first to see the man Eyan said was her father, asking him questions with all the exuberance her two years could muster. Though the midafternoon sun was still bright outside her room, it wasn't long before Jian's eyes grew heavy and her skin took on an unhealthy pallor. She climbed the side of her cot with the stiff movements of an elderly woman, and Eyan had to help her daughter into bed before closing the shutters.

Li Ang sat on a stool beside the bed and stroked Jian's hair, which was thinner and more brittle than it should have been at her age. Once the little girl's breaths grew even, he asked Eyan in a thick voice, "What's happening to her?"

He listened with wide eyes as Eyan told him of the horrible travesty of Jian's birth, how the best efforts of the Imperial hospital could find no way to rid her of the nacre wrapped around her bones. The best Eyan or anyone could do for her was to give her regular thaumatic treatments to cleanse her blood and keep the nacre from getting a hold in her vital tissues.

"I can extend her life and make it somewhat more comfortable," Eyan said. She twined her fingers in her daughter's small hand on the bedclothes. "But I can't remove the nacre from her body, not even with a Pearl."

"There's no cure, then?" Li Ang asked quietly.

Eyan shook her head. "Not yet." She thought of the hours of study that filled her spare time, the thaumatic theory and case histories. And the informal study that constituted her service at the free clinic, risking herself all over again to treat the most intractable diseases—the hopeless cases, each offering its own precious insight into the workings of the human body.

A familiar determination filled her as she added, "There's no cure, but there will be. I'm going to find one."

Nine years later—eleven years longer than she should have lived according to both Varosti and, as she'd learned, Chantic medicine—Eyan's daughter sat up on the bed and rubbed her stomach under her raw silk day dress. Pearl treatment always made Jian a little nauseous. But then she smiled and swung her arms, testing the renewed mobility in her joints.

"Can you stay awhile longer, *mata*?"

"I wish I could, sugar cane. But I have some urgent business today."

A frown appeared on Jian's face, but only for a moment. "That's all right. I can work on my painting, and Chiyi said later on she'll take me around the courtyard." Her voice was overly bright.

Eyan's guilt was salt on her tongue. She would have stayed then and there if not for the two other children depending on her. For all she was the same age, Azka was glass to Jian's diamond—the Maruan girl's self-sufficiency more fragile, ready to snap. She was not yet practiced in enduring hardship.

Reluctantly, Eyan made her goodbyes and left the hospital. She should have an hour yet before Hsiao Len's personal secretary took his break.

"His Excellency Len-sen is not in right now." The secretary did not bother with a greeting or rise from his writing desk. His bow was a mere perfunctory tilt of the head in Eyan's direction, despite the robes that marked her status. Her clothes and Imperial license had been enough to get Eyan past the guard into the antechamber to Hsiao Len's offices, but the nobleman's secretary had obviously seen enough Physicians not to be dazzled by another, especially one who sought his master without an appointment.

"I'll only be a moment of His Excellency's time," Eyan said evenly. "I seek a guest of his, Juvan Trivadi. Some family business has come up which Trivadi-sen must attend to, and I was told your master might know how to reach him."

The secretary tilted his chin up. "I'm sure if his Excellency were hosting any guests he would have informed me. As that is not the case, I must ask you to—"

The sliding door behind him twitched open and an oval-faced man in bright yellow robes looked out. "I couldn't help but over-hear," Hsiao Len said, for it was surely him. "Please come in."

The noble ushered Eyan into an office three or four times larger than the spare antechamber. A writing desk wide enough to make Eyan's own look like a child's toy fronted a large window paneled in actual glass; through the wavy riverine panel, she glimpsed a small square water garden in the courtyard between this office building and the next. Hsiao Len invited her to sit and Eyan sank gratefully onto the crimson silk cushion on one side of the desk. The noble took the other and began stuffing a square pipe with fragrant herbs. He took a long pull, sighing with satisfaction, and said through the smoke, "Whom do I have the honor of addressing?"

"I am Eyan Lin Sung, Excellency, a Physician of the Court of the Descended Moon."

Hsiao Len gave a short chuckle and gestured at her robes. "I can see that. In truth, I am more curious how a Physician comes to my office as a courier. What is this message you have for, who was it again?"

"Juvan Trivadi, Excellency," she said. "I believe he is a guest in your house, as are his niece and nephew."

Hsiao Len tapped his pipe out on its ashtray. He seemed to be searching his memory, or at least making a show of it. "Yes," he said at last. "Trivadi-sen was a guest of mine, but I was under the impression he had moved on some time ago. I don't know his whereabouts now."

Eyan rocked slightly away from the desk, taken aback. Either Hsiao Len was even more removed from the goings-on around him than most nobles she'd met, or he was hiding something. Judging from what Azka had said earlier, she was going to guess the latter.

She spoke carefully. "Do you mean, Excellency, that you are unaware two children are living in your house unsupervised, with no one to care for them?"

That did it—a crack appeared in Hsiao Len's cultivated insouciance. In a lower voice, he began, "But their father . . ."

"I regret to inform you, Excellency, that Toven Trivadi lies dead in your house as of last night," Eyan said. Her voice grew stern. "I am here because his children begged me—begged me—not to report them to the proper authorities while there was a chance his next of kin could be found. However, I am already risking a mark on my record for not obeying protocol. If you can't tell me where Juvan Trivadi is to be found, I will have no choice but to turn them over to foster care."

Hsiao Len rubbed the trimmed whiskers on his chin. "That is sad news," he said, subdued. "Juvan would surely wish to know of his brother's passing. I wish I could tell you where to find him."

"You really don't know?" Surprise made Eyan's voice louder than it should have been. She'd thought the seriousness of the situation might convince Hsiao Len to cease whatever little game he was playing. An uncharitable thought crossed her mind—though the Goddess of Prosperity taught mortals to view everyone equally regardless of wealth, perhaps it was true nobles regarded others' lives as less important than their own.

Hsiao Len shrugged. "The last I heard, Juvan Trivadi was reading among the roses."

For a moment her mind went blank with puzzlement; frustration was quick on its heels. Eyan placed her palms on Hsiao Len's desk, a little closer than propriety allowed. Her voice was low and taut. "A man lies dead and you're talking in riddles? What do you mean by 'reading among the—"

Suddenly his hands gripped her wrists. Eyan stiffened, about to jerk away, and his grip tightened. She was wondering if she should scream when Hsiao Len leaned close and whispered in her ear, "I know who you are, Eyan Lin Sung. I know you have a daughter, Jian, and I know of her illness. If you would know more, find Juvan Trivadi."

Shock and confusion warred in her breast as he released her. With a deliberate movement meant to draw her eye, he turned over one of the papers on his desk to reveal the stamped mark of a black rose.

"I have told you all I can. Words go both ways," he said, still in a whisper. He shot a meaningful look toward the antechamber.

Eyan stumbled through a rote goodbye, mangling the formal phrases on a tongue made abruptly clumsy, and descended from his office to the street in a fog. Fragments of the bizarre exchange hummed through her mind like bees: Hsiao Len had been unsurprised by her visit, had in fact been expecting her. By showing his seal, he clearly meant her to realize he was the one who had summoned her to the house—but why her? How did he know about Jian? And had his words been a threat, or an invitation?

Her feet seemed to guide her of their own volition, until Eyan found herself in the Plaza of Tinkers, staring through a square of white-washed wall at the curling snarl of nacre roses in the Imperial garden without any clear idea of how she had gotten there. Behind her, the plaza was a buzz of voices, creaking wagon wheels, and sandaled feet slapping cobblestones, but she seemed to hear as though through gauze. As the walled garden drew her senses inward, understanding came like a flash of moonlight on water.

"Reading among the roses," she whispered. Eyan slapped the garden wall in quiet satisfaction.

The Rose Wing of the Imperial College Library had been condemned due to earthquake damage for half a year. Eyan waited till it was fully dark, the moon Hsen and fragment Hseia riding high in a deep blue sky, then made her way to the library, sticking to side streets and keeping the shutters closed tight on her lantern.

Wooden placards with warnings painted in bright red Chantic script hung on either side of the high ironwood gate to the Rose Wing. The doors were chained and bolted, set into sheer stone walls ten spans tall. She would not be getting in this way.

Circling back to side streets, Eyan went around the hollow square of the library building till she came to the gatehouse at the front entrance.

"Library's closed," said the guard lounging at the gatehouse window. She opened her lantern and let the light reflect off her white and red robes, keeping her face in shadow. He straightened to attention. "An Imperial Physician; forgive me. How may I assist you?"

"I left a—a . . ." *Idiot!* She should have planned what she was going to say in advance. "A bit of money in the Iris Wing," Eyan finished, her cheeks reddening. She hoped her clumsy untruth would look like mere embarrassment to the guard.

Whether it was her status, her real chagrin, or some combination of the two, the guard seemed to believe her. It was only as he led her into the darkened Iris Wing that Eyan wondered why her instinct had led her to lie at all. Why hadn't she told the guard there was a man hiding in the Rose Wing and gotten his assistance? It seemed Azka's fear and Hsiao Len's caution were seeping into her, infecting her with an unease she could not name.

They rounded the corner into the Iris Wing and Eyan directed the guard to the first reading room on the right. "I think I left the pouch on a table in the back," she said, in a voice that felt dry as sand. Eyan let the guard move farther ahead of her; the light of his lantern left her as he played it over the tables, searching for the fictional money pouch. In the concealing darkness, she slipped her Pearl out of its bag, while inside her a silent voice screamed, *What am I doing?*

Then she thought of Jian, and her mind was reaching for the guard's through the Pearl. She found the ley lines of nerves that regulated his sleep and wakefulness, playing them as a Court musician might play a harp. Watched them dim from bright orange to a dim, slumbering red.

Eyan opened her own lantern in time to see the guard's eyelids flutter closed. She caught him around the shoulders as his knees buckled, but his greater weight brought them both to the floor faster than she would have liked. Eyan cringed as the slap of leather armor against marble echoed through the hall. She waited for a dozen heartbeats, but no other guards came running.

Eyan arranged the sleeping man in what she hoped would be a comfortable position underneath the reading table. A needle of guilt pricked her as she unhooked the keys from his belt. If he were found without them he would be reprimanded, perhaps demoted or even dismissed. Eyan had an hour or two before the guard's thauma-induced sleep wore off, assuming he was otherwise well-rested, but she didn't know how frequent patrols were. She would try to be in and out of the Rose Wing as fast as possible.

The inner door between the Iris and Rose Wings was also labeled with warning scripts and padlocked. Eyan tried several keys before one made the chain fall away. She caught the chain before it hit the floor, her heart hammering. Holding her breath, Eyan pushed the door open on creaking hinges.

Dust swirled in the thin beam of her shuttered lantern before Eyan doused it. Stars and the edge of a moon shone from the skylight that ran down the central aisle, now the only source of light in the chamber. Tall bookcases and walls covered in scaffolding drew themselves on her vision in lines of silver as her eyes adjusted. Eyan shuffled down the central aisle, trying to make as little sound as possible. She suspected by now that for whatever reason, Juvan Trivadi did not want to be found. A belated shiver of fear touched her: a man who had abandoned his relatives might go to any lengths to stay hidden. But the Maruan would not find her defenseless, she thought as her hand went to the Pearl nestled in its pouch.

As it was, she caught him almost too easily. A pocket of light between two aisles led her to a nest-like alcove where books had been piled to create a wall between shelving units. Eyan tiptoed up to the barrier and peeked over.

The sleeping man huddled under a traveler's cloak did indeed share a resemblance to Toven Trivadi, though with skin a healthier deep brown and a bushy black mustache surmounting his upper lip. He'd tucked one hand under his head as a pillow, and the sleeve she could see poking out from the cloak was rumpled as though he'd been sleeping in his clothes for a few days. Long enough to let down his guard and leave his lantern unshuttered beside him.

Eyan stepped back a pace, ready to run, and cleared her throat. The sound was shattering in that quiet. The Maruan's eyes flew open. He jumped up as though a demon had stuck a burning finger in his ear, promptly tangled himself in his own cloak, and fell back down in a jumble of limbs and fabric. Eyan snatched up his lantern before he could upend it and set the whole wing alight.

"W—who are you?" The man stumbled to his feet, making an aborted snatch for his lantern.

"I should be asking that question," Eyan said. Unfamiliar excitement made the words come out low and breathless. "Are you Juvan Trivadi?"

Hesitation flickered in his eyes; then they looked past her. The scrape of a leather sole against marble made Eyan whirl, and the thin yellow spear of a third lantern beam joined the pool at her feet as Hsiao Len stepped into the light. He'd changed from his yellow robes into a black traveler's cloak, leather sandals on his feet.

"It's all right, Juvan," Hsiao Len said. "I called her here. This is Eyan Lin Sung."

"You're Eyan Lin Sung?" Trivadi's eyes widened with something like amazement. "I read your file. What you did in Varost was truly incredible. I'd heard of Physicians assisting their own deliveries before, but—"

The bottom dropped out of Eyan's stomach. "How do you know about that?" she asked, her voice rising. "We've never even met."

"No, you haven't," Hsiao Len said. "But we know you, Eyan Lin Sung. And it's well past time that you learn who we are." He turned from the aisle, black robes sweeping the dust settled in corners. "Come. We have something to show you."

Hsiao Len led the way to a side room. Red warning signs glared from the canvas covering its doorway, but the noble brushed them aside. The room inside looked undamaged. Locked wooden cubbyholes lined the right wall, and a table tall enough to stand at hulked in the center of the room. Hsiao Len took out a key from his robes and removed a long scroll from one of the cubbies, spreading it on the table. The document was a map of the Empire: Eyan recognized the ruff of mountains with New Torj nestled at its base, the squiggles of rivers smoothing into the fertile floodplains of the farther provinces and vassal states to the north, west, and south. Like all maps, it ended beyond the dry eastern coast in a sliver of ocean; the cartographer had not bothered to depict the poisonous wastelands on the other side of the sea.

Yet there was something different about this map. Above the fading red ink denoting the borders and names of territories and villages, Eyan saw several blots of black ink, scattered across the map like—she shuddered. Like blooming deposits of nacre. Squinting, she realized the markings weren't blots at all: each depicted the stylized petals of a rose viewed from above. Every seal lurked near the name of a village, all of them in the vassal territories.

For a time, the two men stood back and let her examine the map. Eyan turned away from it, resting her hands on the sturdy table to steady herself. "What is this?"

Hsiao Len stepped to the edge of the table. "The Empire would have you believe Physicians are the 'healers of the world'. Nothing could be further from the truth." She heard contempt in his voice. "You are tools of Imperial control—for quite some time, the only tools it desired. But that is all about to change."

She was too astonished to speak. Hsiao Len took the opening. "Juvan and I are members of the Black Rose Society. It is a brotherhood that transcends countries, founded just after the war, around the same time as Chane. We are sworn to prevent such a war from ever reoccurring."

He smoothed the rice paper on the table. "Our brothers in the Society created this map. It is a record of villages the Empire has targeted to study the effects of nacre." He tapped the map. "Acene is one of those villages. Over the past few years, Imperial thaumages have been feeding nacre into Acene's soil and water and watching the results—"

She could take no more. "What you say is impossible!" Eyan blazed. "Maybe Old Torj had the power to move nacre at its will, but we've lost that art—"

Behind her, Trivadi barked a hoarse, strained laugh. "Ha! Lost like that Pearl you carry in your pocket?" His next words were choked with grief. "Or are you going to tell me I don't know what my own brother died of?"

At her silence, he nodded. "I already knew what you came to tell me. The Black Rose Society has its own messengers. When did Toven die?"

"The night before this," Eyan said, and blinked at the realization. Had it really been so recently? She held her Pearl up where Juvan could see it; the gem looked suddenly blunt and ugly in the dim lantern light. "Tell me what you meant just now."

It was Hsiao Len who elaborated. "The Empire keeps excellent records. That is its strength and its downfall. It was by tracking those records that our Society recognized a disturbing trend."

Hsiao Len coughed delicately. "By all rights the cases of nacre poisoning in villages with an Imperial Physician posted should have decreased over the years. But the rates of nacre-sickness have remained stable across the vassal states. Do you understand what that means?"

He wanted the words to come from Eyan's own mouth, for her to participate in this madness. She shook her head, her lips pressed together.

"It means Pearls don't destroy nacre," Trivadi said. "They just move it around—from human bodies back into the soil and water. The Empire isn't healing the land; why would they want to, when that would mean relinquishing their control?"

It made an ugly kind of sense. For all that it commanded an empire, Chane did not have a large population from which to conscript an army; its ability to enforce law and order came not from a monopoly on violence, but from the power to give and withhold life itself on a much more fundamental level. And how much greater was that power if it was permanent?

Her whole body felt weak. She slipped the Pearl into her bag before it could slip from her fingers and shatter on the stone. "What about Jian?" She looked between Len and Trivadi. "You said you knew what happened in Varost. If what you say is true, that our thaumages have discovered how to transfer nacre, why haven't they healed her?"

Hsiao Len's face grew grim. "Do you love your daughter, Eyan?"

A sudden rage burned in her. For a heartbeat she wanted to fly at Len's face, claw at his eyes. She bit it back. "Of course I do."

"Then why would the Empire wish to cure her, when they

can use her as a leash to control you?" He smiled in a way that showed more teeth than was proper. "I see you're angry. I'm angry too—at what the country I love is becoming. The Chantic Empire was founded on a promise of peace, but it's twisting itself into something evil."

Trivadi began to roll the map, handling the rice paper with light fingers. "We're not telling you all this just to make you feel powerless," he said quietly. "Len and I wish you to join the Society, if you're willing."

Hsiao Len nodded. "I intend to get Juvan and his family out of the city by dawn tomorrow. It's no longer safe for him here. I'll be a man short after; I could use you as a replacement set of eyes and ears."

Eyan shook her head—not in refusal but in impending informational overload. "What if I refuse? Not necessarily because I don't want to join you, but because I can't? I have duties to fulfill, a daughter to care for—what you propose could endanger all of that."

"It's already in danger," Trivadi said harshly. "You can either continue to live in ignorance of that danger, or you can join the Black Rose and fight back. But know this—either way, if you repeat a word of what we've told you here tonight, the Empire will learn of it and punish you." She started to protest, but the Maruan rode over her objection. "They won't kill you—Imperial Physicians are too valuable—but they will turn all other means in their power to ensuring your silence."

You're lying, she wanted to say, but the words dried up on her tongue. She could see no reason for Juvan to lie. "Is that . . . what happened to you?" she asked instead. "Acene was your home. Did the Empire find out you were with this Society?"

"The Empire does not know the Black Rose Society exists," Len said firmly. "If they did we would not be having this exchange, I assure you."

Eyan laughed tightly. "You're doing a poor job of convincing me to join."

"You've already joined," Hsiao Len said airily, for a moment every inch the carefree noble of their first meeting. "Already stopped being the good little Imperial soldier. Or is the unconscious guard in the Iris Wing nothing to do with you?"

Juvan touched him on the shoulder and whispered something in a language Eyan didn't know. Hsiao Len nodded and both of them went to the draped doorway. "We will withdraw to let you consider," he said, "but when we return I will expect your answer."

Alone, Eyan sat on the chilly flagstones and rested her head against the edge of the table. She cradled her Pearl to her chest like a child's doll and stared into its depths a long time. She felt trapped. But then, perhaps she always had been, and was just now awakening to the bars after spending her whole life asleep.

The canvas rustled and Trivadi and Len entered. Hsiao Len bowed to her and said, "What have you decided?"

Dawn broke over the docks in soft layers of pink and orange. Beyond the swaying keels of ships at anchor, the rising sun colored the bay butter yellow. Eyan stood on the jetty beside Hsiao Len, rough burlap traveler's cloaks covering their fine robes; he had blackened both their faces with a bit of charcoal, to make them look like poorer Chantics who wouldn't be out of place in the rough neighborhood below the Plaza of Sailors.

Two deckhands wrestled an oblong crate up a ramp on the ship nearest them. The crate was labeled rice, but Eyan knew what was really in it. Three figures in traveler's cloaks with the hoods drawn up followed the deckhands up the ramp. One was about Eyan's height, the other two much shorter. The middle figure turned and Eyan caught a flash of a young girl's searching eyes, her mouth forming around a question before the adult figure pulled her back. They reached the deck and Eyan lost sight of them.

She and Len watched in silence as sailors rushed around the deck, loosing mooring lines and poling the ship away from the jetty. Sails opened to the gathering breeze, and the ship turned a red tail to the shore. It was the size of a child's toy on the water when Eyan broke the silence.

"Where will they go?"

A lopsided smile pulled at Len's mouth. "They'll follow the coast for a while, until they're past the most populated coastal areas. Then I imagine they'll set course to cross the sea."

"It's not a wasteland over there, then," said Eyan. She did not inflect the words into a question.

"Not at all," Hsiao Len said. "The Empire has hidden so much from us all. But the truth is a powerful kind of thauma. It can't be created or destroyed, only hidden. And what is hidden can be learned anew."

Eyan nodded. The truth that could heal her daughter was out there. If it took the rest of Eyan's life, she would find it.

Cascadia
Mackenzie Reide

"Cascadia" is inspired by the independence movement for creating a new country of the same name. What if the western states of Washington and Oregon did indeed combine with the province of British Columbia to form a new country? Under the Pacific Northwest Unification Act, Cascadia prospers with renewable energy resources, the western ports, and an influx of tech companies. What if the state of California was given the option to join, but chose to stay behind? The remaining states would become districts in New America and would struggle with the effects of foreign outsourcing as well as political unrest. New America might respond to these problems with severe budget cuts and limitations of individual rights, thus sparking an underground resistance movement.

It was a cloudy day in Los Angeles as Sarah walked quickly across the campus of the University of District Southern California. Spring buds were about to blossom on the trees, which normally she would enjoy, but today she was late for the Monday morning meeting. If she hurried, she could catch the tail end; maybe even grab a donut before the other professors gobbled them up.

She scooted around a group of students holding protest signs. Crowds like this made her nervous, but she couldn't help but glance at the signs. *Fund the Future! Education Does Matter!* The situation on campus was getting worse, she realized. Every day, more students were gathering near the student center to protest the university budget cuts.

At least I'm managing to survive this. She thought of her grant. It was a good way to start her new career as adjunct lecturer and researcher. The other departments weren't as lucky.

As she passed the dean's office, she noticed two men in dark blue suits talking to the receptionist. They seemed out of place with their neatly pressed jackets compared to the casual dress of the students rushing past her between classes. She was glad her department was less formal than some of the other faculties. She missed her student days of wearing only jeans and a T-shirt; now it was dress pants and blouses and annoying heels that pinched her toes. She tugged on a crease in her shirt as she pushed through the doors to the environmental engineering office.

"Dr. Stanford, where have you been?" The receptionist looked up from the paper she was reading. "I've been calling you all morning."

"Good morning, Iris," Sarah answered. "Sorry I'm late, I had a flat tire."

"Oh, dear," Iris said. "I hate it when that happens. I was worried." She put the paper down on her desk.

"I would have called but my phone died. Ever since they started outsourcing all the tech manufacturing, the battery only lasts three hours. It's ridiculous!"

Iris nodded. "Yes, it's like they just want us to be inconvenienced." She held up a small cable. "Here, you can use my charger."

"Thanks." Sarah grabbed it and plugged in her phone.

"No problem. Did you see the new District Homeland agents?"

"District Homeland agents? What are those?" Sarah thought of the men she'd seen in the dean's office. "I saw two men talking to Lois just now, wearing very spiffy suits. Do you mean them?" She stuck her head in the conference room. "What happened to the Monday morning meeting?"

Iris glanced at the paper on her desk. "It didn't happen. The District Homeland agents came in first thing this morning. They wanted to see Dr. Weber, so I told them I expected him to come to the meeting. They waited for him, then they sat in his office and talked for over half an hour. They all left together."

"What?" Sarah poured herself a cup of coffee. "What's going on? What are District Homeland agents?"

"That's what's I asked!" Iris said, throwing her hands in the air. "Apparently, they've reorganized Homeland Security again. They've been assigned to deal with all the protests happening on university campuses across New America."

Sarah frowned. "Are they afraid that we'll end up with the kind of riots we had during the secession vote?"

Iris shook her head. "I don't know. They gave me the creeps. And I don't think they even know what they're supposed to be doing. They seemed very disorganized. They were intent on questioning Dr. Weber, but when they saw my copy of your Seattle itinerary, they suddenly wanted to talk to you."

"Me? Why would they want to do that?"

"I think it has something to do with this." Iris held up the paper she had been reading.

"The student newspaper? What's so special about that?" Sarah took it from Iris.

"Look at the article on page seven."

Sarah flipped through the pages to a goofy caricature of the dean wearing a Statue of Liberty costume, touting an engineering textbook and waving a machete instead of a torch. The caption underneath read: *More budget cuts to come!*

"You know, bad joke aside, that's a good likeness of your father," Iris mused at the drawing.

Sarah's mouth twitched in a smile. "Yes, it does look like him, doesn't it?" Her eyes fell on the article underneath.

The end of the Scribe? Dr. David Nelson, a professor of psychology at Columbia University, was hauled off campus last week by mysterious agents calling themselves District Homeland. No statements are being made at this time, but rumors abound. Is Dr. Nelson our infamous Scribe? Is this the end of our champion of education? What the heck is DH? Stay tuned as The Gazette's *reporters dig deeper for answers.*

"They arrested a professor at Columbia?"

"That's what the rumors are saying," Iris said. She shifted nervously in her chair. "And now Dr. Weber is being taken away. Do you think he's involved?"

Sarah shook her head. "Dr. Weber is one of the top researchers in solar power. He's too busy to be the Scribe. Besides, why would he jeopardize his career? The Scribe's views are very controversial."

"But he does have some good points," Iris said. "Like his article challenging the budget cuts and how important it is not to lose sight of education."

"He also says why bother learning the alphabet if we're only going to be allowed to speak ten words."

Iris laughed. "That was a great article! But seriously, he did warn us that the new government was just beginning to make changes. And now we have DH agents on campus!"

Sarah shook her head at Iris. "The old government made a lot of promises to keep California from joining Cascadia. It will just take some time. There will be bumps."

"Like the fact they want to question you? Do *you* know anything about the Scribe?" Iris leaned forward with a hopeful look on her face.

"No!" Sarah shook her head. "I'm not into that sort of thing."

"That's what I said. But they searched the whole office anyway. They had a warrant, can you believe that?" Iris' hand shook slightly as she fiddled with the mouse. "They asked me lots of questions about your dinner date with Dr. O'Conner next month."

"What? That's not a date!" Sarah felt her face grow hot. "It's for work!"

"Well, I did say that Dr. O'Conner is handsome, but . . ."

"Iris!"

"Well, I was flustered. They made me really uncomfortable. I tried to make them crack a smile but it didn't work. Anyway, I didn't say you were dating, I just said Dr. O'Conner was going to take you out for dinner after your talk at the conference."

"Like I said, that's a work dinner . . . never mind." Sarah sighed. She looked out into the hallway. "Where are the students? They should be on their way to the lab."

"The agents told me to cancel today's classes."

Sarah spun around. "What? They can't do that. We need this lab. We've only got two weeks until the end of the semester!" Sarah stared at Iris in horror. "We've got finals to prep for."

"I tried to explain, but they wouldn't listen," Iris said. "Maybe the Scribe's right, education isn't important anymore."

Sarah shook her head firmly. "No, I refuse to believe that." She clutched her cup of coffee with two hands. "There must be a mistake."

"I hope you're right," Iris said. "Those agents made me so nervous."

"Well, I suppose it's their job to make people nervous." Sarah walked into her office. Her chair should have been nested under her desk, but it was pushed three feet away and rotated in the opposite direction. When she sat down to grip her mouse, the screen lit up. One of the emails from Ryan O'Conner was open—the invitation to dinner.

Sarah felt short of breath. *This can't be happening.* With all the political unrest going on in District California, why would the agents care about her dinner date?

She surveyed the untidy pile of papers on her desk. Someone had rifled through them, so she pulled open all her desk drawers. Same thing. Items were not quite put back in the right places. Sarah felt her pulse quicken. And they'd searched her desk? What for? And why take Howard Weber in for questioning?

She grabbed a pencil from the little cup on her desk and stared at the state grant application in front of her. Ever since the Pacific Northwest Unification five years ago, funding had become increasingly difficult to find. Solar power was not considered research that would bring immediate profits to most companies. That was the prime reason for trying out a joint project with the University of Cascadia. Her father, the Dean, had been reluctant to reach across the new border, but Howard convinced him it would benefit the department. Howard had also introduced her to Ryan, the charming young professor at U Cascadia. She smiled to think of those deep brown eyes and Irish accent. Their first dinner at the tiny sushi place next to the university had been both awkward and funny. Sarah had spilled sake all over Ryan's trousers, but he just laughed and ordered more. For the first time, she'd felt comfortable talking with a member of the opposite sex without charts and data to look at.

She doodled in the margins of the grant proposal in front of her. Could this be related to what happened at Columbia? It didn't make any sense. Why would the Scribe care about solar energy? She remembered Howard being very agitated when she had returned from her last trip to Seattle. She had attributed that to the budget cuts. Then again, Ryan had not been his usual cheerful self, either. Their dinner date had been solemn. His mind seemed to be elsewhere.

A ping pulled her from her thoughts. An email from Ryan had popped up in her inbox. It was marked "urgent".

She stared at the subject line.

GET OUT

She froze. What?

The phone rang in the reception area. Iris answered, "Environmental Engineering office, how can I help you?"

After a short pause, Iris spoke again. "Yes, Dr. Stanford is here now. Can I put you through to her office?"

She stared at the words on the screen in front of her. She typed,

"What?" and hit Return.

The phone rang on her desk.

Another ping.

SARAH GET OUT NOW

Sarah sucked in her breath. She stared numbly at the words in front of her. This couldn't be happening. Not to her.

What the hell was going on?

The phone stopped ringing—must have gone to voicemail.

Iris appeared at her door. "That was one of the agents on the phone." She sounded scared. "They told me to make sure you didn't leave. They want to ask you some questions."

Sarah deleted the last two emails from Ryan. She forced a pretend smile onto her face. "Iris, would you mind closing my office door? I have some work to finish before they arrive."

Iris looked uneasy. "Okay. I'm sure it will all work itself out." She closed the door behind her.

Sarah sat staring at her monitor. She took a deep breath, grabbed her handbag and turned toward the window. "I can't believe I'm doing this," she muttered to herself as she pulled up the pane and pushed out the screen. She crawled through the open window and slid awkwardly to the ground. Swinging her bag over her shoulder, she nodded to the two students who were sitting on a bench nearby, staring open-mouthed.

"Perfect day to skip class," she said, and strode off down the sidewalk.

She reached her car and fumbled around for her keys.

"You probably shouldn't take your car," said a voice.

Sarah jumped. "What?" She stared at the man standing on the

other side of her car. He was six feet tall, with an athletic build that she couldn't help but notice as he leaned forward to rest his elbows on top of her little Honda. He wore a blue dress shirt and jeans. His dark hair was tousled, like he had just gotten out of bed without a shower.

"If you take your own car, you won't get very far. As soon as they figure out you've left campus, they'll start looking for you."

Sarah frowned at the man. "Who are you? Wait a minute . . . aren't you the new janitor?"

The man smiled at her. His blue eyes seemed amused at her confusion.

"Yes, I started with your department two weeks ago. My name's Jason."

"Yes, Jason," Sarah stated back to him. "I know your name."

"Oh." He appeared to feign surprise. "I never thought you'd even noticed me."

"Of course I noticed you," Sarah snapped. "You're . . . er . . . you're the new janitor. A new face, I always notice a new face in the building."

"Ah, but you didn't stop to introduce yourself. That's why I thought you hadn't noticed me."

"Well, I noticed. Now, if you don't mind, Jason, I have to go."

She continued digging for her keys. "What did you mean they'll start looking for me?" A queasiness settled in her stomach. She didn't want to admit it, but the DH agents did not sound like people to mess with. "And what's wrong with my car?"

"Too easy to trace. Why don't I give you a lift in my truck? We can talk as we drive."

Sarah gave up digging through her handbag. "What? Are you

serious?" She stared at him. "You expect me to just jump in a truck with a strange man?"

"Hey, I'm the janitor. You know me . . . sort of."

"Oh, so I'm supposed to just drop everything and get in a truck with the new janitor?" Sarah said. "Wow, that 'sort of' makes it all better."

She shoved her hand one more time into her bag and pulled out her keys. "I'm not going anywhere with you, mister. Now, I'm getting in my car and I will drive over you if I have to."

Jason pursed his lips. His easygoing manner disappeared and his voice got tense. "Look, Dr. Stanford, we need to go now and not in your car."

"*We* don't need to go anywhere!" Sarah said as she opened her car door. "Seriously, I will drive over your foot." She got in and slammed the door shut. As she started the engine she heard Jason mutter, "Dammit!"

He opened the passenger door and slid into the seat beside her. "Fine, you can take your car, but you probably won't make it off campus."

"What the hell are you doing?" Sarah shouted at him. "Get out of my car!"

"No can do, sorry," Jason said as he fastened his seat belt.

Sarah just sat there, stunned. It was not every day that a handsome man jumped in her car, but this was not the day for it.

"You need to go," Jason said firmly. "Drive, Dr. Stanford!"

Just then, Sarah heard shouting from across the parking lot. She looked up and saw two men in dark blue suits walking quickly toward her car. One of the men pulled out a gun.

"Sarah, we need to go, now!" Jason's voice rose in panic.

Sarah shifted the car into reverse. The men started running. Both were holding guns now. She jammed the car into gear and floored it, pulling away just as the agents reached her parking spot. They shouted at her as she sped through the lot, working the brakes just enough to crank a tight turn out onto Main Street.

"They had guns!" Sarah gasped as she drove down the road.

"Yes." Jason's voice shook. "They looked like they would use them, too."

"Who are those men? Are they really government agents?" Sarah gripped the steering wheel tightly. "And what the hell do they want with me?"

"Yes, they're called District Homeland. We need to ditch your car."

"Why? And just where are we going?" Sarah switched lanes. "And who the hell are you?"

Jason fidgeted with his seat belt. He seemed to be checking it to make sure it was secure. "We need to get to the border as soon as possible."

"The border?" Sarah glanced sideways at him. "Are you saying we have to leave California?"

"I'm saying we need to get you out of New America." Jason glanced out the rear window.

"But . . . this is ridiculous. Besides, I don't have my passport with me."

"That's okay, I brought you a new one."

Sarah frowned. "Why? I don't need a new one, mine doesn't expire for another two years."

"Yes, but this one has a new identity on it." Jason looked at the side mirror on the passenger's side. "I don't mean to alarm you, but I think we're being followed."

"What?" Sarah looked in the rearview mirror and saw a black SUV rapidly changing lanes, coming up behind her.

"We need to lose them. Can you do that?"

The queasiness in her stomach morphed into anger. "Watch me." Sarah threw her car into a skid. She swerved to avoid a garbage truck, then maneuvered around two slow-moving cars as she sped down a side street.

"Did you drag race as a kid or something?" Jason looked pale as he gripped the door handle.

"Defensive driving lessons." Sarah concentrated on weaving in and out of traffic. The SUV swerved wildly but managed to follow.

"Oh, yeah?" Sarah said to the rearview mirror. "Try this!" The tires squealed in protest as she turned into a narrow alley.

"I've got a bad feeling about this." Jason's face was now a light shade of green. He reminded her briefly of a former boyfriend who had reacted badly to her fast driving.

"If you feel sick, then stick your head out the window."

"Seriously, you call this defensive driving?"

"Well, there are two agents with guns chasing us, so yes, I call this defensive driving." She paused to navigate between two large cargo containers.

Jason looked back. "They're still on our tail."

Sarah shot back out into traffic. Horns honked as she swerved around a delivery truck. She changed lanes to avoid colliding head on with a BMW. The SUV was still only one car behind her.

"What is it with these guys?" she said in exasperation.

"We have to ditch them!" Jason held onto the armrest with his head jammed up against the window.

Sarah gritted her teeth. "Hang on." She accelerated through a red light.

"Whoa!" Jason's head swiveled back in response to a nasty crunching noise behind them.

"Did we lose them?" Sarah was focused on the cars around her.

"Yes, they just took out the front end of a pickup truck. You drive this car like a weapon!" Jason looked forward. "We need to get to the warehouse district. I have things there that we can use."

"We just lost the agents and now you want to make a pit stop?"

Jason gave her a sly grin. "I think you'll find it worth your while. Besides, we need to switch cars."

"How about you tell me what's going on?"

"Yes, we need to talk." Jason let out a deep breath and seemed to steady his nerves.

"You still need to throw up?"

"No, I'm good . . . really." He gave her a sheepish grin. "That was impressive. You can come to my rescue any day."

Sarah felt her cheeks flush. "Thanks."

Jason pointed through the windshield. "Okay, slow down a little more, please, and pull into that storage lot over there."

Sarah drove through an open rusty gate, then came to a stop in front of a row of doors. "What's in here?"

"Let me show you what's behind door number one." Jason climbed out of the car and wobbled slightly as he pulled open one of the storage doors. He made a grandiose gesture, as if he was presenting something important to her.

Sarah stared in surprise. There, parked behind the open door, was a canary yellow Porsche 911.

"Where did you get this?" She jumped out of her Honda and

ran over to the Porsche.

Jason grinned. "My father collects vintage cars. I borrowed it for the ride down. Much more fun than my old pick up." He pulled the garage door down behind them.

"So . . . you're saying if I go along with this, I get to drive to Seattle in a Porsche?" Sarah frowned at him.

"It's this or the truck I borrowed from Howard. Problem is, that's back on campus. That's why I wanted you to come with me in the first place."

Sarah hesitated. She was itching to get behind the wheel, try it out, but . . . "Okay, wait." She held her hand up. "If these agents are suddenly so interested in me, won't this draw attention?"

"I have a solution for that." Jason reached into the front trunk of the Porsche and pulled out a duffle bag. "I love that Porsche kept the engine in the back. Here, I got you a change of clothes and dye for your hair." He tossed her a box of black hair dye. "The DH is so new nobody knows what's really going on. We can slip through the net if we go now."

Sarah made a face. "You want me to dye my hair black? Can't I be a redhead or something more interesting?"

Jason laughed. "Black's the best camouflage. Your lovely blonde highlights have to go." He gave her a mischievous smile. "Of course, I could cut it all off for you instead."

"Ah . . . no!" Sarah spluttered. "Look, I need some answers. What's really going on?" She placed the box of dye on top of the Porsche and crossed her arms. "Who are you? And why is there a new organization of agents after me?"

Jason leaned against the metal storage wall. "I'm not a janitor."

"Yeah, I kind of gathered that."

He looked at her thoughtfully. "What do you know about what happened at Columbia?"

"A professor was arrested. Rumor has it he's the Scribe."

"Have you read any of the Scribe's articles?"

Sarah frowned. "I've read some of them. Iris loves him. She wishes she could write like that."

A smile twitched at the corners of Jason's mouth. "Good for Iris. So . . . do you have any opinions on what the Scribe writes about?"

Sarah thought for a moment. "Well, he has a point about the budget cuts. But I think he goes too far. The way he talks the entire educational system is falling apart!"

"I see. Have you filled out any of those registration forms that the Bureau of Labor Statistics sent around?"

"I only had to fill out one form. The Stanfords have been on this continent for over 300 years. I thought that was for stats."

Jason nodded. "Yes, they did ask for a lot of stats."

"Look, what's all this have to do with me?"

Jason looked like he was calculating something in his head. "How much have you and Ryan talked about things which weren't work related?"

"How well do you know Ryan? Who are you, really?" Sarah waved the box of hair dye at him. "If you tell me, I'll dye my hair."

Jason smirked. "Okay, Sarah. I teach at U Vancouver. And yes, I know Ryan well."

"Teach what?"

He hesitated before answering. "History."

"History! I'm running away with a history professor!"

"Well, I could go back to being a janitor if you like."

Sarah shook her head. "No, never mind." She sat against the front of the Porsche. "I don't understand why you're here."

Jason took a deep breath and walked over to lean against the Porsche beside her. "I wanted to see firsthand what's going on here. Ryan was worried about you and Howard, and I had vacation days to use, so I volunteered to come. This was a good opportunity to get a feel for the situation."

"You mean the protests on campus?"

Jason nodded. "Yes, I wanted to know how much tension is building against the proposed budget cuts. Especially now that this new District Homeland group is actually happening."

"And you got this by working as a janitor?"

"You'd be amazed at what you learn as a janitor. Did you know Dr. Heller drinks six cups of coffee a day? And Iris has a secret stash of dark chocolate in her desk?"

"No, I did not," Sarah said with a smile.

"Besides, I was a bit of a slacker when it came to cleaning. But I did get a chance to eavesdrop on the students and faculty. Nobody notices the janitor." Jason grabbed the hair dye from on top of the Porsche. "Come on, we can talk more while you stick your head in the sink."

Sarah let out a heavy sigh. "Okay. Fine." She couldn't refrain from making a face at the dingy little sink in the corner of the storage room. "I didn't know storage lockers had running water," she said as she stuck her head under the stream. "Arghhh!"

"Oh yeah, there's no hot water," Jason said, stifling a laugh.

"Why don't you dye your hair?" Sarah snapped at him.

"I'm not the one on the run."

"Hmph. So, why does a professor at U Vancouver care so much

about what's happening on a campus in California?"

Jason didn't answer right away. Instead, he appeared to study his boots. "I was born in San Francisco and stayed there until I was ten. Until my older brother took a rubber bullet in the eye during one of the riots. My dad was so upset that he applied for a fellowship in Vancouver and moved the whole family up there."

Sarah winced. "That's awful. Did he lose his eye?"

Jason let out a choked laugh. "Yes, but he claims that he only needs one eye to look in a microscope."

Sarah smiled grimly. "At least he can have a sense of humor about it. I attended a rally for the secession movement when I was a teenager and almost got trampled when the Swat team charged. Ended up with two broken ribs and a concussion. I was lucky; the kid next to me got his head caved in."

"I'm sorry you went through that."

Sarah shuddered at the memory. "It was terrifying, I felt so trapped. There was nowhere to run. It was a peaceful rally, then suddenly there was tear gas everywhere and people started pushing and shoving. It all happened so fast."

Jason handed her a towel. "I had to sneak out of the house to attend the rallies in Vancouver. That's why I became a history professor. I wanted to know why these things happen. Maybe find a better way to change things."

"I decided I wanted to change the world through science."

"How do you feel about the budget cuts?" Jason asked. "The sciences are being hit now. It's not just the arts and humanities anymore."

Sarah glanced at an old-fashioned clock sitting on a shelf in the locker. She didn't want to leave the hair dye on any longer than necessary. "Not good. The department hasn't been able to secure a state grant for several years. Solar power is not a popular topic. If it wasn't for Ryan's department's contributions, Howard would have to lay off more staff."

"So you've never had any inclination to move up north? The economy's strong."

"Are you kidding? I've always loved living in LA. We've got the best weather, lots of sun for my solar projects." Sarah stuck her head in the grungy sink to rinse out the dye. "Argh! Besides, the Pacific Northwest is very rainy!"

Jason shook his head and laughed. "True, but sometimes living in other communities gives you a new perspective."

Sarah didn't answer as she finished rinsing and grabbed the hair dryer from Jason.

"Just give it a quick dry, then put these clothes on. We need to go." Jason opened the rear engine cover and knelt down. He disappeared from her sight. Sarah smiled to herself. At least he was being polite.

Sarah dried her shoulder-length hair just enough that she could wrangle it into a pony tail. She dressed quickly in the jeans and T-shirt and tossed her dress pants and blouse into the duffle bag.

"Ready."

Jason closed the engine cover and threw open the garage door. He tossed her the keys and then motioned for her to back up. Sarah got in the driver's seat and made a few quick adjustments. She started the engine. It purred like a Porsche should. Her skin tingled.

This is crazy, she thought. *Why am I doing this?* Because

Howard was in trouble and she needed to find out what was really going on. Jason appeared to be her best bet at getting answers. A cold chill ran up her spine at the thought of the agents running toward her car with guns. It had felt just like that day at the rally when her whole world broke apart.

This time she would not get crushed.

Sarah backed up and rolled down her window. "Come on, what are we waiting for?"

Jason looked amused. "Hang on. I want to park your car in the storage unit." He held out his hand for the keys. Sarah hesitated, then handed them over. She felt a pang of sadness as Jason parked her car. Was she saying goodbye to her trusty little Honda? She watched him close the garage door and climb in the passenger side. "Drive casually on the way out of town, please. Try to avoid any more car chases."

"Very funny. And this is from a guy who drives a yellow Porsche while undercover." Sarah took the sunglasses he offered her and put them on. She glanced one more time at the now-closed door. "Where to next?"

"Drive on the old highway until we are well out of town," Jason said. "Oh, and make a quick stop at the drive thru up there."

"Ugh." Sarah frowned. "You know that stuff rots your guts?"

"I have guts of steel."

"Then why did you turn green during the car chase?"

Jason shook his head at her, but laughed. He turned on the radio as Sarah drove past three drive thrus before she finally convinced him to run into a small deli and grab sandwiches.

"See, this is much better," Sarah said with her mouth full of avocado and sprouts as she shifted gears to slow down for a traffic light.

"You are such a granola cruncher!" Jason complained. "You sure you don't want to move to Cascadia?"

Sarah laughed.

They drove carefully through the streets of Los Angeles, though Sarah couldn't help but notice the passersby admiring the car. It was all so surreal. Was she really doing this? Jason switched from station to station as if looking for something. Finally, as they left the city behind and Sarah accelerated on the highway, the news came on.

"An arrest was made at the University of District Southern California this morning. Dr. Howard Weber was taken into custody by the new District Homeland Agency. Students are protesting the arrest of the popular professor. The dean is refusing to comment."

"Howard was arrested? Iris said they just wanted to ask him some questions." Sarah took another big bite of her sandwich, then shifted gears.

The announcer continued. "Dr. Weber is a known colleague of Dr. Ryan O'Conner of the University of Cascadia. The two men are alleged associates of the highly controversial voice known as the Scribe."

"Oh, oh," Jason said.

"Say what?" Sarah said loudly. "Howard is one of the leading engineers in the solar energy field. He's not a troublemaker!"

"Ah . . . Sarah . . ." Jason started to say.

Sarah turned up the radio.

"The police are also looking for another associate, Dr. Sarah Stanford. If you have any information in regards to Dr. Stanford's whereabouts, please call the tip line."

"SAY WHAT?" Sarah shouted at the radio. "I am not! I don't know anything about the Scribe!"

Jason grabbed the radio knob and turned it off. "Look, Sarah . . ."

"Don't 'look Sarah' me!" Sarah roared. "What the hell is going on?" She floored the accelerator. The needle jumped to 90 mph.

"Sarah, not now! Please slow down!" Jason gripped the dashboard with white knuckles.

"What the hell is going on?" Sarah kept driving.

"Okay, okay, there's more to tell you. Just slow down, please? We can't get pulled over for speeding right now. Speeding comes later, okay?"

Sarah glared at the road. Reluctantly, she slowed down and forced herself to drive the speed limit. "Fine, but I want some answers."

"Yes, you're right," Jason said. "What has Ryan told you about his work outside of solar power?"

Sarah frowned. "Not much, really."

"Well, you two are dating, you must have talked about something."

"Excuse me? Those were work dinners!"

Jason smirked. "Worried your dad won't approve of you dating a Cascadian?"

"What's it to you?"

"Nothing." He sat silent for a long moment.

Sarah took a deep breath. "Okay, fine. I just like to keep that part of my life private . . . and my father doesn't know. He blames Cascadia for causing all the riots and now the problems with funding." She passed a tractor-trailer truck. "Is Howard really associated with the Scribe? And Ryan?"

Jason nodded. "Yes." He pointed to a sign ahead. "Please take the next exit. Once we're on the back roads you can let it rip."

Sarah gave him a smile. "You bribe me well." She switched lanes, heading for the exit. "Okay, so the agents came to question Howard about his connections with the Scribe. But why arrest him? Is the Scribe planning violent action?"

Jason shook his head. "No! No violence at all. The point is to educate people about the proposed changes to the education system, not make them riot. There is a group of concerned university professors from both New America and Cascadia that support the Scribe. They're the ones that leak the articles to the student newspapers and to various sources in the media."

"And you're a member of this group? That's why you're spying on campus?"

Jason hesitated before answering. "Yes . . . that is technically correct."

Sarah glanced sideways at him. "What does that mean?"

Jason looked away from her and stared out the passenger window for a few minutes. When he turned back, he looked a little embarrassed. "Actually, I have a very close relationship with the Scribe."

"What does *that* mean?"

Jason took a deep breath and held it for a moment. "I am the Scribe."

Sarah drove silently for a few minutes while she absorbed this. She remembered walking in one day on her students debating the latest news from the Scribe. They paid more attention to his editorial than they did to her lecture.

"Is this because of what happened to your brother? Is that why you write those articles?"

"Yes." Jason nodded. "The Scribe's role is to question everything about the new regulations. And by doing it in a humorous fashion, the students will read it and be informed. I want them to understand what's going on. Like how the budget cuts will really affect them."

"But wouldn't that make them protest more? Aren't you risking a riot?" She shivered inwardly at the memory of the crowd closing in on her.

Jason shook his head. "No, the Scribe is very firm on discouraging any violence or large gatherings. I'm trying to encourage them to take small steps. Write letters to their student unions, stuff like that. If the students feel someone is looking out for them, they're less likely to riot."

Sarah nodded. "Well, it seems to be working, and they love debating the articles." She frowned as it all sunk in. "So . . . Ryan and Howard used me to smuggle information?"

"Yes. You were making monthly trips to U Cascadia, so it was a good opportunity. Ryan embedded the files on your laptop and Howard retrieved them. Then he sent them off to the others involved."

Sarah stared at the road ahead.

"Did you really not know about any of this?" Jason asked. "I thought you volunteered to carry the files."

Sarah shook her head. "No."

Jason looked uncomfortable. "Oh." He shifted in his seat. "Um . . ."

They drove in awkward silence. Sarah slowed down for the

exit, then accelerated into the turn. The last rays of the day poked through the trees as she navigated the narrow winding road while she remembered Ryan first handing her the "research" files for Howard. He had flashed that charming smile as he asked her to carry all the data on her laptop. When she'd suggested using an FTP program, he had simply shrugged and warned her their competition was very good at hacking.

Competitors? Or government agents?

"We're making good time." Jason broke through her thoughts. "I want to hit the border just before the morning shift change."

"How does that help?" Sarah shifted gears roughly.

"Whoa, you okay there?" Jason winced at the grinding sound. "They're less likely to hold us up if they want to go home."

"I see," Sarah said curtly. "Are you planning on telling me my new name any time soon?"

Jason gave her a reassuring look. "You're Dr. Ursula Morsey from U Cascadia, and you just gave a guest lecture on the future of fossil fuels at UDSC."

"Seriously?"

"Yes. We thought you would appreciate staying in the engineering field." Jason pulled a Cascadian passport out of the glove compartment and held it up.

Sarah sighed. "Great, so I'm a dual citizen with a split personality. This will be fun to explain to my dad." She shifted gears smoothly this time. "Did you know the professor at Columbia was going to be arrested?"

Jason shook his head. "No. But Howard heard rumors about a new government organization that was going to clamp down on free speech, such as the editorials by the Scribe. Meanwhile, Dr.

Nelson heard rumors at Columbia that the budget cuts run deeper than just saving money. There's a clause being added to the next round of cuts that will hurt the future of education. Dr. Nelson was investigating it further when the agents picked him up. I guess it was only a matter of time before he told them about the others."

"What about you? You're risking a lot coming here."

Jason shook his head. "No, not really. The only ones who know the Scribe's identity are Howard and Ryan. None of the other professors know."

"So what's this clause that has everyone so rankled?"

"Well, if the cuts go through as-is, the university won't be able to accommodate the students currently enrolled, so there's a bill that limits access to higher education. It mandates that if the parents of a prospective student were not born on New American soil, then that student will be prohibited from enrolling in any degree program. Such as your Environmental Engineering Studies."

"Say what?" Sarah glanced sideways at him for a second.

"Oh, that's just the first step. Once the first bill passes, there will be a second one that revokes the degree of anyone who graduated in the last ten years whose parents were not born here."

"What the hell kind of plan is that?" Sarah shook her head in disbelief. "That would strip the degrees from most people in the country."

"Exactly. It's the beginning of a downward spiral which would result in a class system. It gets worse; there's a conditional clause that states all outstanding student loans are still owed. So, if people lose their degree status they will still have to pay back their student loans, but any company they work for only has to pay them the equivalent of a high school graduate."

Sarah clenched the steering wheel. "That's utterly ridiculous! What idiot came up with that idea?"

Jason let out a heavy sigh. "Don't know. It's a very narrow-minded view."

"There's no way this plan will work! This is not what the government promised California if it stayed with New America!"

Jason put the passport back in the glove compartment. "Well, in a twisted way, it is. The government promised to make jobs and opportunities for those who stayed with New America, but they didn't tell people they were going to redefine what that means. I think the plan is to control education, and thereby one's future. People will be assigned roles as overseen by the government. I think that's what Dr. Nelson found out. And I'm willing to bet it won't stop at recent immigrants."

"I can't believe Ryan didn't tell me any of this," Sarah said. "This is outrageous!"

Jason hesitated. "I don't know why he didn't tell you. I just assumed he had. But when he had my ID made to come here, he made one for you and Howard, just in case things went sideways. I was going to leave them with Howard before I left. It all seemed so ridiculous that I didn't believe it. Part of the Scribe's job is to weed out fact from fiction, and this definitely sounds like fiction. Ryan's more cautious. That's why I brought my dad's Porsche. I wasn't expecting this!"

"Some dinner dates," Sarah muttered under her breath. "What if I went back and told the agents the truth? That I went on a few dates with Dr. O'Conner and that was that. We never discussed anything outside of work. Wouldn't that clear it all up?"

Jason turned in his seat to face her. "Look, Sarah. You could go back to LA and take your chances. Try to convince them you're an innocent bystander. It's a long shot, and it might work. But the fact is, you have incriminating files on your computer. You've gone on dates with one of the leading suspects. Can you really convince them you've never talked with Ryan about any of this?"

He shifted in his seat and looked forward into the night. "Also, can you tell me you honestly agree with the proposed changes?"

Sarah passed a slow-moving car before answering. "No. Not if what you're saying is true."

Jason exhaled slowly. "Then you'd most likely not be okay. Even if they let you go, you would need to stop all association with Ryan immediately, and refuse any contact from him. The agents will be watching everything you do."

Sarah frowned into the darkness. "I don't know what to say."

"For what it's worth, I'm sorry you got dragged into this. If I had known you weren't a willing volunteer, I would have insisted we find another way."

Sarah let out a heavy sigh. "You know, more than half my students would fail under those criteria." Just then she rounded a bend and was blinded by two spotlights from the side of the road.

"Now what?" she said, holding her hand to her eyes.

"Oh oh. It's a roving border patrol." Jason sat up straight.

"I thought they only patrolled the main roads heading south."

"Looks like they expanded their duties."

"What if the agents called them? Are we caught?" Sarah's throat suddenly went dry as the patrol officer knocked on her driver-side window.

"Just act casual," Jason said, though his voice sounded nervous.

The officer leaned over and shone a large flashlight into the car's interior. "Is everyone in this car a New American citizen?"

"I'm New American," Sarah said, trying to keep her voice calm. The officer focused an intense glare on her face. *Does he know?* She could feel beads of sweat starting to form on her forehead.

"I'm from Cascadia," Jason piped up.

The man's attention turned immediately to him. "What are you doing in New America?" he demanded.

"Visiting my girlfriend, sir." Jason gave him a wide smile.

"What? You can't get a girlfriend up there?"

"Can't imagine being with anyone else, sir." Jason gave Sarah's shoulder a gentle squeeze.

Sarah felt her heart skip a beat, and her shoulder tingled where Jason touched it. The officer looked sternly at her. She forced herself to speak. "I'm giving a guest lecture at U Cascadia, so Jason came down for the weekend. We're driving back together."

The officer leaned in close. His breath reeked of cigar smoke. "You know, you could do better than a Cascadian." He stood up and waved her on.

"Gee, thanks a lot!" Jason grumbled as Sarah pulled away. In the dim light, Sarah could see his face had turned red.

"Just don't tell my father I have two Cascadian suitors." Sarah grinned shyly at him.

He laughed. "Whatever you do, don't tell him one of them is a history professor. I can't imagine what he would say to that!"

Sarah laughed too, then said in a more serious tone, "What about the actual border? Do you think the agents will be waiting?"

"That's why you have lovely black hair and a new passport," Jason said. "It'll be okay, just remember your passport says you're from Cascadia and you just gave a guest lecture at UDSC. We're on our way home, nice and simple." Jason leaned his seat back. "I'm going to try to get some shut eye. Let me know if you need to be spelled off."

"I'm fine," Sarah said quietly.

She drove on through the night. A full moon came out that cast interesting shadows along the open spots on the road. Driving fast was her way of clearing her head. What if she turned the car around now? She could slip through the roving border patrol and be back in LA by morning. But, would the agents believe her story? Or would they use her as a means to get to Ryan, and eventually, Jason?

It dawned on Sarah as she spotted a deer standing in the ditch that Ryan might have been planning to tell her everything at their next dinner date. But to drop a bombshell, "Hey Sarah, I'm part of a growing underground movement against your government's new policies. Want to join us? Oh, and would you like more wine?" That was asking a lot.

Then again, using her laptop as a means of clandestine communication was something they were going to have a discussion about. A heated one at that.

Fortunately, the deer was busy eating grass and not concerned with crossing the road, so Sarah accelerated back to her previous speed. She kept one part of her brain focused on the turns in the road while the other part churned away at all this news. *How did I get into this mess?* Ever since that day at the rally, she had always worked hard and never caused trouble. Yet here she was, stuck in the thick of things. And what about her father? How was she going to explain this?

And then there was Ryan: charming, handsome and a smuggler of information. How did she feel about him now?

She thought about the educational clause. Undercutting education was not something Sarah could stand for. Besides, where would it stop? Even if only some of the rumors were true, someone was pulling the strings of New America in a bad direction. She let out a deep breath and shifted gears. Well, one thing was certain. There would be no turning back. She stole a quick glance at Jason, sleeping beside her. A sliver of moonlight shone on his handsome face. No matter how lightly he downplayed it, he was risking his own safety to help get her out. What about him?

Sarah bit her lip. Even if she could go back, she wouldn't be able to ignore the changes around her. Not anymore. She thought of Howard. He had risked his career to help future students. What had she actually done? Never questioning what was said, always doing what was expected of her.

The first rays of the morning sun broke through the trees. Another beautiful day was dawning. She poked Jason hard in the ribs. He woke with a jolt.

"What? Where . . .?" He sat up and rubbed his eyes. "Whoa, it's morning. You drove all night."

Sarah shrugged. "I needed time to think."

"And?" His face looked hopeful.

She gave him a grim smile. "Time to see what's on the other side."

Jason smiled back. "Good to hear." He grabbed the passport from the glove compartment. "Okay, Dr. Morsey, ready to go back to lecturing at U Cascadia?"

Sarah thought of what she wanted to say to Ryan. "Yes, I am."

She hesitated. "Thank you, by the way, for coming all the way to LA for me. You didn't have to do that."

He smiled warmly at her. "You're welcome. And thank you for not handing me over to the roving border patrol."

The early-morning line at the border was short. There was no sign of the black SUV that had chased them or the agents. Sarah smiled politely at the customs officer. He seemed more interested in the Porsche than in her, though he drilled her with questions about what she had or had not purchased. Finally, he let them go with a grunt and a warning that the duty free was going to be disbanded so "buy now".

As she drove away from the border, she felt relief, but also a strange sensation, like she was seeing the world in a different way. Colors were brighter, sharper somehow. Had she really been looking the other way for so long? What was she going to see now?

"Time to eat," Jason said. He pointed at a drive thru.

Sarah sped up. "Yes, I'm hungry, too. But when you ride with me, you are required to eat real food."

He laughed and shook his head at her. "Fine. You're in the driver's seat."

"Yes, I am." She laughed too.

They stopped at a coffee shop and sat down for a breakfast of egg whites and granola. Jason insisted that Sarah should try to get some sleep, so she reluctantly handed over the keys. She leaned her seat back and watched the trees go by as they drove through the roads of what was old Oregon. She remembered driving up with her father when she was a little girl. They had stopped at a fruit stand outside Ashland, and she had loved the smell of the fresh apricots. Even though the trees still looked the same, something felt different. Whenever she crossed the new border now it was like crossing into a new world. The people were still friendly, but they were more reserved. Tension between the two nations was growing. The secession itself had not been an easy one. Families had been divided over what to do. She fell asleep thinking of how angry her father was going to be.

Sarah slept fitfully in the passenger's seat. She woke up at a rest stop south of Portland. It was all she could do to grab a cup of coffee on the way back from the restroom. Her head was woozy and she felt slightly nauseated, but it wasn't from car sickness. She decided to let Jason drive another leg.

This time, she woke up to see Mount Rainier standing majestically over the horizon. "We made good time," she said as she sat up. She glanced at her watch. It was late afternoon.

"You're not the only one who likes driving a Porsche." Jason smiled at her. "I suppose you want the next leg?"

"Hell, yeah." She grinned.

They switched at the next rest stop. Sarah slid back behind the wheel. As soon as she pulled onto the highway, she felt her nerves calm. Something about driving fast made her feel better. Maybe it was the illusion of control. Whatever it was, it helped.

They drove on past drive thrus and fruit stands, though they did stop for apricots. Jason visibly relaxed as they got closer to Seattle. He was almost home, Sarah realized. It was only three hours to Vancouver and no border crossings. But for her . . . home was getting farther and farther away.

It was evening as they pulled onto the campus of U Cascadia. Sarah felt her pulse quicken. What was going to happen now? Where was she going to stay? She hadn't even thought of that.

Jason had called Ryan on his cell phone after they had crossed into old Washington. She had pretended to be asleep so she didn't have to talk to him. Now, here he was jogging up to the visitor's parking space with a concerned look on his face.

"Sarah, Jason! Thank goodness you're all right!" he said in his thick Irish accent. He leaned in the driver's window. "After what happened to Howard, I was worried you'd both get caught in the net."

"We need to talk," Sarah said curtly.

He nodded as he opened the car door. "Yes, my dear, we will. Please, let's get some food in you."

"Got any whiskey?" Jason said. "I think she needs a dram."

Ryan laughed. "That I have. I made arrangements for you to stay at the faculty guest house, Sarah. But first let's go to the office." He gently touched Sarah's elbow to give her a little nudge toward the sidewalk. "Your hair looks just as beautiful black as it does blonde."

Sarah bit her lip and started walking. Questions were flying in her head, but she was suddenly tongue tied. *I'm just tired*, she thought.

Ryan prattled on about the unusually sunny weather Seattle was having as they walked across the campus. The setting sun cast an orange glow on the windows of the engineering building. The campus was quiet. Not like UDSC where the students stumbled around at all hours of the night. Here, they tucked indoors. But she knew they must be noisy somewhere. Ryan's voice filled the quiet night. It was soothing somehow, even if he was just making small talk.

Jason walked quietly behind them. "That Irish accent is so not fair," he grumbled under his breath.

They sat in Ryan's office, a bottle of whiskey between them. Ryan fussed over Sarah and produced food from a mini fridge. She noticed it was sushi from the little place where they'd had their first dinner date. Jason downed his dram in one gulp, then stood up.

"I'll let you kids talk." He grabbed a salmon roll and walked out.

Sarah started to protest, then caught herself. She stared at her glass. Suddenly, she felt like being back on that first date. She took a sip. "Why didn't you tell me about the articles?" She took a bigger sip. The smooth whiskey went down easy. Ryan had pulled out the twenty-year-old stuff.

"Sarah, I owe you a huge apology." He topped up her dram. "I didn't want to bother you, not with what happened when you were a kid. I thought if you saw the good the Scribe was doing, then I could ask you if you would carry the files. You'd feel better about it."

Sarah set her whiskey down with a thump. "Wait a minute, you deliberately used me to carry information to get things started, *then* you were going to ask me? Did you have any intention of telling me about what you're doing now?"

Ryan hesitated. "Well . . . no . . . not exactly. I thought I was making it easier for you."

"You call being chased by DH agents easy? They had guns, Ryan! They chased my car. They arrested Howard!"

Ryan looked pale. He took a sip of whiskey and shook his head. "We never . . . I never thought it would escalate like this. Jason's articles are political, yes, but satirical. Meant for the students. We're not trying to start a movement, we're trying to prevent it!"

"By keeping them informed, I get it," Sarah said. "But you had no right to use my laptop without asking. What's going to happen to me? My job? Good grief, what am I going to tell my father? He's going to have a fit!"

"I guess this is not a good time to tell him about our dinner dates?" Ryan gave her his charming smile.

Sarah glared at him. "No." She stood up. "I'm not hungry. I'm going to my room. We'll talk more tomorrow." She grabbed her handbag and walked to the door. "Oh, and you owe me some new clothes."

A light patter of rain on the window woke Sarah the next morning. She lay in bed listening to it. *Sounds like their sunny streak is over*, Sarah mused. Suddenly, she felt homesick. What was going to happen to her? How much trouble was she actually in? And what about Ryan and Jason? Would Howard give up their names?

She wrinkled her brow in thought as the rain pounded harder on the window. Was she stuck here forever? What if she couldn't go back? It was all fine for Ryan and Jason, this was home, but what about her? A sickening thought occurred to her. Was she going to be Ursula forever?

A knock on her door interrupted her thoughts. She glanced at the clock by the bed, 9:00 am. Guess she'd got some sleep after all. She had lain in bed fuming most of the night. The knocking continued. She threw off the covers and stomped over to the door. She was still wearing her clothes from the night before.

"I'm not ready to talk to you yet, Ryan . . . oh." Sarah started as she opened the door.

"That works for me." Jason gave her a big smile. He was standing there holding two cups of coffee, the duffle bag hanging off his shoulder. "Peace offering?" he said as he handed one to her.

Sarah felt her cheeks grow warm. She took the cup from Jason. "Thanks." She took a sip. "Mmm . . . wait a minute, how do you know how I like my coffee?"

Jason laughed. "Perks of being a janitor."

Sarah shook her head at him. "So . . . where is Ryan?"

"Teaching two lectures back to back," Jason said as he followed her into the quaint apartment. It was a cute little one-bedroom with an open kitchen and living area. Sarah liked sitting in the bay window attached to the kitchen. It was reserved for all visiting professors, but Ryan always seemed to manage it so she could stay there.

"I brought your clothes from yesterday," Jason continued, dropping the duffle bag onto the counter. "Though they're a bit wrinkled and smell like, well, oil actually." He took a sniff. "Think the Porsche needs a tune up." He grinned playfully at her. "I like your new hair style."

Sarah ran her fingers through her disheveled hair. "You know, this is all the rage on campus."

"Yes, you have mastered the all-nighter-passed-out-in-my-clothes look." Jason laughed.

Sarah looked down at her clothes and felt her face grow even warmer. She noticed Jason was nicely showered and wearing a light blue shirt that accented his eyes. "Yes, I seem to be having problems with my wardrobe."

"Then let's solve that, shall we?" Jason said. "Care for a bit of Seattle shopping?"

Sarah gulped down her coffee. "Know any good places?"

Jason pulled out a small notepad. "No idea, so I asked Jan in the office." He flipped open the notepad to show a list of stores. "Apparently, you have lots of options."

Sarah laughed as she took the pad. "Thanks. Just so you know, shopping with me is not a pretty sight."

"It's the least I can do." He gave her an apologetic grin. "It's my fault you're here."

"Actually, that's Ryan and Howard's doing, isn't it?"

Jason shook his head. "No, this whole thing starts with me. I'm the Scribe." He took her gently by the shoulders. "We will find a way to resolve this. I won't stop until we do."

Sarah stared into those deep blue eyes and saw worry and sadness there. She sighed inwardly. How were they going to fix this? "Come on," she said as she grabbed her handbag. "But don't say I didn't warn you. I shop like I drive."

They hit most of the stores on Jan's list in less than two hours. Jason complained he had whiplash from watching her shop. Sarah ignored him and cranked a tight turn into a vintage shop parking lot. There was one more item she wanted to get. She found a faux leather jacket and modeled it for Jason. He gave her a thumbs up. By the time they got back to campus it was lunch time.

"Ready to face Ryan for a lunch meeting?" Jason asked her.

She took a deep breath. "I guess so."

They dropped off her bags. Jason busied himself putting away groceries they'd bought, while she grabbed a quick shower. "You really don't have to do that," she called from the bathroom.

"Oh, I do," Jason answered. "You're humoring my guilt trip very kindly."

"I'll get really mad when the shock wears off," she quipped back.

"That's what I'm afraid of," Jason said quietly.

It felt good to put on new clothes. She paired a crème-colored long-sleeved shirt with new jeans and a belt, topped with her faux jacket and comfy yet stylish sandals. In spite of the strangeness of the situation, Sarah couldn't help but feel curious about what was going on. She had to find a way to help Howard and learn more about the proposed changes. If Jason, a.k.a. the Scribe, was right, the education system really was falling apart. Sarah had always believed learning was the key to a better future. Her father called it the cornerstone of a decent society. She had to find a way to stop the damage from happening.

Ryan was deep in conversation on the phone as they walked into his office. He looked up as he ended the call. "Sarah! I see you found your way to the shops. Nice jacket. Let me know the cost, I'll pay for everything."

"Too late, we already had that argument," Jason said. "I managed to pay for half."

"Then I must cover the rest," Ryan insisted. "I'm the guilty one here."

Sarah waved her hands in frustration at both men. "It's not the clothes or food I'm worried about. It's my job, my career, my home we're talking about! Are you going to pay for that?"

Ryan pointed at the two chairs in front of his desk. "You're right. Let's get to work figuring this out, shall we?"

A red-faced Jason sat down. He looked at his hands as Sarah took the chair beside him.

"Okay, I just got off the phone with one of our contacts in LA.

Howard is being held for questioning, but as they have not found any incriminating files as of yet, all they have is circumstantial evidence."

"Where's the laptop?" Jason asked.

"You mean mine? In my handbag." Sarah pulled it out and put it on the desk. "I took it home for the weekend to review some data. *Actual data.*" She gave Ryan a pointed look.

Jason reached over and tapped the cover. "First thing we need to do is wipe the files. Then they'll have no concrete evidence that Sarah or Howard ever smuggled the articles."

"Except for whomever Howard gave the articles to at the student newspaper," Sarah said.

"Howard delivered them anonymously," Ryan said. "Until now, the students all thought the Scribe was another student just like them."

"Maybe a little wiser," Jason added.

Ryan gave him a smirk. "Have you told Sarah about the Scribe's first article? About your investigative technique that had us hiding out on a window ledge on the fourth floor of the administrative building?"

Jason cleared his throat. "As I said, a little wiser now."

Ryan laughed. "There was a rally on campus about foreign tuition fees more than doubling, which as you know affected me greatly, so Jason decided to record the meeting of the deans and the administrative board. Great idea until we almost got caught planting a listening device and ended up spending the next two hours on a cramped window ledge!"

"Nobody saw you?" Sarah looked incredulously at the two men.

"You'd be surprised how few people ever look up. And we had

a bit of tree cover," Jason said defensively.

"It was three branches!" Ryan laughed. "Anyway, we got what we needed and leaked it to the press via the Scribe."

"Did it stop the tuition increase?"

Jason smiled. "It slowed it down. The Scribe managed to rally enough students to sign a petition for it to be reviewed."

"And we got an increase in scholarship funding by a private tech company that was inspired by the Scribe," Ryan added proudly. "So it can make a difference. You just have to reach the right people with the right words."

"So the DH is afraid that the Scribe could rally enough students against the educational clause that they could shut it down?" Sarah said.

"I think we've gone beyond that," Jason said. "No, we've stumbled upon something bigger than just budget cuts."

"If what Dr. Nelson heard is true, then yes." Ryan nodded. "We need to be careful. I wiped all files pertaining to the Scribe from my computer. What about yours?" He looked at Jason.

"I have an external drive with all the articles saved on it stashed away in a safe place in Vancouver. But that's not the worry. This is." He held up a small thumb drive. "I've been writing the educational exposé while in LA. I was waiting for Howard to give me the info from Dr. Nelson."

"So the article's almost done?" Ryan asked.

Jason nodded. "Yes, but it's not pretty, and I don't have any suggestions on how the students should react."

Ryan thought for a moment. "We need to tell the students to stay calm. Even if we don't know what to do. Can you finish the article as best you can while I figure out what our options are here?"

Jason leaned forward. "What about Sarah?"

"Howard knows Sarah knew nothing about the articles. I'm willing to bet he claims he picked them up directly from me."

"Except it's Sarah who's been traveling back and forth every month. That's why they want to question her."

"What about you, Jason? Are you in danger?" Sarah said to him.

Jason shrugged. "Dr. Nelson doesn't know who the Scribe is and I doubt Howard would tell them. It's you who's in the uncomfortable spotlight."

"Which we will figure out," Ryan insisted. "For now, Jason, you need to finish that article!"

Jason groaned. "Okay. Fine. I'll kick my muse into high gear." He stood up and looked at Sarah. "What about your father? What do we do about him?"

Sarah swallowed hard. "Ah . . . yeah. That, I need to deal with."

"Just blame it all on Ryan."

"Thanks, Jason." Ryan frowned at him.

"What are friends for?" With that, Jason walked out.

"This is all going to be okay, Sarah, I promise," Ryan said.

"You're not the one on the run."

"Not today, but when I was in high school in Ireland I attended a meeting for students who wanted to change the O level/A level system to make it less restrictive. We got raided by the police."

"What happened?"

"I spent two days in a maximum-security prison thinking I was never going to see the rain again. Fortunately, the powers that be decided I was not a threat, and I was released with a stern warning and a mark on my record." Ryan leaned back in his chair. "All because I cared about access to higher education."

Sarah swallowed hard. Would she have a mark on her record? "What did you do?"

"Kept my head down long enough to graduate, then applied to U Cascadia. Been here ever since."

"Is that why you help Jason with the Scribe?"

Ryan nodded. "Jason was writing articles for the student newspaper while we were grad students, under the Scribe alias. He really has a way with words." Ryan leaned forward and put his hands on his desk. "You should have seen how the students reacted to his articles. Some thought they were funny, others ignored them, but a lot of them listened. Jason was able to diffuse several potentially bad situations. Then after we graduated, Jason got a fellowship at U Vancouver and I stayed here. The Scribe retired, so to speak."

Ryan took a deep breath and continued, "When Howard approached us with the joint project at UDSC, we were already hearing rumors of changes to the education system. I convinced Jason to start writing articles again to keep the students informed here, but when you started making your trips . . ." He smiled his charming smile at her. "Howard saw the opportunity to bring the Scribe south of the border. But with your father being the dean, well, we thought a few practice runs might be a good idea. That way we could gauge the students' interest and see if it was worth doing."

He reached out and took one of Sarah's hands in his. "The students not only got on board, but the news spread to other campuses. The articles started to get reprinted all over New America. So Howard set up an underground channel to get information, as accurate as possible, to Jason."

"So each trip I carried information up and the articles down." Sarah kept her hand still.

Ryan seemed to sense her doubt. He gave her hand a gentle squeeze. "We believe there is a danger of violent protest if the students are suddenly told they can no longer study. They will find themselves stuck with a large debt and no education to show for it. If we can get Jason's articles into the student papers before the budget legislation is passed, then the students and the educators can lobby with all the facts. Try to stop it from going through."

"But who's to say the people behind these proposed changes won't just stop the papers from being printed?"

Ryan looked thoughtful. "Once the articles appear in some format, the words will find a way to travel. And the students know that the Scribe doesn't make things up. That's why they're trying so hard to get to the Scribe first. Rumors don't hold as much weight as his words."

Sarah gently pulled her hand away. "You still should have told me first."

Ryan nodded. "You're right. And I'm really sorry. Now, we need to fix things. Do you have any vacation time you can use, or a sabbatical?"

Sarah sighed. "I have two weeks of vacation owed me."

"Great! Let's start with that." Ryan grinned. "Seattle's really nice this time of year."

"What about my students? We're two weeks away from finals!"

"Can you tell them you're visiting a sick relative or something? Have your teaching assistant run the tutorials and answer the big questions online?"

Sarah thought about it. "Yes, that could work. But it's not

ideal."

"It's a start. We need to buy Jason time. How he says things can mean the difference between logical action and a riot."

"I understand. Now, what about my father?"

Ryan suddenly looked embarrassed. "That, I'll leave to you."

"Great," Sarah grumbled.

"Maybe a little lunch first?" Ryan flashed his charming smile.

Sarah shook her head. "No, I had better deal with this now."

A deep sense of dread pooled in Sarah's stomach as she neared her guest apartment on the other side of the campus. What was she going to say? A flash of light caught her eye. She turned just in time to see a figure duck behind a tree. Had someone just taken a picture? Sarah felt her heart turn cold. Had the agents followed them here? Had Howard told them about Jason?

No, she told herself firmly. Howard would never do that. He could be very obstinate when he wanted to be. He'd kept on course when convincing her dad to team up with U Cascadia, he could do that with the agents and their questions. But what if someone was following her looking for clues? She and Jason were not the best at being discreet. A shiver ran up her spine.

She strode as casually as she could to her apartment. Inside, she let out a deep breath. First thing, call her father. Try to ease whatever worry he might have. She made herself a cup of coffee and took a few sips to steady her nerves.

She called Iris and was relieved to hear her voice. Iris was as confused as ever about Howard's situation, but agreed to arrange with Sarah's TA to teach the last few classes and tell the students a family member had a medical emergency. Then she called Lois at the dean's office and asked her to book Sarah's vacation days. If

Lois thought it was an odd request, she didn't show it. She spoke in her friendly businesslike voice like she always did when Sarah brought up U Cascadia. Sarah smiled. Good old Lois. She, like Iris, thought Dr. O'Conner was a good match for Sarah.

Then Lois said, "Shall I transfer your call to the dean?"

Sarah could feel the question underneath the words. *Do you want to talk to your dad?*

"Yes." Sarah took a deep breath and steadied herself.

"Sarah! Where are you? Are you all right?" His deep voice sounded concerned.

"Yes, Dad, I'm fine," she answered, keeping her voice as light as possible. "Dad, there's something I want you to know . . . I'm dating Ryan O'Conner."

"You're dating the Irish professor?" her dad exploded into the phone. "He talks funny! I can barely understand him!"

On the other end of the line, Sarah gave him a wry smile. "I'm beginning to understand him better. Look, Dad, I took a trip to U Cascadia. Ryan and I are discussing our relationship."

"Now? Good grief, Sarah, now is not the time! Wait until the semester is over. Besides, we have a problem with Howard."

"What happened to Howard? Is he okay?" Sarah felt her gut twist.

Her father sounded terse. "Some agents calling themselves District Homeland took him in. Do you know anything about this Scribe?"

Sarah mentally crossed her fingers. "You mean the writer my students think is wittier than me?"

"The one who's causing all this trouble! I told them they're being ridiculous. Who cares if a student is letting off steam? It's a student newspaper! It's supposed to be annoying."

He thinks the Scribe's a student, good.

"Listen, Sarah, we need you back here. I don't know how to talk to these kids. The students are up in arms about Howard. You can discuss your . . . er . . . relationship with O'Conner after the semester ends. Okay?"

"Okay, Dad. I'll see what I can do."

Her father sounded relieved. "That's my Sarah. By the way, do you know anything about a new janitor? Apparently he's not very good."

She sucked in her breath. *Jason.* "I saw a new face recently, but I never stopped to introduce myself."

"Never mind. I'll deal with that later. Now please hurry. Oh, and tell that Irish bloke we need to have a chat."

"Dad, that's my business!"

"Hmpf!" was all her dad said.

"Love you, Dad. We'll get this sorted, I promise."

He grunted his reply and hung up. Sarah put the phone down with shaking fingers. The agents hadn't pressed the issue with him, at least not about her involvement. Why?

And, he had yet to find out that Ryan was on their watch list. That might buy her a little more time. Sarah made herself a second cup of coffee and curled up in the bay window. Okay, so Howard was still in custody but should be all right. He'd probably made it very clear that Sarah had no idea what was going on. That she'd run because they frightened her, not because she was guilty. But how long before her dad heard the rumors? What about her students? What were they thinking about all this?

A thought occurred to her. They had asked her father about a new janitor. Suddenly, Sarah's pulse quickened. Of course they'd seen Jason in the car with her! Even if it was only for a few seconds. The man behind the tree, would he follow Jason too?

She dropped her coffee mug in her haste to grab her rain jacket. The rain pounded harder on the window. *How do they stand all this rain?* she thought absently as she ran back across campus. She kept an eye out for the mystery follower but didn't see him.

She barged into Ryan's office just as he was leaving. "Sarah, what's wrong?" He caught her in his arms; she hesitated for one second, looking into those deep brown eyes, then blurted out, "Jason, where is he?"

Ryan raised his eyebrows. "Probably tucked away in the top nook of the library. He likes to write there." He held her for just a second longer, then let go. "What's wrong?"

"I think a man was following me when I went back to my apartment. I think he took a picture. When I called my dad, he said they were asking about the new janitor."

"We need to find Jason!" Ryan grabbed his coat. "If he's in the library, he'll have his cell turned off."

They ran out the front doors, narrowly avoiding colliding with two students who had their heads down because of the rain.

"Hey, watch it!" one of them grumbled.

"Done your lab assignment?" Ryan quipped back as they took off down the sidewalk.

"Sorry, Professor!"

"Gets them every time," Ryan said as he ran with his phone to his ear. "Come on, Jason, pick up. Damn! No answer. He's got to be in the library." Ryan ran faster. Sarah ran beside him as they cut across the grass and ducked through the humanities building.

They burst through the doors of the library, ignoring a disapproving clucking sound from the librarian. Ryan led the way up the stairs, taking them two at a time.

They reached the top landing and ran into the reference room. It was like an old attic, with slanted walls lined with comfy couches. Students were dozing on the soft cushions. A few had their noses buried in their books and didn't look up. Almost all of them were plugged into their headphones.

Jason was sitting at a small table nestled in a window nook on the far side, overlooking the whole campus. The rain clouds hung low in the sky. He was typing with a look of concentration on his face.

Sarah recognized the man sneaking up behind him as one of the agents who had run toward her car.

"Jason!"

Jason looked up just as the agent jabbed a needle into his neck. He let out a surprised yell and yanked it out. Ryan tackled the man and they both crashed to the floor.

"Jason, are you all right?" Sarah glanced at his neck. Blood trickled where the needle had broken the skin.

"What the hell?" Jason gasped as he held his neck with his fingers.

Sarah jumped out of the way as Ryan and the agent rolled across the floor, grappling with each other. She took a step to the side and back, watching the fight closely. Ryan grunted and tried to get the man in a headlock, but he punched Ryan in the gut. The two men pulled apart and staggered to their feet. The agent took a step back toward the door, but as he turned to make a run for it, Sarah's well-aimed fist clocked him in the temple. He slumped back against the wall with a look of surprise on his face.

"Nice punch!" Ryan looked at her in admiration.

"Huh?" Jason mumbled as he slid to the floor with a thump. "Did you learn that in defensive driving class?"

Ryan grabbed him before his head hit the floor.

"Quick, I need some rope," Sarah said, looking around. All she could see was books.

"Shoelaces?" Jason made a waving motion with his hands at his boots. He seemed to be having trouble coordinating his limbs.

"Here, I'll help." Ryan set Jason gently on the floor, where he curled up in a ball.

Just then the stranger let out a loud groan. "Don't hit me! DH!" He held his hands protectively over his head as Sarah took an aggressive step toward him.

"That's exactly why I should hit you again!"

"I'm a government agent! Please!" He pushed against the wall and stood up slowly.

"Government agent? You just shot a needle in my friend's neck!" Ryan stood beside Sarah with his fists balled. "What kind of agent does that?"

The DH agent held up his hands. "Easy." He looked at a couple students who were sitting quietly watching. One of them held her cell phone in her hand. "It's okay, no need to call campus security."

She looked at Ryan doubtfully.

"Tell them Dr. O'Conner is dealing with it and will call them later," Ryan said to her. She put the phone down slowly on the table. The rest of the students were still asleep on the couches.

"Look, is there somewhere we can talk privately?" The agent was rubbing his head.

"My place," Sarah said, still standing with her fists balled.

Ryan hesitated. Jason dragged himself across the floor and tugged at his trouser leg. "Ryan, I can't get up."

"Hang on." Ryan quickly shut down Jason's computer and pocketed the thumb drive. He swung Jason's bag over his shoulder, and together with Sarah's help, they heaved Jason off the floor.

"You know, you look really good in that jacket . . ." Jason swayed to the side as they staggered down the stairs. They refused any help from the agent.

"Jason. Shut up. You've been zapped with something," Ryan warned him.

"Oh, you shut up, you and your fancy accent. It's not fair you know," Jason babbled to Sarah. "Always gets their attention, the girls, you know. They love the accent . . ."

"But they love to read your words, Jason, I can't do that." Ryan shifted his grip on Jason to keep him from tumbling down the stairs.

Jason seemed to contemplate that thought. "Yes," he said. "I write! You talk and I write."

"That's what makes us a great team," Ryan grunted as they stumbled out the doors. The rain had slowed to a fine drizzle which helped perk Jason up just enough that they made it across campus without falling on their faces. They dumped Jason on the couch in Sarah's apartment, then Ryan turned on the agent.

"What the hell do you think you're doing?"

The agent winced. "After we got ditched, I figured they'd come here." He turned to Sarah. "You drive a mean line."

"I almost threw up." Jason giggled from the couch.

"We thought you were the Scribe, given your history in Ireland," the agent said to Ryan. "But it's him, isn't it?" He pointed at Jason.

"What were you planning to do with Jason?" Sarah said. "You have no jurisdiction here."

"Dope him up so I could smuggle him back across the border."

"Jason's a Cascadian citizen, you can't do that!" Ryan was so outraged his face turned beet red.

"Once he's across the border, I can do anything."

Sarah balled her fist. "I think I am going to punch you again."

"Do you even know what the Scribe's doing?" Jason piped up from the couch. He was lying on his side watching them. "You don't, do you." Jason flopped his arm at Ryan. "Show him the article."

"Nobody's admitting to anything, Jason. It's all circumstantial."

"Show him the article," Jason insisted.

"He doesn't care what happens to the students," Sarah said.

The agent frowned. "I have my orders. I don't need to know what you wrote."

"Yes, you do." Jason got partway up, then laid down again with a groan. "I'm going to throw up."

Sarah stood in front of the agent. "What's your name?"

"Call me Ted."

"All right, Ted, what if I told you that students whose parents were not born in New America are going to be prohibited from enrolling in any degree programs by an unconstitutional clause. After that, any student who graduated in the last ten years whose parents were not born here will find their hard-earned degrees stripped from them. How do you think they're going to react?"

Ted's brow furrowed as Sarah continued, "The Scribe, whomever they might be, has been developing a relationship with the students and faculty at universities across the country. If you cut that voice off, you will get protests. Remember what happened at the secession rallies? Do you really want that again?" She remembered the terror as the crowd closed in.

Ted stood there glaring at Sarah.

"Do you need a degree to work at District Homeland?" Ryan asked. "Because you look about the same age as us."

"Where were your parents born?" Sarah crossed her arms.

Ted looked back and forth between them. "Norway. But . . ."

"But what? You're in the same category!"

"Wow, she really gets it." Jason looked up dreamily at Ryan. "She's so awesome. She can rescue me any day."

Ryan put his hand over Jason's mouth. "There's more. We think Dr. Nelson at Columbia found out what comes after the degree clause. There's a plan to control what education a student gets and what jobs they will be assigned to. It's the beginning of serious controls on the population."

Ted frowned. "This sounds like rumors and craziness. That's the kind of message that gets people to panic and cause riots . . . the Scribe's dangerous!"

Ryan shook his head firmly. "No. The Scribe is a voice that can calm the populace."

"You should be investigating what the real intentions are behind these rumors, not drugging history professors," Sarah said. "The Scribe is trying to sort out what's important and inform us so it doesn't blow up."

"If what you are saying is true, nothing will calm people." Ted looked skeptical, but Sarah could see his mind was churning away at the facts.

"Mmmmpppffff," Jason tried to say. Sarah wasn't certain, but it sounded like he was cursing Ryan's ancestry.

"Let's just say we've seen it work before. Better to have some outlet for voices than none at all," Ryan grunted as he struggled to keep his hand on Jason's mouth. "You'll thank me for this later," he said in Jason's ear.

"Can't you talk to Dr. Nelson?" Sarah said. "He can confirm our story."

Ted looked reluctant to answer. "Dr. Nelson went into the hospital a few days ago, heart complications . . . I think."

"And you don't think that's suspicious?" Sarah was horrified. "Oh my god! What about Howard?"

"Dr. Weber is being held at an undisclosed location, but as far as I know he's just fine," Ted said hastily. "Like you said, it's all circumstantial, based on Dr. Nelson's statements."

"And you were going to do that to me?" Jason managed to squeak out from behind Ryan's fingers.

"My orders are to bring you in for questioning," Ted said.

"Yeah, and then he develops a mysterious heart condition," Ryan growled. "We all do."

"Look, we don't know all the facts yet," Sarah said. "Nether does Howard. But we can help as things unravel. That has to be worth something."

Ted pulled a chair from the kitchen table and sat down. He rubbed his temples. "Why did I leave my desk job at the CIA?" he muttered to himself. "You realize this sounds preposterous. According to you, I could lose my job because my math degree would be void because my parents were born in Norway. That's utterly ridiculous!"

"Wouldn't be the first time in history that people in powerful places make decisions with disastrous consequences," Jason said, sounding more like himself. "Especially when they start impinging on basic rights and freedoms."

"And it's just the beginning of something bigger," Ryan added.

Ted sat glaring at his fingers. "This is not what I signed up for." He sat, silent, for a long moment. "I have friends at the CIA that I trust. I can ask them to look into what you believe to be true."

He ran his fingers through his cropped hair. "I've taken on the assignment of watching you." He nodded to Sarah and Ryan. "I can continue with that."

Jason sat up straight. "Does that mean Sarah can go home? Without being arrested?"

Ted nodded, frowning in concentration. "Yes, I can report that I followed Dr. Stanford to Cascadia but didn't find enough evidence to make any arrests or conclusions. I'll say I want to keep watching. Hope for a lead." He leaned forward, sounding more excited. "Right now, nobody knows who the Scribe is. I can report that I believe Dr. O'Conner is not the Scribe, which is true, that he is just another professor in the article loop."

"What about Jason?" Ryan asked.

"Well . . ." Ted hesitated, then seemed to come to a decision. He looked at Jason. "What would you say to extending your janitorial career? Think you could pull a sabbatical from U Vancouver?"

Jason stared at Ted in surprise. "You seriously want me to work as a janitor? For real?"

"If what you're saying is true, we'll need your words. I would like to keep you close by. You've already set up your cover story, we can use that."

"What about Ryan?"

"Dr. O'Conner is good right here. Play the red herring. You're the talker, right?" He laughed at Ryan. "So talk to people, see what you can learn."

Ryan rubbed his chin in thought. He had a light five o'clock shadow starting. "This could work. But can you guarantee Sarah and Jason's safety?"

"Right now, I can't guarantee anything, but I think it's our best option."

"Does this mean I have to clean toilets?" Jason sounded horrified.

Ryan burst out laughing. "And take out the trash! I had to do all of that when we were roommates," Ryan said to Sarah.

"You're a neat freak," Jason grumbled.

"You don't have to do this, Jason," Sarah said.

He looked at her for a long moment. "I'll do it."

"You sure about this?" Ryan asked him.

Jason exhaled slowly. "No, but I want to help. Something is happening that needs to be stopped. I can survive the summer as a janitor."

"I want to help too." Sarah nodded to the agent.

"Sarah?" Ryan raised his eyebrows at her.

"I have to help Howard and my students."

"What about you, Dr. O'Conner?" Ted waited for his answer.

Ryan crossed his arms. "Well, I'm not the one on the front lines here." He looked at both Sarah and Jason. "But if you're in, I'm in." He slapped Jason on the back. "I guess we're back to hanging out on a window ledge!"

Jason and Sarah laughed. Ted looked confused. "Nobody's hanging out on window ledges. Just act normal, like you usually would."

With that Jason, Sarah and Ryan all burst out laughing. "Think we had all better take some defensive driving lessons!" Jason quipped.

Ted shook his head. "Let me talk to my CIA contacts first. Then my bosses at DH. Need to sell them on my report."

It took Ted the rest of the week to set up what he called OS, for Operation Scribe. Sarah did an online tutorial with her students and was relieved to find the TA had handled things well. So well, in fact, that she found herself at loose ends with no papers or lab reports to grade, so she poked around Pike Market with Jason. Ryan seemed determined to make up for his info-smuggling gaffe by taking her out to the best restaurants in Seattle. It was the first time Sarah had ever found herself the center of attention of two handsome gentlemen. She smiled to herself as she packed the duffle bag on her last morning there. She decided to enjoy the attention and let the boys sort it out later. After all, it was both their faults that she'd ended up in this bizarre situation in the first place.

Ryan gave her a gentle kiss goodbye, and insisted on opening the driver's door for her as Jason jogged up and threw his bag in the front trunk of the Porsche.

"Ready?" Jason asked as he handed her a new pair of sunglasses.

Sarah put them on. "Ready." She fired up the Porsche, enjoying the purr of the engine.

"All tuned up and ready to go," Jason said as they backed away from Ryan, who flashed his charming smile at her as if to reassure her everything was going to be all right. She smiled back and gave him a little wave. As she pulled out of the parking area, she caught a glimpse of Ryan still standing in the parking space, this time with a look of worry on his face.

The weather cooperated almost all the way through old Washington, though they got nailed just south of Portland with heavy rains. Sarah drove at a more leisurely pace and even stopped at a drive thru, where Jason gleefully got himself a burger and fries. Jason took the night shift for driving while Sarah tried to sleep. Ryan's worried face greeted her when she closed her eyes.

What was waiting for her when she got home? She felt like she was driving into a void where she couldn't see what was in front of her. Her whole life had been planned out, from soccer practice to the tenure track as professor. Now, it was a blank canvas.

As they crossed back into New America, Sarah thought about Howard and how he'd risked his career to help future students. What had she really done? Ever since that day at the rally, she had kept her head down and worked hard. Never questioning what was going on. Now here she was, a burgeoning spy for a DH agent and the CIA.

Her heart beat faster as she shifted gears, passing a slow-moving truck. No back roads this time, now they were front and center. Let them watch. She was done doing what she was told; this time she would decide what she supported and what she believed. This time, she would stand up front and lead the crowd.

She took a deep breath and let it out slowly. What about Ryan? He'd blown her trust by not telling her about the files. Though a part of her could understand the logic, her heart took it personally. A slight snoring sound came from the seat next to her. Jason shifted in his seat and settled his head against the door. Even with the seat pushed back as far as it could go, he was a little cramped with his long legs. What about him?

Jason had risked everything to keep her out of harm's way. Now he was going to push a broom for the summer. What would have happened to him if she had refused to drive that day? If the agents had snatched him up along with her, the Scribe might have been silenced forever. She felt queasy at the thought.

She rolled down her window and smelled a gentle whiff of pine as she maneuvered the Porsche off an exit ramp. Suddenly, she didn't feel the need for speed. Instead she drove along the old highway, enjoying glimpses of the coastline as she drove by. Maybe she'd ask Jason for a walk on the beach when he woke up. Sarah smiled; yes, she'd like that.

She didn't know what was going to happen to her or her students, and that frightened her, but one thing for certain was that she was not going to face it alone. There were people who cared out there: from a group of professors to a DH agent to the students themselves. Together, with the Scribe, they would make a difference.

About the Authors

Michael Ben-Zvi has had a long-standing love of science fiction and fantasy adventure ever since his first time watching *Star Wars* as a child. He has participated in several New York-based writing groups and critique sessions over the years, gradually honing his ability to put into words where his mind has always chosen to wander. Residing in Manhattan, but a refugee from suburban New Jersey, Michael is a graphic designer and presentation specialist with a history in Corporate America, and is now seeking to explore ever more strange new worlds.

He is currently developing his own collection of speculative short fiction for an independent release in 2018.

Shirley Chan has been writing and telling stories all her life—don't all writers say something similar? Storytelling is her creative outlet. After the science Ph.D., and then the cat-herding job of digital strategist and project manager, she spends her time either consuming stories or trying to spin her own. A few hard-learned truisms: saying you'll do it and doing it are not the same; unemployment, while unwelcome, can certainly be a huge catalyst to creative productivity.

Jennifer Graham was born and raised in Brooklyn, NY, but spends a great deal of her vacation time in Barbados or the United Kingdom with family and friends. She has also traveled to Canada and spots along the eastern coast of the U.S.

Jennifer's first published story, "Intelligence", appeared in the anthology *Beacons of Tomorrow*. Her story "Burden of Proof" appeared in *Nights of Blood 2*. Under the name Jacqueline Zest, her sci-fi romance novella "Star-filled Wishes" is set in the *Future Jinn* universe. Previous jobs include: a chemist, a programmer, a data processor in a financial firm and an administrative assistant.

She continues to write stories of sci-fi, sci-fi romance and adventure.

Caitlin McKenna's formative years were spent immersed in science fiction and fantasy, and she's been dreaming up faraway worlds ever since. A dedicated traveler, she has visited three continents and lived in Vancouver and New York. By day, Caitlin is a freelance editor and writes articles about the intersection of technology, media, and society for Yellow Bear Media.

Her science fiction novel *Absence of Blade* was published by Scoria Press, and her near-future SF tale, "Where the Water Meets the Land", appeared in the anthology *49th Parallels: Alternative Canadian Histories and Futures* (Ottawa: Bundoran Press).

Mackenzie Reide is a mechnical engineer, writer and adventurer. She also dabbles in aerospace so, yes, you can call her a rocket scientist. She loves to see strong girls in stories which is reflected in her middle grade novels, *The Mystery of Troll Creek* and *The Mask of the Troll*, which are the first two books in the *The Adventurers* trilogy. She is currently working on the third book. If you like alternate history, you can read her short story "Shifting Gears" in the anthology *Altered States of the Union*. For more information, check out her website at www.mackenziereide.com.

CPSIA information can be obtained
at www.ICGtesting.com
Printed in the USA
FFOW03n2138090218
44916967-45146FF